DARK ALCHEMY

Also by Laura Bickle

Embers
Sparks

As Alayna Williams
Dark Oracle
Rogue Oracle

For Young Adult Readers
The Hallowed Ones
The Outside

DARK ALCHEMY

LAURA BICKLE

HARPER
VOYAGER
IMPULSE

An Imprint of HarperCollins Publishers

This is a work of fiction. Names, characters, places, and incidents are products of the author's imagination or are used fictitiously and are not to be construed as real. Any resemblance to actual events, locales, organizations, or persons, living or dead, is entirely coincidental.

EPub Edition MARCH 2015 ISBN: 9780062389862

Print Edition ISBN: 9780062404923

10 9 8 7 6 5 4 3

For my husband Jason, who is always behind me

DARK ALCHEMY

DARK ALCHEMY

CHAPTER ONE

BURIED

The raven saw it first.

His dark eye scraped the horizon, scouring the earth for movement in the lengthening shadows. The shadows crawled across the scrub and the sage, wrapping around lodgepole pine trees and flickering through bits of grass. A hot breeze ruffled the raven's feathers, pulling him higher over the land. He sensed something old, something malevolent sliding under the fences and over the rocks.

Old magic, gathering, dispersing.

By the time the first evening star burned in the sky,

the raven had spied it: a tangle of paleness, nested in the grass. Diving down, his claws grasped the safety of a pine tree. He bounced on the branch once, twice, cupping his wings against the turbulence. He turned his head right and left, as he did when he'd spotted something shiny that made his heart pound in the light cage of his chest.

This was more than something shiny, something more terrible. His gaze took it in, eyes dilating to suck in all the available light.

The raven squawked. His call rattled through the tree branches, over fields and between the hooves of cattle. It bounced off a barn and echoed against the side of a truck in a hoarse whisper.

A man heard the raven's call. He stood with his back to the horizon, eyes closed. He was dressed as an ordinary ranch hand: flannel and jeans and scuffed leather that smelled like earth. An old black hat shadowed the man's angular face. His arms hung loose at his sides. Though his left hand was open, the right was missing. From the wrist down, the sleeve of his shirt flapped like a rag on a clothesline. He stood motionless, not breathing, not so much as a pulse leaping through the skin under his neck. Gabe was focused within, on the darkness behind his eyelids.

Gabe's eyes snapped open, gleaming gold.

The raven's call was answered by others, taking up the cry of alarm. Gabe climbed inside his pickup truck and slammed the door, awkwardly cranking the ignition with his left hand and shoving the gearshift into reverse with his knee. He worked the steering wheel with his left hand, watching the horizon. Dark outlines of birds were gathering. Not the twilight gathering of chattering birds coming home to roost, but raucous panic. He followed them, knowing that the contagious call would summon others.

Night fell swiftly as the sun dipped below the mountain. The truck bounced over the ruts in the fields, and Gabe did not turn on the headlights. He avoided spiky stands of weeds and deep rills in the land with practiced turns of the wheel. Like any worker in these remote parts of Wyoming, he knew the land well. And all its secrets. Or so he'd thought.

He slammed on the brakes as bulky shadows appeared before him. A half dozen cows in a tight knot hauled ass back toward the main part of the ranch. His eyes narrowed. Cows shouldn't be on the move this late at night. Something had spooked them.

He turned the truck back west, his foot lighter on the gas this time. Beyond the edge of a ruined fence, he could make out the figures of men in the field, standing in a circle. They were thin as scarecrows, their clothes seeming to dangle on lopsided stick frames, many missing limbs. They were also dressed as ranch hands, but Gabe knew that was simply cover, like a thin coating of dust on a rattlesnake. Silently, their heads turned toward Gabe. They'd been standing in the dimness, not one of them carrying a flashlight or lantern. Gabe's men were, among other things, good at seeing in the dark.

Gabe shut off the engine. Coolant continued to tick inside it, like a watch, as he climbed out of the pickup and approached the cluster of men. Ravens perched on the ruined barbed wire fence cawed at him softly. There were dozens of ravens. One was his. Some belonged to the other men. And the rest . . . well, those were compelled to come, summoned by curiosity and a flicker of magic to gather and gossip at the spectacle.

Gabe lifted the empty sleeve of his right arm. A raven separated from the mass of birds and flew to him. It slipped up his sleeve, meshing with flesh in a flutter of darkness.

Gabe flexed his right hand, whole and unmarked. His skin felt cold from where the evening chill had begun to seep into the bird's feathers, dew now glistening on his skin.

Feathers flashed, slipping into a flurry of shadow as the ravens left their perches and surrounded the men. The birds poured into them, plumping their shadows and filling their outlines. They had the appearance of full, healthy men now.

And the spectator ravens, the ones that belonged to no one, fled in a panic, screaming.

Gabe strode to the edge of the circle and peered down.

Two skeletons lay in the grass. But they weren't simply corpses, plucked clean by vultures. These were ivory-white, twisted into unnatural shapes, the bodies facing each other and knitted together. One was frozen midfall, with its head turned backward over its spine. Delicate spires of bone reached out from the fingers like icicles, sheets of what looked like cartilage wrapped around splintered ribs. Black eye sockets melted in wavering shadow, rimmed with a rusty stain of blood. They looked like something cast out of papier-mâché, barely recognizable as human.

Gabe crossed back to the pickup truck and keyed the CB radio. "You need to see this, Boss." His voice sounded hoarse as it warmed, remembering human sounds.

After a beat of silence, a voice crackled back at him. "God damn it. Do you know what fucking time it is?"

"You need to see this," Gabe repeated slowly.

A static-punctuated breath blew over the radio. "What's your twenty?"

"West edge of the property, beyond the new fence. A hundred yards north of the road as the crow flies."

He disconnected the call and rejoined the others, to wait in the silence until Sal Rutherford arrived.

They saw him coming from a far distance, Sal's headlights bucking over ruts and scaring the cows.

His glossy new pickup pulled up beside Gabe's. Sal popped open the door, grabbing his shotgun from the rack, a flashlight, and a box of shells. He left the engine and the lights running. Sal was not one of these men, and he knew it.

"Gabe. What the hell did you wake me up for?" he growled, rubbing the sleep crust from his eyes as he plodded toward the group.

Gabe was unarmed. His men didn't need weapons

"Dead cattle?" Sal demanded. He didn't wait for an answer, broke down the shotgun and fed it shells. "Was it wolves?"

Silence dragged. Gabe shook his head. "Come see."

Sal followed him to the men staring down at the ground. The truck headlights cast their shadows long over the scene, like negative images of ghosts.

"Shit," Sal swore. Gabe could see the sweat prickling the back of his neck.

"Those human?"

Gabe stared down at the twisted remains. "Looks like they were, once upon a time."

"Did you boys have anything to do with this?" Sal demanded.

"No, Boss."

Sal mopped his brow with a meaty palm. "Shit."

From the tangled skeletons, a sound emanated: a splintering bleat that caused Sal to jump and aim his shotgun.

One of those once-upon-a-time humans moaned from deep within the prison of bones.

"Jesus fucking Christ," Sal hissed. "It's still alive."

Gabe turned his unblinking stare at it, nonplussed. "Seems so."

Sal ratcheted the shotgun and shot the creature in the head. Bones shattered like broken ice under the roar of the blast. Sal waited for the echoes to recede, staring at the fragmented skeleton, seeming to dare it to make another sound.

The husk was silent, and Sal nodded. He turned back toward the truck, climbed in, and slammed the door.

"What do you want us to do with them?" Gabe called. These bones were like any other secret on this land: writhing pieces of darkness that had to be shoved further back into shadow. Forced back before they acquired form and volition.

Sal set the truck into reverse and rolled down the window with a shaking hand.

"Bury 'em."

"This is odd land," Mike Hollander said, glancing sideways at his passenger. Petra couldn't tell if he meant it as conversation starter or a warning.

"That's what they tell me, Ranger Hollander. Everyone says the Yellowstone region is one of the most geologically interesting places on Earth." Hot air whipped through the open windows of Mike's Forestry Service Jeep, blowing long strands of Petra's dark blond hair into her mouth. It still tasted like sea salt. She shaded her eyes against the sun dazzle with a hand, her gaze tracing the distant horizon of mountains and scrub plains. This was as far from the water as she could get.

Hollander shook his head, smiling. "The early Indians and trappers said that this was the place where hell bubbled up."

"I can see why they might think that." Petra wasn't much in the mood for idle conversation, but Hollander seemed too chatty to let her ride to their destination in peace.

"So you're a geologist?"

"Yes. Taking soil samples for the U.S. Geological Survey."

"Most of the geologists are gone by spring. What did you do to get sent all the way out here this late in summer?"

Petra's mouth thinned as she tugged her sleeve down to cover the handprint-shaped scar on her forearm. "Just looking . . ." She paused, weighing how much to tell him. "Looking for a little solitude."

Hollander fanned his fingers over the wheel, casting hand-puppet shadows in the molten light. He laughed. "Point taken. Most people out here are either looking for something or running from something. You'll fit in fine."

Petra jammed her chin on her fist and stared out the window at the tassels of grasses flashing past in the dust. The wind felt soothing on her sunburned freckled face, and she let her eyes slip shut. Maybe she could pretend to sleep, and Hollander would give up.

"Look, I don't mean to be nosy. Strangers are rare enough around here, except for the tourists. And we don't pay them much mind."

Petra opened one eye. "I appreciate you picking me up from the airport. Really."

"No problem. Tourism's down this year, and there isn't much to do at the station. This kept me from spending the day hauling winter gear up to the ranger cabins."

"Sounds like fun."

"Forestry is a glamorous business."

"Are there any other scientists around?"

"Some. There's a group of biologists that will be here in a few weeks to track wolves. I'll introduce you when they show up."

"Thanks." Petra wasn't sure how social she felt. But she appreciated the effort.

Hollander pointed through the dirty glass. "Here's your new home sweet home."

A sign perched by the side of the road announced that they were entering "TEMPERANCE—Pop. —412." Beyond it, Petra could make out a main street with a gas station. There were no stoplights. They drove past a bar, pizza parlor, canoe rental, and a post office.

"Small town," she remarked.

"Temperance is at a crossroads," Hollander said. "We're at the intersection of an Indian reservation, Yellowstone Park, and ranch land."

"It's a tourist town, then?"

"Nah. It's been around since the Gold Rush days. Legend says it was founded by an alchemist who was determined to turn dead rocks into gold."

"Judging by the size of the town, he wasn't too successful."

"I guess not. He disappeared when his house burned down. The town hung on by its fingernails after that, but it never really flourished." Hollander turned the Jeep down a gravel road and west into fields. "How the heck did you find this place?"

"The Internet."

"Well, here it is."

The Jeep pulled up to a beat-up Airstream trailer parked in a broad plain about two miles out of town. The trailer's amenities consisted of an electrical pole tied off at the mast and a rusty charcoal grill leaning beside the front door. Petra opened the door of the Jeep and stepped into the field. The tall, brittle grasses lashed around her ankles. Hollander picked up her bag from the backseat—a military-style duffel containing her only possessions.

"Look, I can take you to the lodge at the park . . ." he began.

Petra ignored him. She tugged the Airstream's door open and fumbled inside for a light switch. Fluorescent lights flickered, illuminating faux wood paneling, a futon covered in a plaid quilt, and a small refrigerator. The floor creaked as Petra walked to the back, where a small bathroom was tucked away. The trailer was blisteringly hot, so she reached for a window.

"I can take you to the lodge," Hollander repeated. He hadn't set her bag down yet.

Petra shook her head. "Thanks, but . . . this'll be fine." She gave him a reassuring smile.

Hollander frowned. "These really aren't accommodations fit for a woman."

Petra laughed, and tried to smother it with the back of her hand.

"What's so funny?"

"I've spent the last two years working on an oil rig. This is . . . luxurious by comparison."

"Okay." He set her bag down on the futon. "Look, if you need anything, you have my cell number."

Petra nodded. She surveyed her new domain, finding the keys to the Airstream's door on a small fold-down table next to a preaddressed envelope for the rent. She'd seen worse, much worse. She could make this work.

Hollander frowned some more at the surroundings, thumbs caught in his belt. "You got a gun?"

"Airline is sort of a bitch about traveling with weapons these days."

"I'm not leaving a gal out in the middle of nowhere without protection." He smiled. Hollander had a very nice smile. A smile that took out some of the sting of being called a "gal." He reached into his boot, pulled a gun out of a hidden holster. " 'Specially not a gal with a handprint-shaped scar around her wrist."

Piss. Cops were cops, no matter where she went. She tucked her arm behind her back, tugging down her sleeve again. "The Forest Service is well armed," she observed, to change the subject.

"We're out in the wilderness without anyone else for miles around. You bet we're well armed." He held out the gun, but she didn't move to take it. "You know how to shoot one of these?"

"Yeah. That's a five-shot Ruger SP-101 .38. Nice piece."

"I'm impressed. A gal who knows her firearms." He set it on the fold-out table.

"Hollander, I don't want to take—"

"You're borrowing it, until you get your own. This isn't my federal-issue sidearm. I've got others."

Petra bit back a snide remark. But she was conscious of the shadows drawing down outside, knowing that it would be dark soon in unfamiliar territory. "Okay. Thanks. I'll get it back to you as soon as I get one of my own."

Hollander tipped his hat and headed for the door. Petra stood in the doorway and watched him drive away into the melting light. When the dust plume had faded, she closed and locked the door behind him. The door didn't fit exactly square in the frame, and she had to bump it with her hip to make sure that it shut properly.

The heat was thick, sticky like caramel. Petra opened the rest of the creaky windows. She was glad to be rid of Hollander. He was a nice-looking man, but Petra had had enough of nice-looking men to last a lifetime. And the alpha-male types, too. Tears blurred her vision as she set about opening her duffel bag. Her fingers clasped around the pendant that knocked less of the new world fall over her as it fell over the land, hoping that it would obliterate her thoughts and grant her a dreamless sleep.

Petra jolted upright. For a moment, she forgot where she was. Expecting a long drop from her bunk to the floor, she misstepped, turning her ankle as she scrambled out of the futon and the tangle of covers.

Something was howling outside. She squinted through the window into the inkiness beyond, shivering. Cold had invaded the trailer.

Was it a wolf? She'd never heard one before. This animal's voice sounded higher pitched than the wolves she'd heard in movies, punctuated by yips and owl-like hoots.

A dog? It had to be a dog, she decided.

She peered into the dark. Was it hurt? Worry gnawed at her.

There would be no sleep while it was carrying on. She reached for her boots and a flashlight. As an afterthought, she reached for Hollander's gun. She hoped that the dog wasn't hurt badly enough that it would need to be put down. That would just be icing on the cake.

Petra dragged the door open and stared out into the night. Night here was different than on the ocean. The ocean was black, capped with white waves, but the lights from the drilling platform and boats obliterated most of the stars.

against her collarbone. It was cast in the shape of swallowing the sun, a gift from her father. Her finger moved from the pendant to the scar spiraling around her wrist, a mark left by the last man who'd touched her. The puckered edges were flattening, turning white with time. She feared what would happen when it faded—would she forget?

But coming here was for exactly that—for forgetting. She wanted this to be the biggest, widest oubliette in the world. Petra savagely tore through her clothes and stacked them on the futon: jeans and casual shirts, T-shirts, tank tops, sunglasses, an olive military-style jacket, boots stained with oil and crusted with brine. A shockproof plastic case held her tools: compass, binoculars, picks, flashlights, chisels, hand lenses, rock-climbing gear. And six fat envelopes full of cash. She stuffed five of them behind a piece of loose plastic paneling in the wall, and put the sixth on the table next to the rent envelope. That was for a gun. And a car—probably a truck. But those were tomorrow's worries.

She stretched out on the futon, watching the light drain from the day. The thin mattress smelled of tobacco smoke. The light seeped away from the field, sucking shadows toward the distant mountains. A rim of brilliant gold outlined the craggy, snow-covered peaks until it faded like the corona of an eclipse, leaving violet sky behind. Crickets and cicadas chimed and buzzed in a soothing melody. Not like the sussurance of the waves, but a landlocked lullaby all its own.

This place was all earth and dirt. She let the black-

Here . . . here was different. Night held sway over everything else. The only light was the one in Petra's hand and the glorious spill of the stars overhead. She sucked in her breath, taking in the white shadow of the Milky Way stretching from horizon to horizon.

She stepped down, onto the ground. Her weight shifted beneath her, and she nearly tripped, craning her neck to see upward. She was too accustomed to the swell of the tides—solid ground was screwing with her sense of balance. She spread her arms out for steadiness, staring up at the sky again.

The Big Dipper shone overhead, and she could pick out the sickle of Leo low on the horizon. Her father had taught her about the stars when she was a little girl, before he disappeared. Her throat closed around the memory.

The howl sounded again, to the east. Clutching the gun and the flashlight, Petra swept the beam across the field of spiky grasses and stones. She whistled, and the howl cut off, midnote.

"Come here, puppy," she called, feeling moronic. Her breath made ghosts in the air before her, and the chill cut through her tank top and cargo pants.

The keening began again. Resolved, Petra clomped through the grasses and gravel to the source of the sound. She swatted away mosquitoes determined to make a meal of her, whistling for the dog.

Twenty yards from the trailer, her whistle froze and fell flat in her mouth. A pair of shining gold eyes peered through the grass at her.

Petra edged the flashlight to the eyes, raising the gun. The light outlined a small, reddish-grey creature with big ears and a bushy tail. Not a dog, not a fox. Coyote.

"Hey," she called, wondering why the coyote wasn't running from her. "You okay, little guy?"

The coyote blinked, lifted his head, and sniffed in her general direction. He yipped conversationally, then presented his rump to her. He dug with his front paws in the sandy earth like a dog searching for a bone. Judging by the size of the hole, he'd been at it for a while.

"Whatcha got there, little guy?" Petra tried to peer into the hole. It was about a foot and a half deep that she could see, but the coyote was enthusiastically kicking up enough dust to make her cough.

The coyote ignored her, continuing to dig. Petra backed away, deciding to leave the coyote to his business. Perhaps it was den-digging season, or he smelled a delicious vole. Whatever he was into, he didn't want human involvement.

Suddenly, the coyote broke off and scampered a couple of feet from the hole. He looked her straight in the eye and gave a soft, lilting whimper.

"What? I don't want your dinner. I had pretzels on the plane."

The coyote laid his forelegs down on the ground and yowled at Petra.

Petra shined her flashlight down into the hole. Something metallic glinted in the dirt.

"Oh. What did you find?"

She looked back at the coyote, to find that he'd vanished like a puff of smoke in the sere landscape. She held her breath. She couldn't hear him moving in the undergrowth. He was gone, swallowed into black.

Petra laid down the gun and reached into the hole, hoping that there was nothing inside that would bite her. Snakes would be just perfect. Blackened wood crumbled under her touch. A tarnished metallic plate was jammed in the side of what looked like an old building beam, turned up at an odd angle. Petra dug into the flaking wood to free it.

The metal was about the size of her palm, round and ornately engraved. She rubbed at it with her filthy hand, and her heart leapt into her mouth. It looked like a compass with numbers and the cardinal directions carved around the rim, and in the center was an image of a lion devouring the sun. Her fingers fluttered up to her necklace. No, it couldn't be. Too damn weird.

She stood up yelled for the coyote. "Hey, come back here!"

Her voice startled the nearby crickets into silence.

The metal cut into her palm, but the coyote didn't answer her with as much as a yip.

CHAPTER TWO

TEMPERANCE

Petra woke at dawn and squinted at her diver's watch. Six thirty. Light crept into the trailer, illuminating the strange medallion she'd left on the floor next to her bed after she'd staggered in the night before. She had wanted it close at hand, suspicious that it would dissolve in the morning like a muzzy dream. But it remained.

She got up to rinse the worst of the grime off the medallion in the bathroom sink. Though pitted and scuffed from age, the compass gleamed soft and yellow. She could now see that its numbers were out of sequence between the cardinal directions, with seven rays emanating like the spokes of a wheel from the center, and there were Latin words she didn't recognize surrounding the lion. The rays corresponded to none of the cardinal directions, seeming to fan out randomly to the edge. She scraped the edge of it against the glass of the bathroom window. The metal didn't scratch the glass, though the window left a small mark on the rim of the artifact.

Gold. The corner of Petra's mouth turned upward. Though the old prospectors in this town had failed, she seemed to have struck it lucky in less than a day. She shook her head. No such thing as luck. If she believed in it, she'd have to believe that the only luck she'd ever attracted had been bad. And then she'd have to believe that there was a reason the men on the rig had called her "Jinx," and it wasn't just because of old superstitions about women at sea.

She tucked the artifact into the trailer wall with her money, then turned her attention to the tiny bathtub. It was barely two-thirds the size of a standard tub, with a handheld shower set. But a hot bath was a luxury. She'd made do with lukewarm four-minute showers at sea, knowing that a dozen men were waiting in line for her to get the hell out so that they could take their turns.

She unscrewed the tap, which spat brown water for a couple of seconds before grudgingly emitting a thin stream of hot water. Petra nodded in satisfaction. The Internet ad for the rental said that the unit had running water and electric heat. She didn't need much else.

Petra worked her hair free of the rubber band that held it out of her face and poked around the cabinets. She had a toothbrush and toothpaste, but she needed to buy soap. She found the dried-up remains of lemon dish detergent and ran the water into the plastic bottle, letting the it float and spin in the bath as bubbles foamed. She peeled off her clothes. Freckles dotted the milky-pale skin on her chest and legs that wasn't sunburned. She scrunched into the bathtub, hissing as the hot water touched her skin. She fiddled with the shower sprayer, succeeding in blasting herself in the face before she managed to get a steady stream that she could use to rinse her hair.

As she stood to allow the water to sluice down the drain, she imagined the last particles of salt being rinsed away. The last residue of the sea.

Leaving wet footprints behind, she dug in her bag for her toothbrush and toothpaste. She let the water evaporate from her body as she brushed her teeth, adding towels to her list of things to buy when she made it to town. She stared out the window across the field. Town was about two miles away, a manageable trek on foot.

Her hair still hanging wet over her shoulder, Petra dressed in a tank top, cargo pants, and her work boots. She didn't carry a purse, and was at odds what to do with Hollander's gun. She settled on jamming it into the hip pocket of her cargo pants. She had no idea if concealed carry was permitted here, but she was beginning to get the impression that there wasn't much law enforcement around. Except for Hollander. And so far, she was on his good side.

She pulled a white long-sleeved linen shirt over her shoulders to hide her scars and a hat and sunglasses to keep from being further crisped by the sun. Keys in hand, she left the Airstream and struck off across the field to find the road.

There was no sign of the coyote or the hole he'd dug. Petra squinted at the flat landscape. She knew that the hole was here, somewhere. She wondered what it was he'd found—part of a house? What had been here before, this far from town?

Her fingers brushed the amulet at her throat. She would find out.

She headed south and west, toward the gravel road that Hollander had driven down the night before. In daylight, the Rockies were cool shadows in the distance, green pines and yellow aspen crowded at their feet. The sky glowed blue overhead, broad and wide as it had been above the sea. Bleached grasses rippled in the breeze, and if Petra closed her eyes, they almost sounded like waves. Almost.

She'd been walking for fifteen minutes when the roar of an engine sounded behind her. She smelled dust and burning oil before it came, and she stepped off the road into the ditch. The car slowed behind her. Petra set her jaw and didn't turn. If it was Hollander, come to check up on her, he could pick up the damn phone. She didn't need to be hovered over like a tourist wandering too far off the marked trail.

"Hey, baby."

She glanced behind her. A dirty red Chevy Monte Carlo tooled at her heels, keeping pace on the one-lane road. The car was full of young men, thin and stringy as a pack of wolves. She turned back to the road before her, ignoring them.

"Hey, I'm talking to you."

Petra didn't answer, but her heart hammered in her throat. She stepped farther into the ditch, out of reach of the driver.

"You wanna party? I've got some crank."

"No thanks." Out of the corner of her eye, she caught sight of the driver's pockmarked face. His decayed grin was missing a tooth.

Great. Meth heads.

"Leave her alone, Justin." A sullen, goth-looking kid in the passenger's seat crossed his arms over his black jacket. Underneath spiked hair, a silver ankh earring gleamed. "We've gotta find Adam and Diana."

"In a fucking minute. I'm busy." Justin the meth-mouth leaned out the window. "You too good to party with us?"

She shook her head and said nothing. Her gaze flicked to the field to the left of the road, and her fingertips brushed the flap on the pocket of her pants. She weighed her options. She could call for help on her cell phone, but she had no idea how long it would take for help to arrive in a place this remote—she'd seen no police station in Temperance. She could draw on them, but she knew that she was too chicken to contemplate really pulling the trigger. The gun might frighten them off, assuming they weren't armed themselves.

"Justin, quit fucking around." The goth kid punched the driver in the arm. "We don't have time for this shit."

Justin shook the kid off. "We've been looking all night. Shut your yap."

Petra squinted ahead. Temperance was about a half mile up the road. She could cut through the field at an angle, where the car couldn't follow her. That was the way the nature channel on TV always said to avoid alligators—run at an angle. If she took off through the field, perhaps they wouldn't follow. And if they did, they might be faster . . .

"I don't want any trouble."

Justin turned his attention toward Petra. "Too bad, Freckles. Trouble found you."

Petra heard crunching gravel as the tires stopped, the click of an opening car door.

In that instant, her analysis of the situation drained away, and instinct kicked in.

Run.

Petra lunged into a run, slamming her heavy boots into the thick soil. She flew, laces snapping around her ankles, fists pumping in time with her steps. She kicked up clods of dirt as she surged through the grasses and leapt over rills in the land. Her breath burned shallowly in her lungs.

Damn it. The land around the Rockies was almost eight thousand feet above sea level. Her breath was shorter at this altitude, whistling at the back of her throat. She looked back.

The driver, Justin, was out of the car. Almost. The goth kid had leaned across the seats and grabbed onto the sleeve of his T-shirt. Justin turned and slugged him hard enough that Petra could hear him squeak as he fell to the floorboards.

Petra turned her gaze forward, swung left to avoid a low-growing tree . . .

. . . and jammed her right foot into a chuckhole.

She pitched forward and landed hard, twisting her ankle as her elbows and knees scraped the gravel. Still tasting dirt, she flattened to the ground, scrambling for the gun in her cargo pocket. Hopefully, they wouldn't be able to see her at this distance through the scrub . . .

Justin stood at the shoulder of the road. The goth kid was leaning out of the open car door and spitting blood on the ground. The young men in the backseat howled in amusement.

"Look at what you did, you ass clown. We lost her."

"We didn't need her, anyway." The goth kid wiped his mouth.

"She mighta had money, you tool!"

"Yeah, well, she's gone now."

Justin shoved the goth kid back into the car. He turned back to the field and yelled. "We'll see you again real soon, Freckles."

Petra gave him the middle finger, assured that he was too far away to see her or her gesture of contempt. The car engine started, and the Monte Carlo rumbled slowly down the road in a cloud of dust.

Petra struggled to her feet. Her ankle pounded painfully against her tight bootlaces. She gingerly poked at it. Probably nothing broken. Just one of those annoying injuries that would hurt like hell for a few days.

She blew out a shaking breath and limped the remaining distance to town.

Temperance didn't quite live up to its billing.

At first, it seemed peaceful enough. Petra hobbled up to a convenience store and gas station. Bears carved from tree trunks flanked the entrance that announced that she'd arrived at Bear's Gas 'n Go. She opened the door decorated with jangling cowbells.

A lottery counter and cash register sat to her right, with aisles of overpriced convenience foods to her left. A few dusty tourist tchotckes were mixed in: T-shirts, water pistols, sunglasses, postcards, magnets, and plush grizzly bears. Above the cash register, a huge stuffed black bear's head and paws crawled out of the wall. Moose antlers hung above the dairy case full of ice cream.

Petra's stomach grumbled. She hadn't eaten since a flight attendant had slipped her extra pretzels on the plane yesterday. She noticed a diner counter stretched across the back of the store and a deli case full of potato salads, sandwich meats, and cheeses. Petra parked her butt on a red vinyl stool repaired with duct tape.

A large man dressed in a flannel shirt and apron appeared behind the counter. His salt-and-pepper ponytail was tied away from his face, and his beard grew nearly white. He was built like a well-fed former linebacker.

"Good morning, young lady. What can I do you for?"

Petra smiled. "You must be Bear."

"I am." Bear's blue eyes crinkled. "And you must be our new geologist."

"News travels fast here. I'm Petra Dee."

"Like they say, news and the dead travel fast." Bear stuck a meaty paw over the glass counter. "Pleased to meet you, Petra."

"Likewise." She eyed the stuffed bear over the cash register. "This is a great place you've got, here."

Bear chuckled. "That's Daisy. She's my good luck token. Scares away robbers and keeps the lottery tickets lucky. I've sold a state-jackpot-winning ticket here every year since I hung her over the register."

Petra laughed. "If I believed in luck, I'd have to start playing."

Bear grinned. "You've come to the right place for changing luck." He slid a photocopied menu across the counter at her. "You look like you had to chase your breakfast."

Petra looked down at her dirty sleeves. "Um. Yeah.

Ran into some guys who were a little too friendly. Tweakers."

Bear's mouth thinned. "I know the guys you're talking about. Red Monte Carlo?"

"Yeah. Charming."

"It's Justin and his posse of wannabe thugs. They kept trying to buy cold medicine from me to cook that crap up." Bear gestured at a locked case holding medicines behind the register. "Once I figured out what they were up to and threw 'em out, they must have found another source."

Petra smiled to imagine Bear forcibly throwing the young men out of his store. "Must have."

Bear's gaze darkened. "You got a gun?"

"You're the second person to ask me that." Petra dodged the question, ambivalent about the gun. She suspected that once people knew she was packing, she'd go from being the new girl in town to something else entirely. And she didn't want to know what that was. Instead, she said: "What I'd really like to get a line on would be a vehicle. Car, truck . . . doesn't matter, as long as it runs."

Bear rubbed his beard. "I'll check around for you. Shouldn't be too difficult to find a ride in a day or two."

"Great. Thanks." Petra looked at the menu, trying not to salivate over the list of sandwiches, salads, and sides. "What's the house special, Bear?"

"Bear's Bacon Buffalo Banana Pepper Bacchanalia. Number 42. Comes with slaw and potato salad. I also recommend the root beer. Local brew with extra sas-safras."

Petra slid the menu across the counter. "Hit me with the Bacon Buffalo Bacchanalia and the root beer."

The Bacchanalia almost did Petra in. A half hour later, she was wobbling on the stool like a stuffed tick. Bear had given her a bag of ice to prop her ankle up on. Grudgingly, she slipped from the stool and foraged among the aisles for provisions. Bear rang her up and sacked her groceries in a brown paper bag. Petra thanked him and lifted her groceries. She could get back to the Airstream with this load, but she'd have to take it slow.

He looked out the window and pointed. "That's Maria Yellowrose's truck. Looks like she's got a FOR SALE sign on it."

Petra peered out the window to see a huge, rust-colored midseventies Ford Bronco parked on the street. The back window had been painted with white FOR SALE lettering and a phone number.

"Thanks, Bear."

"Don't thank me." Bear pointed upward. "Thank Daisy. The luck's all hers."

Petra grinned and clanked through the door with her sack in hand. She crossed the street to get a better look at the Bronco. Rust had chewed through some spots in the wheel wells, but the tires still had enough tread on them to last until winter. It was no doubt a gas guzzler, but Petra didn't mind the idea of visiting

Bear's deli on a regular basis to get gas and Bacchanalia sandwiches. The Airstream kitchen was not made to produce three-course dinners.

The Bronco was parked on the curb in front of the Compostela, a bar that looked like it had stood since the Gold Rush days. The faded wood building was pierced by gothic windows and shutters, fronted by a porch with creaky floorboards. Petra guessed that it might have originally been a church. Perhaps as a nod to its origins and the name of the town, a wooden cross was hung over the door. A sign in the window announced beer and appetizer specials for happy hour.

Petra glanced at her watch. It was almost 2 P.M.—a bit early for drinking. Maybe Maria Yellowrose worked here.

Shuffling her groceries to her left arm, Petra pushed the door open into the shade of the bar. It took a moment for the red sun shadows of the day to resolve themselves. This place had, indeed, been a church in a prior incarnation. The gothic windows still held colored glass that played on the scarred floor in kaleidoscopic colors. The effect was no doubt spectacular under the influence. Church pews had been cut up and reassembled as booths and table seating. The altar area had been converted to a bar. Pendant lights glittered over a slab of highly polished wood that looked to have been cut from a single tree.

There was something pragmatically blasphemous

about the whole setup. Petra didn't believe in anything that couldn't be quantifiably recorded. Religion held the same sway over her that fairy tales and New Age crystals did. But she still found it amusing.

The bar was sparsely populated at this hour. A group of old men sat playing cards in the corner, and a half dozen other patrons were silhouettes in the pews. Petra made her way to the altar. The bartender was a blond man about twenty years older than Petra, dressed in black. The wall behind him gleamed in a pattern of stars hammered out of tin.

"Can I help you?" Petra could feel his gaze sizing her up.

"Hi. I'm looking for Maria Yellowrose."

The bartender pointed behind her. "She's over there. But now might not be a good time."

Petra turned. At one of the pews, a man and woman were arguing. Or, rather, the man was arguing, and the woman was attempting to reason with him.

". . . not going anywhere," the man slurred. He was dressed in jeans with a loose button-up shirt, and his hat lay before him on the table. His skin was pale, and his wizened hands curled protectively around an empty glass.

The woman stood beside him, hands pressed to the table. Black hair dusted her shoulders, and she wore a long lace tunic over a gypsy skirt. She spoke low, so low that Petra could barely hear her.

"It's time to come home, Frankie," the woman said. "I'll take you."

Frankie shook his head. "I'm not going home to listen to any more of that bitchin'."

"You can't stay here. You've already been cut off."

Frankie stared into his empty glass. "No."

"You can either come willingly, or get thrown out." The woman's eyes slid to the bartender.

Frankie slammed down his glass. "Let me take a piss first."

"Okay. Then we'll go."

Frankie stumbled out of the pew and wandered away to the restrooms. The woman sat at the edge of the pew and rested her heart-shaped face in her hand. Her sloe eyes were fixed on Frankie's empty beer glass.

Petra hated to intrude, but she didn't relish the idea of roaming the countryside without the protection of a steel skin around her. She screwed up her courage and approached the pew.

"Excuse me, are you Maria?"

The woman blinked and looked up. "Yes?"

"Hi. My name's Petra. I saw that your truck was for sale. But if this is a bad time . . ." Petra's gaze slid to the men's room.

Maria shook her head, and her silver earrings shivered. "There's no such thing as bad timing. I need to get that beast sold before insurance is due on it this fall."

"Tell me about it?"

"It's a '78. Three hundred sixty-seven thousand miles. New water pump and fan belt, old tires, air-conditioning doesn't work. Put a battery in it last year. But it runs. It's never left me stranded."

That squared with what Petra had observed. Her ankle throbbed, and she was reluctant to walk all the way back to the trailer. Even if the truck was a lemon, it might be fixable. "What are you asking for it?"

"Eight hundred, firm."

"Let's go look at it."

Maria nodded. She glanced back toward the men's room, where the sounds of vomiting could be heard. She caught the eye of the bartender.

The bartender didn't look amused. "I'll send him out when he's done."

"Thanks."

"Sure."

Petra followed Maria out to the sunlight. The beast of a truck cast a shadow on the gravel, seeming to give Petra the once-over through dirty headlamps. Maria opened the driver's side door, popped the hood. Petra stood on tiptoe to look in at the dusty engine as Maria started it. The engine vibrated with a satisfying idle, deep and loud enough that Petra had to shout to be heard above it. "Smells like oil."

"Yeah. It burns about a quart every three months. Wasn't worth it to track down the leak."

Petra nodded and dropped the heavy steel hood down with a puff of dust. Maria shut the engine off, but the sound still roared in her ears. Petra stepped up on the running board and peered into the interior. The vinyl seats were intact, and a fist-sized charm made of citrine beads clicked from the rearview mirror. But she was more interested in the shotgun in the backseat.

"Is that for sale, too?"

Maria shook her head. "Sorry. But the pawn shop could probably hook you up."

"Where's that?"

"Two streets over. Stan's Dungeon."

"Sounds like an S&M shop."

Maria cracked a smile. "Nah. Though you can probably score some handcuffs there, if that's your thing."

Petra shook her head. "I'll pass. But thanks for the info." Her fingertips lingered on the hot dashboard. "Eight hundred bucks? Can I take it today for cash?"

"Eight hundred bucks and a ride back to the reservation," Maria amended.

"Deal." Petra extended her hand, and Maria grasped it, bracelets chiming.

At that moment, Frankie came stumbling from the bar into the street. He patted his pockets, looked right, left, and then fixated on a box truck parked on the curb ahead of the Bronco. A man in jeans and a black cowboy hat was loading fence posts and coils of barbed wire into the back from the hardware store next door. In this heat, he was wearing long sleeves, buttoned at the wrist. A raven paced on the roof of the truck, watching the man in the hat work.

"Hey, you!" Frankie stabbed a finger at the man in the black hat. "Shouldn't you be back at the ranch, sucking Rutherford's cock?"

The man in the hat ignored him, throwing sharpened fence posts into the back of the truck as if they were foam pool noodles and not hardwood four-by-fours. The raven stopped pacing, turned its unblinking obsidian eyes toward Frankie.

Maria grabbed the old man's arm and dragged him toward the Bronco. "Time to go, Frankie."

But Frankie wasn't through shooting his mouth off. "You digging graves for him? He got you digging your own?"

The man at the truck looked up then. Under the shade of his hat burned the coldest, most distant look Petra had ever seen. Petra had only seen a look that remote on a corpse.

"Watch your mouth, old man. Or the next grave could be yours." His voice was barely a whisper, but the threat in his amber eyes chilled Petra's blood. The man turned his back to them and continued to load the truck, while the raven continued to stare at Frankie, fluffing its wings.

"Frankie," Maria hissed. *"Shut the hell up."*

"He ain't right. Rutherford's boys aren't natural. The raven told me." Frankie flailed as Maria attempted to shovel him into the car.

Awesome. She forgot that the drunk guy was coming along for the ride, too. Petra hoped he didn't barf in the Bronco, since she was pretty sure that the mess was now hers.

"Get in the truck, Frankie," Maria said, slamming the door after him. Frankie wormed to the other side and slithered out the opposite door. Petra saw him snatch a fence post from the ground. The raven cawed, a harsh, raw sound.

"Look out!" Petra shouted.

Frankie swung on the man in the hat. The fence post crashed into his back with an audible crack. The stranger slumped against the side of the truck. Frankie swung and struck the man again, hitting so hard that the man's shoulder dented the side panel of the truck on impact. Blood spattered on the dingy paint. The raven fluttered down from the roof of the truck, skittering helplessly along the perimeter of the fight.

"Jesus, Frankie's gonna kill him." Maria dug in the back of the Bronco for the shotgun, scrabbled in the glove box for loose shells.

In the doorway of the bar, Petra spied the bartender. He stayed in the shadow of the door, watching.

"Help him!" Petra shouted.

The bartender shook his head. He watched with detached interest, like a vulture watching a predator make a kill that he could pick over later.

The taillight of the truck broke under the impact of one of Frankie's blows, glittering red in the spatters on the pavement. The stranger was on the ground, and Frankie slammed the fence post into the man's ribs. The stranger's hat lay on the pavement, broken plastic shards glittering on the leather. The raven paced beside the hat, wings spread, shrieking.

Petra stepped up to Frankie. "Leave him alone."

Frankie paused. Petra marveled at the power of her voice, that Frankie was willing to stop midstrike, bloody fence post lifted over his head.

Then she looked down, saw the pistol in her hands

and the barrel pressed against the base of Frankie's neck. The pressure seemed to keep the gun from shaking.

"Holy shit," she breathed at herself.

The raven looked up at Petra and cawed hoarsely, as if challenging her to act. Or pleading.

CHAPTER THREE

BLUFFING

A shotgun shell ratcheted noisily into its chamber somewhere behind Petra. She held her breath, tensing to receive a load of buckshot in the back.

"Do as she says, Frankie," Maria snarled. "Drop it."

Frankie let the stained fence post clatter to the ground. Sullenly, he turned to Petra and Maria. Spittle ran down his chin and flecked the front of his T-shirt.

"Last chance. Get in the truck, Frankie."

Frankie, grumbling, shuffled toward the Bronco. He vomited in the street and collapsed upon reaching the truck, passing out against the fender.

Petra knelt before the beaten man. His dark hair was matted with blood and dirt. Petra rolled him on his side, saw the purpling bruise already swelling on the right side of his face.

"Are you okay?" It was a dumb question. He clearly wasn't.

"Mmmph," he said.

She dug her cell phone out of her pocket and called 911. The call rang twice, then disconnected.

"Hey," she shouted over her shoulder at the bartender. "Call an ambulance."

The bartender disappeared. Petra didn't know if he'd make the call, if there even were ambulances out here.

Petra pried open the man's good eye. The pupil in his shimmering amber iris contracted in the sun. That much was good. The eye began to roll back into his head.

"You." She shook him. "Stay with me. What's your name?"

The man coughed a mouthful of blood up on Petra's shirt. "Gabriel."

The raven paced before them, rustling its feathers in agitation. Petra tried to shoo it away, but it hopped back, making sketchy tracks in the blood with its claws.

Petra turned Gabriel's stubbled face toward her, examining the bruise covering the right side of his cheek. His skin was oddly cool, like stone, and he smelled like metal. No heat emanated from the wound, nor from the blood that covered his skin. Petra rubbed her hand on her pants, conscious of the risk of blood-borne contagion.

Gabriel touched Petra's collar. "Sorry about your shirt."

Her gold pendant necklace spilled out from under the fabric, and Gabriel immediately brushed his fingers against it in fascination. "The true green lion," he rasped,

"What? You know about this?"

His amber eyes fluttered shut, and she reached for his wrist to take his pulse. Her fingers sought an arterial thump of blood. But she didn't feel a thump . . . she felt a buzz. Like placing her fingers on a stereo speaker that was playing only static. "Paramedics will be here soon."

Gabriel shook his head. "No paramedics." He shifted his weight, struggling to get his hand under him to climb to his feet.

"You need a doctor."

"No. Help me up."

"Absolutely not. The squad will—"

"*Medicines are our poisons, and poisons our medicines. Even the New Testament can be poison,*'" Gabriel muttered.

"What are you talking about?" That sounded like something a whackadoodle would quote to avoid treatment. "The Bible?"

"Paracelsus. He wasn't an idiot on *all* counts."

Something seemed to move under his shirt. She thought it was a trick of the light, but something like black feathers twitched at the edge of his collar.

"What—?"

Gabriel shoved her hands away and hauled himself to his feet. The raven cawed at him, lighting on the driver's side mirror as he stumbled to the cab of the truck.

"You can't drive. You'll pass out," Petra yelled at him. The absolute gibberish he was spewing suggested that he had at least a concussion, maybe a skull fracture or a brain bleed. The raven buzzed the airspace near her left ear, startling her into stepping back.

Maria Yellowrose grasped her arm. "Don't follow him."

Gabriel's truck chugged to life and rolled down the street. The raven took wing overhead. The truck and the bird disappeared in the bright, dusty sunshine.

A man from the hardware store, wearing an apron and a name tag, came outside. He cranked open the valve to a garden hose spigot and began to rinse the blood from the street, as if someone had spilled a milk shake, and he wanted to rinse the stickiness away before it attracted wasps.

"**W**hat the hell was that about?"

Petra rode in silence for the first ten miles in the shotgun seat of the Bronco before she spoke. Hot afternoon air slid through the open windows, rattling Maria's car charm against the windshield. She could taste the red dust on the breeze. In the backseat, Frankie stretched out, sleeping off his bender with a crust of vomit drying around his lips.

Maria glanced sidelong at her. "How about you start with what the hell you're doing here, at the ends of the Earth?" Maria had the shotgun wedged up next to her, between the door and her hip.

Petra tried a half-truth. "I got a job. I'm a geologist."

Maria watched her. "The economy's that bad, that a geologist would come all the way here?"

"Yellowstone's an exciting place. It's the caldera of an active volcano. Hot steam geysers, noxious gases, mudpots . . . for a geologist, it's a playground."

The smell of fetid breath came in a gust from the backseat as Frankie wobbled upright. He spoke in a dreamy singsong. "Runaway from water. Runaway from fire. Runaway looking for her daddy."

The fine hair on Petra's arms stood upright in the heat. "What did you say?"

Frankie slid back down to the seat as if he'd been deflated.

Petra turned her face to the window, bit her lip. The blood was drying on her shirt. She was trying not to imagine what microbial creepy-crawlies were in it. The gun felt hot in her hip pocket, drawn twice today.

Maria stared straight ahead at the road, which was stained red from bits of iron ore in the asphalt. "Frankie is clairaudient."

Petra blinked. "What?"

"Frankie hears things. But only when he's drunk, and he forgets all about them when he's sober. Which isn't often." Maria stared at her. Hard.

Petra looked out the window at the shimmering heat. She rubbed her temple, mindful to try to keep the blood on her sleeve from smearing on her face.

Maria laughed. "You aren't fooling anyone."

"You clairaudient, like Frankie?" She couldn't keep the skepticism out of her voice.

"No. I'm a social worker. I've seen more than one domestic violence case in my time." Maria gestured to the mark on Petra's arm.

Petra opened her mouth to protest, closed it, and tugged the sleeve down on her wrist. Maybe it was better if Maria thought it was that simple. Something in the other woman's expression had softened, and maybe that was a good thing.

"It's not what you think. I just . . ." Petra shook her head, and she could feel the quaver in her voice. "I don't think I'm ready to talk about it. Not yet."

Maria nodded. "Fair enough."

"You're a social worker?" Petra turned a question back on her.

Maria nodded. "Yeah. I work at the Family Center on the reservation. This far out, people have a lot of problems that get swept under the rug."

"Like Frankie?"

Maria shrugged. "Frankie's my uncle. I've gotta take care of him."

Petra's brows drew together, and she glanced in

the side view mirror at the lump in the backseat. They looked nothing alike. Maria was dark and exotic to Petra's eye, while Frankie looked like a wrinkly white cast-off from a Florida retirement colony.

"We're related by marriage," Maria said, and it had the feeling of a confession, the way she said it. "He was my uncle's . . . aunt's . . . er. They met at Burning Man in the nineties. It's complicated."

Petra glanced at the shotgun tucked up next to Maria's skirt. "Would you have shot him?"

Maria chewed her lip. "No," she admitted. "But I would have shot in his general direction. He was swinging at one of Rutherford's men like it was the ninth inning with bases loaded."

"He said his name was Gabriel." The name tasted odd and metallic on Petra's tongue.

"I'm surprised that one of them spoke to you. They're a quiet, creepy bunch. They work for Sal Rutherford, the owner of the biggest ranch around here. Ranch hands."

"I take it that you don't think much of Rutherford, either?"

The corner of Maria's lip turned down. "Sal's got money. Lots of it. And he gets what he wants. His family's been here for generations, old cattle barons. They were always pissed that our tribe got land here. He moves his fences forward every year. We move them back." Maria gestured with her chin to the green sign beside the road that said: WELCOME TO RED ROCK INDIAN RESERVATION. Pavement dropped immediately to gravel with an audible *thunk* of the Bronco's tires. At least the shocks didn't squeak.

Maria's mouth thinned. "This may go to Rutherford, sooner or later, I think. The reservation populations have been dwindling as more and more people move away to look for work. Someday, this land might belong to the federal government. Or to Rutherford's descendants."

The Bronco churned through a small town like any other in the West: convenience stores, fast food, gas station, a Laundromat. Down one side street, Maria pulled a U-turn and parked the Bronco beside a white two-story house that probably dated from the 1930s. Flowers bloomed in carefully tended window boxes, and laundry was drying on a clothesline in the side yard. The paint on the porch was curling a bit, suggesting that traditional women's work was going on as usual, but the men's work was slipping a bit. Maybe Maria was doing it all.

Maria shut off the engine. Valves continued to ping loudly against the backboard hood as Maria reached into the backseat. "Frankie. Frankie, get up. We're home."

Frankie groaned and climbed upright enough to ooze out from the car door. Petra inspected the backseat with a sharp eye, searching for vomit.

Frankie muttered to a grasshopper resting on the mailbox, then to the birds perched on the roof gutter, before sinking down into a porch swing.

Maria rolled her eyes. "He thinks the animals talk to him."

"They do talk to me," Frankie insisted. He pointed at Maria. "That one could be a most excellent shaman, if she would stop talking long enough to listen."

"Frankie, take your pills." Maria groaned, rubbing her forehead, before turning her attention to Petra. "He knows nothing about shamans. Look, you wanna come in and avoid the heat? I need to dig out the title on this beast. And you can get cleaned up."

Petra self-consciously climbed out of the truck. She peeled her shirt off, but the tank top she wore beneath was still stained in places and showed off her scars. A mess, no matter which way she looked at it.

Petra followed Maria to the porch. Sweetgrass surrounded the foundations of the house, and a garden heavy with tomato vines and nodding sunflowers stretched to the west side. Sparrows were busily attacking the sunflower heads in a quest for seeds. A small grey and white cat lurked in the dirt, tail lashing, waiting for an opportunity to pick off one of the tiny brown planes.

"Leave those birds alone." Maria gave the cat a stern look. The cat blinked and ignored her.

Petra smelled sage as she followed Maria into the house, noticing that the door was unlocked. She wondered if Maria was that trusting, or whether her fearsome reputation with the shotgun was enough to keep intruders at bay. Plants had overtaken the interior of the little house, as well. Maria punched a button on the window air conditioner, and the artificial breeze stirred a strand of bells and devil's ivy growing from pots suspended from the ceiling. The main room was a small living area dominated by a slipcovered couch on one end, kitchenette on the other. Cast-iron pots dangled from a rack, where more plants reached from the kitchen windowsill. Herbs were stuffed in bottles and laid out to dry beside empty canning jars. The walls were painted a cheerful yellow, scarred wood floors covered in colorful carpets.

"I'll get you a clean shirt." Maria disappeared into the back of the house.

Reluctant to sit on the furniture with half-dried blood on her clothes, Petra stood awkwardly in the center of the floor with her arms crossed, listening to the air-conditioning hum. She jumped when the front door creaked open, but it was only the small cat, pushing the door with her front paws. The cat sauntered into the living room and looked up at Petra.

Petra knelt and let the cat have a sniff of her fingers. The cat thrust her head under Petra's hand, emitting a rusty purr. By her size, Petra had judged her to be a half-grown cat, but closer inspection showed the sinewy muscle of age.

"Pearl likes you. And Pearl's not usually very fond of strangers." Maria returned to the living area with a small bundle.

Pearl looked up at Petra and emitted a meow that sounded like she'd smoked six packs of cigarettes a day.

"Is she your watch cat?"

"Pearl does what she wants." Maria handed Petra a shirt. "This should fit you."

"Thanks. I'll bring it back to you."

Maria shook her head. "No need. It shrank in the dryer, and makes me look pretty slutty if I try to wear it. There's soap and washrags in the bathroom."

Petra looked down at her shirt.

"Don't worry about getting blood on anything. The towels are old. Feel free to use the shower, if you want."

"Thanks," Petra said. She was grateful to be directed to the bathroom and to shut the door behind her. She placed her red-speckled hands on the faux marble countertop and let out a quavering breath. She stared at her red knuckles, reached for the squeaky tap. Hot water scalded her shaking hands, and she scrubbed viciously with cedar-scented soap.

She yanked her tank top over her head, taking three tries to peel it over her face without the red touching her lips or eyes. It had soaked through to her bra and skin. She pulled the rest of her clothes off, reached past Maria's daisy-patterned shower curtain for the shower tap, and stepped in.

She scrubbed until her skin was raw and pink, letting the water and the soap do its work. Gradually, the scent of the cedar soap permeated her skin, calmed her. No red—it was gone.

When she stepped out of the shower, she surveyed her clothes. The bra and tank top were ruined, but her pants seemed fine and she pulled them on. Maria's shirt, a gauze peasant top, wasn't designed for a bra, anyway. It was a chocolate brown color, off the shoulder, with smocking that wrapped around her waist. She had to admit to herself that it was pretty. Petra hadn't owned feminine clothes in years. This felt . . . different. It didn't smell like salt, unlike everything she owned. This smelled like land, like it had been dried in sunshine and kept in a closet with lavender sachets.

She padded out of the bathroom in bare feet, the ruined shirt and bra balled in her hands.

"Feel better?" Maria stood at the kitchen counter, chopping herbs. Pearl perched on top of the refrigerator, taking a bath. Her tail tickled the colorful kitchen magnets studding its surface.

"Yes, thanks. I hope I didn't use up all your hot water."

"There's always more. You're welcome to stay for dinner."

Petra shook her head. She didn't believe in Frankie's supposed special powers, but didn't trust her reactions around Frankie's drunken fishing. "I appreciate it. But I should get back."

Maria nodded, wiping the knife off in a dish towel. "Truck title's on the table. Sign off, and I'll notarize it."

"You're a notary, too?"

"I wear a lot of hats. Pearl will be our witness."

Petra signed while Pearl watched from her perch until her attention was arrested by a refrigerator magnet that was fun to push around the surface of the fridge. While Maria stamped the document, Petra fished her money out of her cargo pants and handed eight hundred to Maria. The other woman didn't bother to count it, stuffing the wad into a cookie jar on the counter. She opened one of the upper cabinets and dug around for a blue bottle about the size of her hand with a screw-on cap. Sunlight glistened through the bottle, outlining a shadow of plant matter inside. She handed the bottle to Petra.

"Take this."

"What is it?"

"A sleep potion. I call it 'Liquid Dreamcatcher.' Nothing harmful or illegal. Just herbs and rum."

Petra swirled the contents of the bottle around. "I look that rattled?"

"You look like you need to sleep. That will help. Two sips should take you to dreamland." Maria took a card off the counter and handed it to Petra. Her brown eyes were warm. "This is my card. If you need anything, and not just with the truck . . . Call me."

The card was plain white, with Maria's name and the LISW designation below it, listing her address and phone number at the Family Center. On the back was a number scratched in red pen. "That's my cell number, when you're ready to talk."

"Thanks. A lot. I mean it. And . . . I will call."

And it felt like she meant it.

CHAPTER FOUR

BLOOD

"Look what the cat dragged in."

Gabe slammed the truck door and leaned heavily on the fender. His fuzzy vision settled on a figure outside the barn holding an axe.

"Boss." Gabe tipped his hat with his bloody knuckle, leaving a wet smudge on the brim.

Rutherford approached, inspecting Gabe's injuries. He poked Gabe in the shoulder with the axe handle. Gabe winced.

"What the hell happened to you?" Amusement lit in Rutherford's voice—amusement and curiosity. Sal

Rutherford believed that he was the only one who knew the vulnerabilities of his silent ranch hands. If others knew, his power over them might be diminished. Might.

"Lucky drunk took a couple of swings at me with one of your fence posts." Gabe told him the truth. There was no need to lie.

Gabe walked heavily into the barn, Rutherford following on his heels. The light was lowering on the horizon, sliding through the chinks in the barn in golden slats. Dust motes were suspended in the light like daytime fireflies.

"*Hnh.*" Rutherford seemed to chew on what Gabe had said. He blocked Gabe's way with the axe. "Where you think you're going?"

"To ground." Gabe paused, fixing Rutherford with his amber gaze.

Rutherford shook his head. "I've got work for you boys."

Gabe narrowed his eyes. "Not tonight, dear."

Rutherford swung the axe. Gabe raised his arm to block it, and the blade of the axe embedded itself in his palm. Gabe looked serenely over the blade, wrenched it away from Sal.

He pulled the axe blade from his hand. It was like pulling a paring knife from an apple: no blood, no sign of pain. He cast the axe to the floor of the barn, and it skidded away in the straw.

Rutherford smiled. "You boys always amuse me. I can shoot you, burn you, stab you, and you'll remain standing. But whack you in the knees with a baseball bat, and you go down like everyone else. Makes me wonder what would happen if I skewered you, like that Vlad the Impaler guy . . ."

Gabe was on him in two swift steps. He grasped Rutherford by the throat, lifted him with one hand. Rutherford's feet kicked up straw dust, and he wrapped his hands around Gabe's wrist, gurgling and flailing.

Gabe leaned in close to whisper in the boss's ear, his breath ruffling the grey hair of the boss's muttonchop sideburns. "You'd do well to remember that you've got more weaknesses than we do. Many more. And there are more of us than there are of you."

Rutherford smiled and croaked, "You could kill me. But I have the tree. The Hangman's Tree is on my land. All it takes is one can of gasoline over that thing and a book of matches, and you're done. And that's exactly what the Rutherfords will do if anything happens to me."

Gabe dropped Sal, gasping, to the floor. He turned on his heel and walked away, into the field beyond the barn and the sunset. Closing his eyes, he felt the warmth of sun on his skin and the tall grass flickering through his fingers as he walked. He could find his way back to the tree without looking, had counted these steps over and over in his mind for more than a century.

A lone elm stood alone in the center of the field, gnarled with age and reaching toward the sky with bent and twisted branches. It had been here ever since he could remember, which was a very long time. The cool shadow of it pressed on his face, the breeze rustling through its leaves. Somewhere above, a raven perched, cawing to its fellows. They came here at sunset, the ravens, all to this place. Men like Rutherford called it the Hangman's Tree. It still bore scars in its lower branches where ropes had scraped away the bark.

But Rutherford had little idea of what it really was, beyond knowing that Gabe and his men needed it. The Alchemist had called this the Lunaria, the Alchemical Tree of Life. Where its branches stretched to heaven above, its roots reached into the earth in perfect symmetry.

"'As above, so below,'" Gabriel muttered. The Alchemist had said it first.

The ravens gathered in the molten light, cawing to themselves, roosting in the tree by the dozens. Black wings flapped in the leaves, and the Lunaria took on the impression of something more intensely alive than a singular tree, moving, shifting in that pure breeze and cacophony of black feathers.

Gabe knelt, feeling the dry grass prickle his palms as he searched for the door. He found a hidden root, pulled open a rusty door covered with turf and dirt. He climbed inside the hole, away from the light and grass and the cackling of ravens.

It smelled like damp earth here, like a root cellar kissed by floodwater. The fingers of roots brushed Gabe's face as he dropped below the surface. This place was one of many rabbit holes the Hanged Men had dug over time to go to ground. Rutherford had little knowledge of the warren of tunnels that worked beneath the field, the barn, even his own house. As far as he was concerned, the boys disappeared and re-emerged at will.

Gabe's vision gradually adjusted as he stepped into the dark. He could see the dirt walls and uneven floor of the tunnel as he wound deep into the earth. He looked down at his clothes. They were streaked with golden light, like frozen sunshine. He could taste it in his mouth, and he spat it out on the floor of the tunnel.

The tunnel opened up to a chamber directly beneath the tree. Roots reached out in all directions. Gabe could feel the pulse of water and light through the living wood as tendrils dug through the earth, worming after nutrients in the soil.

The other men were already there. They dangled motionless from the ceiling of the chamber, roots wrapped around their necks and arms, the grotesque fruit of the Lunaria. Gold light pulsed through the silent roots into their bodies, feeding them, regenerating what seemed to be corpses buried underground. Gabe and the rest of Sal's men could stay away from the Lunaria for a day, or even a handful of them. But they always needed to return, to feel the embrace of the tree.

Gabe reached upward, feeling the roots wind around his hands, shoulders, and throat. As the Lunaria lifted him into itself, he awaited the cold sunshine dripping into his veins, bringing with it the chill of sleep.

"*As above, so below.*"

The coyote was waiting for her back at the trailer.

The sky had purpled like a bruise by the time Petra returned to her new home. The Bronco chewed through the gravel road, kicking up stones that rattled against the undercarriage. She was more than halfway back before she noticed that Maria hadn't removed the beaded charm from the rearview mirror. Perhaps Maria was trying to lend her some luck. Petra promised herself that she'd return it. Even if there was such a thing as luck, she wasn't sure that any of it would stick to her.

She cranked up the windows and shoved down the locks, stuffing the keys into her pocket as she approached the trailer. She balanced her groceries awkwardly on her left hip and held her bloody clothes in a ball at arm's length. She'd seen no sign of the meth heads on the way over, but she was still wary. In the falling light, she thought she saw movement, and her hand twitched to her side, to the heavy pocket on her right. But, as her eyes adjusted to the darkness, she saw that it was only the coyote.

He sat upright on the creaky wooden steps to the trailer door, watching her with shining eyes.

"Hello, again."

The coyote cocked his head. One of his ears was black and speckled in gold, as if he'd been painted by a child with a short attention span. He seemed very comfortable in this place.

"You've probably been living here a lot longer than I have."

The coyote stuck his hind foot in his speckled ear and scratched.

"I'm harmless. Really."

The coyote looked at her and blinked.

"I'll make you a deal. You can keep living here, if I can keep living here."

The coyote looked at the sack in her arms. His nose twitched.

Petra set the bag down. She'd picked up some lunch meat that was probably ruined by now. She dug through the provisions for the package of salami, ripped it open. She crouched before the coyote and extended a piece of meat to him.

"Seal the deal with a gift?"

The coyote's nose quivered. He slunk down the steps, body low to the ground and ears pressed back. He approached slowly, shied to the left, and snatched the piece of meat from her hands. Then he trotted away with his catch.

Petra fished the trailer key from her pocket and climbed the steps to the door. A piece of paper was taped to the glass. It was a man's handwriting, all capital letters:

SOME CRATES OF EQUIPMENT FROM USGS
CAME FOR YOU AT THE TOWER FALLS
RANGER STATION. YOU CAN COME BY AND
PICK IT UP MONDAY MORNING.
CALL IF YOU NEED ANYTHING.
                                            —MIKE HOLLANDER

Good, she thought. She'd be able to get to work right
away. Petra stuffed the note in her pocket and jiggled
the key in the lock. She heard a rustling behind her,
and spun in alarm.

It was the coyote again, head buried in the grocery
sack.

"Hey!" she shouted.

The coyote dragged his head out of the bag with his
jaws closed around the package of lunch meat. Seeming to grin, he sprinted away into the dark.

"Little thief."

Petra's hands balled into fists as she went to retrieve
the bag. The coyote drove a steep bargain. She guessed
that she'd be playing by his rules, not hers.

Petra carried the sack and her ruined clothes into
the stifling heat of the trailer. She switched on the
light and opened the windows to get the air moving.
Everything seemed as she'd left it. Her money and
the engraved compass were still tucked behind the
wall.

She emptied her pockets of the gun, her cell phone,
and money. She set her groceries out on the small

kitchen table, pleased to have accomplished the acquiring of essentials, like toilet paper and soap.

Maria's blue dreamcatcher bottle felt warm in her hand. Hesitantly, she unscrewed the cap and sniffed. It smelled like alcohol and something bitter.

"Two sips to dreamland," Petra repeated. She took two slugs from the bottle and grimaced. It tasted metallic, like a mouthful of aluminum foil, burning on the way down. She beat feet across the tiny space to the bathroom for her toothbrush to scrub the taste from her mouth.

The overhead light was attracting bugs through the window above the futon. That window was missing a screen, and Petra had the unenviable choice of roasting alive or being covered in mosquito bites. She turned the light off and stretched out on the futon, propping her sore ankle up on the futon arm. A cool breeze trickled over her face as she waited for Maria's potion to kick in. Her eyes roved around the unfamiliar shadows of the trailer.

Back on the oil rig, there had always been light—light to ward away ships and to summon helicopters. The rig had glowed like a small city in the darkness as the waves scraped its steel skin. It had been easy to believe that the rig was a world unto its own, a little planet floating in space.

But something gleamed here, too, in the black. Not the fireflies swimming outside, nor the stars overhead. Something gold and phosphorescent on the floor of the trailer near the door.

The hair on the back of Petra's neck lifted. She climbed off the futon to study the pulsing light. It looked like glow-in-the-dark slime from a child's toy store, the kind that parents inevitably found ground into shag carpet. Warily, Petra turned on the overhead light.

The glow drained away. All Petra saw was her wadded-up bloody clothes on the floor of the trailer.

She shut the overhead light off again, backtracked to the bathroom. She turned the light over the sink on, just enough to trickle into the main area. She crossed back to the floor and stared at the incandescing pile of clothes.

Petra knelt and poked at them. Where the bloodstains had spattered her shirt, the fabric looked as if it had been covered in phosphorescent paint, a bit of gold glitter that seethed in the light. Light that gave off no heat.

Fear and curiosity blended in her. She'd never seen anything like this, not even in books and material-safety data sheets she'd read about radiation. Curiosity won out. She dug in her equipment bag for her hand lens, peered through the magnifying glass at the surface. The closest thing it resembled was cave lichen; it had a curiously granular appearance.

Petra tucked the clothes into the empty grocery sack and sealed it up as tightly as she could. This bore some analysis, she vowed. But in the morning.

Maria's dreamcatcher potion was taking effect; she could feel her thoughts slowing and running together.

She washed her hands, climbed back into bed. She felt a tingling in her fingers, and the numbness spread to her face. Petra remembered feeling this way when she'd been given a heavy dose of Klonopin after the accident, after everything on the oil rig fell apart . . . .

"You sure that there's something down there?"

The shift supervisor yanked off his hard hat to wipe sweat from his filthy brow. In his oilman's jumpsuit, the big man was roasting, even with the cool breeze coming off the water. The sky had been white-hot and clear, the sea calm and smooth as bathwater, but tensions were boiling on the mobile offshore-drilling unit. They had been drilling for weeks, all on Petra's assurances that dead dinosaur fluid was roaming somewhere under the seafloor. These assurances were becoming increasingly expensive.

The drill ship *Cassandra* had been anchored in the Gulf for days, the drill in its hull pounding away at the seafloor. The mighty engine thrummed an unceasing buzz through the soles of her feet and in the back of her dental fillings.

"It's there." Petra stood with her arms crossed over her clipboard. "I was on the survey ship and sent out the hydrophones myself." She stood her ground. Shift supervisors like this guy always thought they were right, despite what geologists could show in data. No one had ever gone out this far before on this range. It was risky, but she knew that there was oil to be found here.

The shift supervisor squinted at her under a receding hairline. "We should have hit it by now. I don't know whether your calculations or the buoys were off, but we're getting nothing but mud."

"She says it's there. Keep drilling." Des had come up behind him. Even though his jumpsuit was streaked with silt, he cut a handsome figure. Time outdoors had weathered his skin to a golden tan, and green eyes behind sunglasses crinkled at the corners when he smiled. Blond hair had been bleached by the sun to nearly the color of wheat.

"I don't like drilling this close to a fault," the supervisor growled. "It's dangerous."

"The fault is where the oil is," Petra insisted.

"You're only humoring this twit for a piece of ass." The supervisor glared at Des. It wasn't out of jealousy. The supervisor hated anything that he perceived as screwing with his crew's smooth operation. That could be anything from taking long breaks to actual screwing. In his mind, a woman was an unnecessary distraction on a rig.

Des grabbed the supervisor's lapel in his fist. Though the supervisor had at least forty pounds on him, Des was all sinew. She knew every inch of that muscle, and knew that the supervisor was on thin ice. "Shut the fuck up. Take a break. I'll watch the crew for a while."

The supervisor glared at Des, then at Petra. Des was the lead engineer on the ship, the installation manager, and the two could only push each other so far. He shrugged out of Des's grip and stomped away across the deck. Gulls scuttled away as he approached, squeaking protests.

Des lifted his hard hat and ran his hand through his sweaty hair. "Look, I'm sorry about him."

Petra shook her head. "Forget it." She'd worked around roughnecks long enough to know that the bigger you made an issue, the bigger an issue it became.

The corner of Des's mouth turned down. "He needs to mind his own damn business."

Petra resisted the urge to kiss the corner of his frown. The rest of the men were milling about, and though there were no secrets on a rig, they did their best to keep others out of their affair. Instead, she clasped her hands behind her back with her clipboard.

"I'll deal with him, later," Des promised.

A shout from the spire of the derrick snagged Petra's attention. "Hey, we got something!"

"What is it?" Des strode to the men at the turntable. Between segments of pipe casing, a spray of dark fluid was beginning to spurt.

"It's not mud!" Des gave her the thumbs-up, grinning, his teeth gleaming white in his tan and dirty face.

Petra let out a breath she hadn't known she'd been holding. She grinned, vindicated. Maybe the supervisor would finally shut the hell up, and they could get to work.

Before she could suck in another breath, her smile faded. The kick of oil spewing out of the casing increased. The blowout-preventer valve must have failed. She shouted at Des, who turned in enough time to see the drill string being forcefully ejected from the hole, shooting upward with a tearing sound.

As the metal and rock sheared upward, a spark ripped through the drill string. A deafening roar rumbled through the boat, pitching the deck. An orange fireball raced through the hull of the boat and up the derrick, the heat scorching Petra's skin.

She screamed for Des in that fireball, not seeing him, buffeted by the men running and the pitching of the deck. She ran for the fire, but the blaze drove her back. Through tearing eyes, she could see the figures of burning men flailing near the stack. Shrapnel rained from the sky, and black smoke poured over the deck. Klaxons sounded, and she smelled chemical fire-suppressant foam, charred oil, burned meat . . .

The orange plume raced high into the air, dissipating in charred black edges. The captain of the vessel was calling on the crew to abandon ship. Petra scrabbled around the edge of the fire, fell to her knees beside a smoldering lump of canvas and blood. It was so hot that she could feel the heat through her gloves when she turned it over to see a blackened face. A blackened face with the plastic of sunglasses and white hard hat melted to a shock of straw-blond hair.

Petra turned away and retched on the deck.

Someone grabbed her wrist. Hard. Petra cried out, her vision blurring. Des had grabbed her wrist with a grip that burned like hot oil. Her skin sizzled under his touch.

"Des!" She reached to turn the ruins of his face to hers, to give him CPR. But no breath rattled from his lungs. His chest didn't rise and fall under his blackened jumpsuit. She pounded on his sternum, forced air past his seared and blackened lips.

But it was no use.

The firefighters found her sitting beside Des's body, his fingers curled around her wrist and baked into her own flesh.

She shut her eyes, sobbing. She couldn't bear to look as the medics separated them.

Petra opened her eyes.

Cold morning light streamed through the window above the trailer futon. Her heart pounded in her throat, and she swallowed it down to her stomach, waiting for the roar of blood in her ears to recede. She scrubbed her sleeve across her eyes. The sea was gone. So was Des. No matter how potent Maria's dream-catcher potion was, no matter how real the dreams were in the dark, they were gone in the daylight.

It had been six months since the accident. Six months of being deposed in lawyers' offices and taking walks along the beach. Vitrum Oil, the holding company that had owned the rig, quieted the press by lining the pockets of reporters. The official explanation given for the blast was a failure in the pressure seals, an engineering product failure.

But Petra knew. She knew that it had been her fault.

She'd picked the spot. Even though she wasn't legally culpable, she knew that Des would be alive if it wasn't for her. As time passed, that certainty grew, sank past the shock into the marrow of her bones. Though the edges of Des's face seemed to grow fuzzier in her dreams, and her scar was fading, she still felt that hurt in her chest when she took a deep breath.

She shivered a bit in the chill, tugging the tobacco-scented blanket closer around her. Her feet felt curiously hot, and she wiggled her toes. Her ankle seemed better. She missed the warmth of sleeping beside Des, how he let her put her cold feet in the crook of his knees in the cramped bunk.

Something moved at the foot of the bed, and it wasn't her.

Holy shit.

Petra scrambled bolt upright, reaching clumsily for the pistol on the floor. It rattled away from her fingers, skidding under the futon.

A gold-flecked ear lifted above the blanket. Then a black one. The coyote turned his golden eyes, half-lidded in sleep, toward her.

"What the hell are you doing here?"

The coyote yawned. He was curled up around her feet, not much larger than a big house cat.

"Okay, I get that you were asleep. But how did you get in here?"

Petra's gaze flicked to the open window. She didn't know that coyotes could jump. Hell, Maria's dream-catcher must have knocked her entirely out for her not to have noticed a coyote scrambling into her bed. No matter how much he looked like a dog, Petra was conscious that he was a wild animal. With teeth.

The coyote stuck a foot in his ear and scratched. Jesus, she hoped he didn't have fleas.

Petra extended her hand gingerly. She had no idea if she could get a rabies shot within a hundred miles of this place. The coyote didn't *look* sick . . .

The coyote sniffed at her hand. She reached for his head to pet him, but he ducked. She didn't push it. Eventually, he let her touch the back of his head. His fur was rough and coarse, not the soft coat of a domestic animal. He was nervous; she could hear a fine whistle in his chest as his breathing quickened. She took her hand back.

"Are you sticking around, then?"

The coyote climbed to his feet, stretched. He placed his paws on the windowsill, scrambled over it with claws scraping on the metal. He landed in the dirt with a huff and vanished under the trailer.

Petra looked after him, resting her cheek on her arm. Perhaps it wasn't such a bad thing to have something to keep her toes warm, someone to watch over her. Even if it was only for want of salami.

CHAPTER FIVE

THE ALCHEMIST

Cal hated disturbing the Alchemist at work.

He hesitated on the basement steps, his knuckles white on the railing. He avoided coming down here, hated everything about it: the creak of the steps if he forgot and walked down the middle of the treads; the smell of sulfur; the snap and crackle of fire. It reminded him of hell. Maybe not hell with capital letters, not *the* Hell, but certainly a bit of the outer reaches of it.

He waffled, contemplating going back.

"Who's playing on my back stair?" The Alchemist's

voice drifted up the steps, the craggy voice of a man who'd smoked a lot of cigarettes. Among other things.

Cal shut his eyes. *Damn.* "It's me . . . Cal."

"Come down, Cal."

Cal's boots clomped on the rickety wooden steps, laces flapping against the risers. He put his sweaty hands in his pockets as he reached the last step and looked around for the Alchemist.

Glass bottles lined innumerable shelves, creating a maze that flickered in blue light from a furnace in the corner. Wooden apothecaries leaned against the crumbling walls of the basement. Powders and books and bits of bone were strewn across uneven worktables made from cinder blocks, mismatched table legs of scrap wood, and doors torn from the upstairs rooms of the house. Paint peeled from the elaborate six-panel doors. Mason jars held silvery liquid that seemed to quiver in the uneven light. A hot plate glowed red in the darkness.

"Stroud?" Cal called. He thought he spied movement in the furnace. Through the grate, a tiny salamander wriggled. It dropped to the ground and scuttled across Cal's shoe. Cal started, jumping back as the creature slipped away.

"Here, child."

Cal saw him then, nearly motionless in this hoarder's nest. Stroud was sitting on a stool, measuring powders on a postal scale. He was old enough to be Cal's father: a stringy sinew of an ex-hippie hunched over his work. His blond hair was fading to grey at the temples, but his eyes shone fever-bright blue. He looked over the round rims of his glasses at Cal.

"I'm sorry to disturb you." Instinctively, Cal took a step back.

"It's all right." Stroud's lips peeled back over a smile. He cocked his head, observing Cal. Cal squirmed. He always tried to avoid Stroud's notice. Getting Stroud's attention usually meant trouble. For the young women, that meant being tied up in his bed. For the young men, it meant dangerous assignments that often landed them in jail.

Cal swallowed. "Adam and Diana are missing."

Stroud took off his glasses, frowning. "How long?"

"Three days. Justin and I went out to find them . . ." Cal shrugged, his hands open. "We can't find them. All their things are still here, at the Garden."

Stroud drummed his fingers on his makeshift workbench. A bead of mercury rolled off the edge to the floor. The bead veered around Cal's foot into spiderwebs beneath a shelf.

"I sent them to spy on Sal Rutherford." Stroud's gaze was distant. "I hope that Rutherford didn't find them."

Cal's fists clenched. "I'll go look for them there."

"No." Stroud shook his head. "Not yet. Not alone. Give them more time to come back."

"What did—" Cal bit his tongue. He knew better than to ask the Alchemist questions. If he asked, he got answers he would never forget, answers that would keep him awake at night.

Stroud regarded him. "Can I trust you with a secret?"

Cal bit his lip. He wanted to say "no." He didn't like secrets. But he had no choice. "Yes."

"Rutherford has magic."

Cal frowned, processing. "Magic like this?" His thin fingers sketched the lab. "You're the only one who makes the aqua vitae, the Elixir."

Stroud's gaze burned like the blue of a gas flame. "He has something else. A piece of the puzzle of eternal life."

Cal didn't ask any more questions. He didn't want to know how Stroud had come upon this shiny bit of information.

But Stroud was going to tell him anyway. The Alchemist opened a battered leather journal that seemed to be disintegrating under the weight of mildew. His fingers flickered through the fragile pages. "I have Lascaris's journals. He left something there, on Rutherford's land, that yields immortality."

Cal could see spidery sketches, strange symbols, and words in Latin, but could make no sense of it. "If Rutherford has the secret, why isn't he using it?"

Stroud smiled. "I don't think that he knows *how* to use it."

Cal's fingers knotted nervously in the chain to his wallet. "I'm worried about Adam and Diana."

"We'll find them," Stroud said soothingly. "You've been up all night?"

Cal nodded miserably.

"And got into a fight, I see."

Cal touched the side of his swollen face self-consciously. "It was nothing."

"Rest first." Stroud handed him a glass vial.

Cal stared at it.

"Go ahead, take it. It's the Elixir."

Cal stared morosely down at his shoes. From the corner of his eye, he could see the escaped salamander swatting around the errant mercury bead. "I haven't got any money."

"It's okay. It's a gift."

Cal swallowed hard and took the vial. "Thanks." He didn't like owing the Alchemist anything.

Stroud smiled. "I'll send someone to search for your friends. You rest."

Cal nodded. "Thank you." The vial burned coldly in his hands.

Stroud turned back to his measurements, and Cal retreated back up the steps. Back into the light.

The kitchen of the old farmhouse was bathed in glorious golden sun, illuminating a sink full of filthy dishes. A cereal box scuttled across the floor until a turned-around mouse emerged with his cheeks full of Froot Loops. Beer bottles were lined up against the window, casting green and amber shadows on the sticky linoleum.

Upstairs, Cal could hear somebody fucking. He banged through the torn screen door, past a limp figure in a plastic lawn chair who smelled as if he'd pissed himself.

Outdoors sprawled the Garden. At least, that was what Stroud called it. Cal thought the old man must have a secret sense of humor. Trailers were parked in uneven rows around the old farmhouse, bounded by woods, corn, and blond field grasses. A chicken wandered by, ignoring a skinny dog chained to a clothesline post. The only thing that resembled a garden here was a bit of Indian paintbrush growing wild in the field.

Cal found a downspout at the corner of the farmhouse and shimmied up it to the sheet-metal roof of the porch. He sat down on the hot steel and fished his pipe out of his pants pocket. He tapped the contents of the vial that Stroud had given him into the bowl of the pipe, and reached for his lighter to heat it.

Cal waited impatiently for the liquid to begin to fade to vapor and crystallize against the glass. He inhaled deeply, holding his breath and staring up at the clear blue sky.

This was what Stroud called the Elixir. A piece of immortality. As the ghost of the Elixir soaked into his brain, he began to feel a sense of peace steal over him. This sensation, this presence, was what Stroud said that yogis and bodhisattvas chased.

The past—the fight with Justin, the miserable conditions of the Garden—fell away.   The future—worry for what had happened to Adam and Diana—fell away.

He was one with the sky and the heat of the day radiating from the metal at his back. He was one with that clear blue. Feeling nothing but the rise and fall of his chest and the beat of his heart. Thinking nothing.

A sublime smile curled the corner of his mouth, and Cal sank into oblivion.

He didn't see the raven perched on the edge of the gutter, watching.

Stan's Dungeon was not what Petra expected.

Bells tied to the iron-laced door chimed as Petra pushed into the gloomy pawn shop. The shop was stacked floor to ceiling with shelves, dusty glass cases, and gun racks. It smelled of new tobacco and old gunpowder, and racks of military surplus clothing cluttered the floor.

But there was more here than just guns, old musical instruments, and militaria. Stan was apparently a collector of antiques. A cigar-store Indian stood just inside the door. An old saddle was suspended by rope from the ceiling, and cases of coins and grainy photographs of the Old West hung from the walls.

Petra paused to look at the collection of photos in metal frames. The sepia-toned posed shots showed wooden buildings on a dirt street and men and women in hats and bonnets. She saw some familiar contours to the buildings and layout to the streets. People in dresses and shiny boots stood around a building she knew. Church clothes, she realized. The Compostela's earlier incarnation as a house of worship.

"You like old photos?"

Petra turned to see a man who had appeared behind the counter. He leaned against the glass by an old-fashioned red dial telephone. Petra hadn't felt his eyes on her, had no idea of how long he'd been sizing her up. He was stooped and wizened like a tree, albeit a tree clothed in flannel. His voice issued out from beneath a carefully waxed grey moustache that was as shiny as pewter.

"These are really fascinating. How old are they?"

"Some of those go back to 1852. Got a whole cabinet of 'em. Some wet collodion, some dry plates. Old newspapers, too."

A smile crossed Petra's face. "This isn't just the town pawn shop, is it?"

The old man shook his head, and Petra heard bones creak and pop. "No, ma'am. I'm also the town historical society—a society of one."

"Then I'm in the right place." Petra approached the counter and extended her hand. "I'm Petra Dee. I'm new to town."

"The geologist. I heard that you were coming. I'm Stan." Stan's moustache twitched when he smiled. "What would you like to know about Temperance?"

Petra's smile thinned. "Everything."

Stan rubbed his moustache. "Temperance was founded in 1852. Rumor has it that it was founded by Lascaris Aldus, a self-proclaimed alchemist."

"Yeah, people have mentioned him. I didn't know that gold was mined here, though."

Stan shrugged. "Lascaris found gold, somewhere.

Or conjured enough of it to keep the town thriving for ten years. He vanished in 1862, when his house burned down. Most people assumed that he died in the fire, though his bones were never found. The town hung on until Yellowstone was established as a national park in 1872."

Stan pointed at a tintype perched on the wall. "That's old Lascaris."

Petra squinted at the disintegrating photo. A man stood before a faded, underdeveloped landscape. He was dressed in long coat and tall boots, his shirt dirty and rumpled. A battered hat perched above decidedly patrician features. His gaze was distant, faraway. Petra knew that look. She'd seen that look in her father's eyes before he'd disappeared.

Petra tore her gaze away. "He was a good-looking man, in a sort of crazed way."

Stan chuckled. "He was definitely thought to be a nutbar recluse. Some think that he still haunts Temperance, looking for hidden gold or the Philosopher's Stone. Depends on who's doing the telling."

"That's a nice ghost story."

"Lascaris was a mysterious man. If anyone had unlocked the secret of eternal life, it would have been that old alchemist."

Petra chuckled. She'd believe ghosts when she saw them, but didn't want to go out of her way to offend the old man who was giving her the tourist spiel.

"Don't tempt them, young lady." Stan winked at her. "Temperance is a strange place."

Petra looked at the glass case beneath the register, full of handguns displayed on threadbare velvet. "Are those for sale?"

"Everything's for sale, for the right price." Stan pressed his hands to the glass. "What are you looking for?"

"Something small. Manageable." Petra had nothing to prove by carrying a bazooka on her hip.

"A girl gun?" Stan pulled out a tiny Derringer from the case that fit into his weathered palm. The handles were a pink-tinted mother-of-pearl. "I've also got one that's barely bigger than a lipstick case around here, somewhere . . ."

"Cute, but I'd like something a bit more substantial. I'm thinking something like a .38."

"Six-shot or automatic?"

"Six-shot." Automatics made Petra nervous. Too many moving parts to fuss over if she needed it. And if yesterday was any indication, she'd have to become very familiar with the new toy.

Stan fiddled with his moustache and grinned. "I've got just the thing for you. Stay right there." He disappeared into the back, leaving Petra to browse.

She pawed halfheartedly through the racks of military jackets, camo coveralls, and khaki shirts. She found a couple of shirts and a pair of fatigue bottoms that looked like they might fit, and heaped them on the counter. Work clothes. She picked up a sturdy-looking military backpack and a black canvas ammo bag for her tools. It was the closest she would ever come to carrying a purse. It slung comfortably over her shoulder, and had enough loops to hold her picks.

She bypassed the musical instruments, coins, and sporting equipment. Pausing at the clothing racks, her nostrils flared at the rich scent of leather.

"Oh, my," she breathed, in spite of herself. She pulled out a knee-length brown leather coat, worn in to buttery softness. Unlike the other clothes she'd chosen, this was clearly a woman's coat. Probably dating from the 1970s, it was flared with a broad lapel and full skirt, studded with tortoiseshell buttons. She reached inside it, finding a zip-out lining. She held it at arm's length, staring at it. Fall would be coming soon, and she had no coat.

"Try it on." Stan had returned, was fussing behind the counter. "There's a mirror over there." He gestured to a corner of the room, where a cheap door mirror had been propped up.

Self-consciously, Petra shrugged into the coat. It smelled of leather and tobacco. She peered at her reflection in the cheap glass. It fit her like a glove. She had to admit, she liked the swashbuckling silhouette it gave her.

After a moment's hesitation, she stepped out of it, placed it on the counter with the rest. For winter, she told herself.

Stan had pulled out a wooden box that looked as if it had survived a flood. He opened it, and Petra wrinkled her nose at the smell of moldy velvet.

Stan lifted two silver pistols to the light. They were

tarnished, free of embellishment except for pearl grips. "How about these?"

Petra lifted one dubiously and peered down the long barrel. She estimated that it weighed about four pounds. Underneath the tarnish, there was no pitting or buckling, so it was unlikely to blow up in her face. "That's a lot of gun, Stan."

"That's an 1881 Colt Frontier six-shooter. It's a .44. Need cleaning, but they're a nice set."

Petra considered the weight of it in her hand. It had a reassuring heft. The long barrel would give her more control over the larger caliber bullet, but still . . .

"I don't know that I need two guns." She checked that the barrel was empty and pulled the trigger. The action was a hard pull. It wouldn't go off accidentally—no featherlight trigger here.

"I'll cut you a deal on the set." Stan rummaged around in the box. "Also comes with the gun belt." He held up a decrepit piece of leather. "It's a fine antique."

Petra tried on the belt. She had to wrap it exactly twice around her body to get it to fit. The leather needed oiling, and the buckle was tarnished black.

"That makes you look like a proper cowgirl." Stan said, approvingly. "Try it with the coat."

Petra made a face. She didn't primp. But she had to admit that the coat with the gun belt made her look like she belonged here . . . like Annie Oakley. Maybe the meth heads would leave her alone.

"Hm. How much?"

Stan rubbed the edge of his moustache. "Two thousand."

Petra removed her hands from the belt as if it were hot. "Two thousand?"

"Those pistols are worth good coin. I'm cutting you a deal."

Petra frowned and set them back down on the glass case. "I don't really need an antique."

Stan reached under the counter. "I've got this one." He placed a cheap Saturday night special on the glass. "Fifty bucks."

The piece felt cheap and flimsy in her hands. Not like the smooth, warm pearl. Her eyes slipped longingly back to the Colts. "You got ammo for those?"

"How much you want?"

"Two boxes of .44s." She hoped to God that she wouldn't need more.

"So . . . Seventeen hundred, then."

"Uh-uh. A thousand," she countered. "Cash."

Stan smiled. He knew he had her. "Fifteen hundred."

Petra's index finger circled her pile of clothes. "Fifteen hundred for everything."

Stan shrugged. "Cash? Deal."

Stan went to the back to rummage around for ammunition, and Petra continued to poke around the store. She found Stan's jewelry case, which was a bit saddening. Old wedding rings and new engagement rings sparkled under the artificial light.

But her attention was snagged by a piece of black jewelry at the bottom of the case. A moon was inlaid on it in gold, surrounded by four tiny bits of cut glass. The style reminded her a bit of the necklace her father had given her. She waited for Stan to come back with the ammo and asked him, "Hey, could I take a look at that?"

Stan obligingly opened the case and handed the brooch to her. "That's an onyx mourning brooch. Back in the 1900s, they were quite the thing."

Petra turned it over. The back of the brooch was black, an intricately woven texture as glossy as a raven's wing behind glass. A gold serpent coiled around the border, swallowing its tail. "What's this made from?"

"Hair. Widows would weave and braid hair of the deceased into the brooches."

Petra nearly dropped it, imagining fondling hundred-year-old hair. "Ugh."

"They were a sentimental lot."

But it was pretty, in its way. Petra fiddled with it, and a spring popped open. The interior of the brooch was a locket, holding two minute tintypes that swiveled in their frames. They'd corroded severely; she could barely make out the face of a blond woman on one side. On the other was the shadow of a man, his profile nearly eaten away by time.

Petra squinted at it. There was something strange about that profile, something familiar.

"That's pretty much ruined. You can have it for ten bucks."

Petra clasped it in her fist. "Sold. By the way, I found something pretty interesting the other day. I was wondering if you could tell me about it."

"Sure, I'll take a look at it. What is it?" Stan paused in bagging up Petra's finds and leaned forward.

"Some kind of compass or sundial, I think." Petra pulled the compass from her pants pocket. She watched Stan's reactions carefully. He blinked when he saw it, picked it up, and turned it over.

"Where did you find this?"

"I'm renting a trailer just north of town."

"The old Airstream off Ember Ridge?"

"That's the one. I guess. Unless there's more than one old Airstream around here."

Stan smoothed his moustache with his fingertips. "That's where Lascaris used to have his house, before it burned down. If I had to guess, I'd say it belonged to him."

Petra's eyes narrowed. "What makes you say that?"

The shopkeeper pointed to the symbols. "Those are alchemical symbols, and the markers of the cardinal directions associated with the ancient elements: earth, air, fire, and water."

Petra's heart leapt into her mouth. "What about the lion and the sun?"

"In the symbolism of alchemists, the lion is tied to the sun. This is the true green lion, and his devouring of the sun symbolizes the transformation of unpurified material."

Petra swallowed. She'd heard that before, from Gabriel. Unconsciously, her fingers flitted up to the medallion from her father, hidden beneath her shirt collar. "What is it?"

Stan shook his head. "I don't know. Some kind of ward or talisman, maybe. There's somebody I can ask to appraise it, though, if you want to leave it here."

Petra didn't like how the old man's hands curled possessively around the edges of the compass. "I'll bring it back later," she said, prying it from his fingers. She tucked it away in her pocket and gathered her bags.

"Thanks for your help, Stan."

"Sure. Come back anytime."

The door banged shut behind her with the chime of bells, but Petra couldn't shake the feeling of the old man's gaze on her back. She stood to the left of the door, listening, the hair prickling on the back of her neck. There was a space of silence, the sound of a rotary-dial phone churning, and then Stan's voice.

"Stroud, this is Stan. I saw something today that I think you'd want. Something that would fit right into your collection."

Stan began to describe the piece and where it had come from. "It looks like a compass, but with the Prima Materia lion in the center. Cardinal directions, the seven rays on it. Looks like gold to me. Customer said that it was found on Lascaris's old property. I dunno if she'd sell it." There was a pause, and what

Stan said next was unintelligible. Then she heard him say, "With the new girl. Petra Dee. Yeah. Her last name is Dee. So?"

The man named Stroud must have hung up, because there was a very long pause after that, followed by the sound of the receiver being put down and Stan muttering, "That girl's gonna need those six-shooters."

Petra slunk away from the shadow of the store, unable to shake the chill of sweat tracing down her neck.

CHAPTER SIX

FOOL'S GOLD

"Hey. Get your asses to the south field."

Gabe wound barbed wire tightly around a fence post, looked back to see Sal Rutherford clomping toward him. Ravens pecking at the shiny wire coils skittered away at his approach, fluffing their feathers and cawing. The rest of the ranch hands working on the fence, setting posts and winding wire, stopped. They turned silently toward Sal, then looked to Gabe.

Gabe stripped off his gloves. "We're not done here."

"Doesn't matter. We've got a problem in the south field."

Gabe's eyes narrowed. "What problem?"

Sal's mouth thinned. "We're shorthanded. I lost a dozen balers."

"Lost?" he echoed.

"They left. Deserted, after they found another corpse."

"Like the last one—skeletonized?"

Sal looked away. Gabe could see sweat trickling down his brow. He reeked of fear. "The balers took off before getting too close to it . . . they didn't say. They were seasonal workers." Seasonal workers came and went on the ranch. There weren't enough of Gabe's men to do all the work this time of year. Gabe knew Sal disliked having outsiders around, but it was a necessary evil.

Gabe tucked his gloves in his belt. "What do you want us to do about it?"

"Take care of it. And when you're done, finish where they left off. Bale the hay they left standing out there before it rains."

Gabe stared at him. The other men didn't move. They didn't look to Sal first for direction. Instead, they watched Gabe. There was a curious vacancy in their gazes, as if some of the soul behind their eyes had been drained out. Some, more than others. But they were useful, in their way. Labor for Sal. Company for Gabe, of a steadfastly silent sort.

Gabe gave a curt nod, and the men left their work behind, climbing into the backs of pickup trucks. They left the barbed wire where it lay, in coils snaking around loose posts. Gabe sat in the back of one of the trucks, wondering at what they might find.

He rubbed the side of his face that had been bleeding just yesterday. His skin had been knit whole, smooth and tanned as if he'd never been struck. He ran his fingers over the skin, willing himself to feel some of that pain. It had hurt, to be sure. Maybe that's why he let it happen. It had been the most exhilarating, real sensation he'd felt in a very long time.

Almost. The curiosity the woman had piqued in him was just as real. He'd seen the alchemical symbol on the medallion she wore before, mostly in the hands of strangers who occasionally came to Temperance searching for Lascaris's alchemical secrets. Those people inevitably became sucked into the Alchemist's mysteries and vanished.

But this woman had none of the metallic tang of magic about her. She seemed . . . ordinary. And Gabe wondered what she wanted.

The truck bumped over the fields, rattling tools and teeth as it went, toward the south field. The hay had been mown, and much of it baled. Gabe directed the driver to stop where the line of bales faded away into the fallen grass line, where the balers had abandoned their work. Pitchforks and baling hooks glimmered where they had been cast aside.

His mouth pressed into a grim slash. He hoped that after telling Sal about the body, the deserters had just left, in silence. He hoped that they wouldn't linger around town, that they wouldn't talk. Because if they did, he was certain that Sal would order Gabe's men to take care of them, too. And there would be more bodies to bury.

He hopped down from the back of the truck, snatched a pitchfork. He scanned the golden field, searching for what had spooked the men. Ranch workers—of any kind—were a hardy sort. Death was common enough out here. It had to be bad to convince them to flee.

Hay had been pushed by the wind into jagged rills and valleys. Gabe waded through the field, smelling the sweetness of grass and sunshine. But he could sense magic beneath the straw, moving and flowing, something foreign. Something that didn't belong here.

A raven waddled before him, poking through the fallen grasses for something to eat or something shiny to hoard. The bird stuck its head into a stand of grass, ducked back into the light. It shook out its tail feathers and looked back at Gabe with obsidian eyes.

Gale paused before the spiky structure the raven had been investigating. The raven scuttled away from it, hopping and flapping. It cawed an alarm to its fellows. The birds in the field took wing, squawking as they took to the white sky.

Gabe poked at the uneven hay with his pitchfork, gently moving the stalks aside. As if he were an archaeologist excavating a mummy, he brushed aside tendrils of grasses to reveal . . . a scarecrow. That was the closest word in his vocabulary that could describe it—a scarecrow bent by a windstorm. The suggestion of the shape of a man was twisted in the grass, rendered in pale bone that splintered and twisted like ocean coral, pocked and fused at unnatural angles. There was no skin, no flesh or meat, as if it had been picked clean. Grotesquely elongated fingers wound around ribs that melted together. Grass poked through the eye sockets and the spaces between vertebrae. It was as if someone had left the wax figure of a man in the sun for hours and pulled it apart, like taffy.

Gabe touched the brittle sculpture with his pitchfork. There was no telling how long this body had been here, but this one was well and truly dead. He thought back to a ranch hand who'd disappeared a couple of months ago. This might be him, might not. There was no way of telling.

But what Gabe was certain of was that there was something out here. Something other than the cows and the grass and Gabe's men with their raven familiars.

Something even stranger.

Petra was determined to tame her corner of Temperance with every tool at her disposal. That might not be much now, but she could build something out of chewing gum and tinfoil.

Petra dumped a paper sack of supplies on the Airstream's tiny kitchen table. The hardware store had yielded many treasures: aluminum tape, X-acto knives, a piece of PVC pipe, razor blades, and rubbing alcohol.

She'd picked a cardboard box out of the trash behind the post office and found a handful of CDs for free tax software that postal patrons had thrown away.

She had everything she needed to build a crude spectroscope.

With the X-acto knife, she cut three holes in the box: an oval hole to hold the PVC pipe at an angle for a viewing port; a round hole on the adjacent side; and a small rectangular cut opposite the small hole. She taped two razor blades over the rectangular slice, allowing only the smallest traces of light to enter. She affixed the CD on the side with the round hole, the unmarked side facing the interior of the box. It was a crude diffraction grating, but it would do. Using the aluminum tape, she affixed the PVC pipe at an angle in the oval hole, then carefully taped the box sides and seams so that no additional light could enter.

The finished project looked like a grade-schooler's sloppy rendition of a spacecraft. She drew all the blinds and peered through the pipe viewport at the fluorescent kitchen light. Light trickled through the slit and struck the back of the CD. A rainbow of colors appeared, with a couple of weak orange lines and strong green and blue ones. That was right for a mercury-vapor light: lines in the spectrum between four hundred and five hundred nanometers. The calibration was roughly what she'd expect for such a crude device. The contraption worked.

Petra found the bag containing the bloody shirt, opened it. In the darkness of the bag, the spatters still glowed. She peered through her makeshift spectroscope at the dim glow.

Her brow wrinkled. She saw some of what she expected to see: iron, green and red lines. Iron was common in blood. And some copper. But the configuration she was seeing was unknown to her. It suggested phosphorus. And something else.

The strongest lines were in the violet end of the spectrum, which would correspond to around 270 nanometers—that was right where gold would be.

Gold? Phosphorus? In blood? She frowned. Not possible. Was Gabriel suffering from heavy-metal poisoning? She discarded that thought. It was unlikely that a blood sample would show enough of a trace element to show up on a spectrogram, let alone give off its own light.

Gabriel. Who the hell was he? Or . . . what?

She sighed in frustration. This equipment was too crude for her to draw a conclusion. Perhaps she could wring some better tools from the USGS, but they might be a long time coming. They'd likely only sent her surveying equipment and sample tubes for soil, to be mailed away for analysis at a more sophisticated lab. She drummed her lower lip with her fingers. Maybe she could sneak a fragment of this to them for analysis, wait for the lab's inevitable "What the fuck?" call when they discovered she'd sent them a contaminated sample.

It sounded like the best plan she had, for now. She closed the paper bag containing the luminescent blood sample and opened the blinds. The coyote was sitting outside the trailer, waiting patiently with his tail scuffing the dust.

"Did you decide to knock, this time?" Petra asked him through the window.

The coyote looked up at her, licked his chops.

She opened the door, and the coyote sauntered in. He flopped down on the linoleum before the refrigerator, slapping his tail on the floor.

Petra obliged by feeding him part of the sandwich she'd picked up from Bear's Deli. The coyote delicately dismantled the sandwich with his nose and ate it one layer at a time. When he was done, he yawned and looked toward Petra's futon.

"I take it that you're staying, then?"

The coyote looked at her levelly.

"You need a name, in that case."

He flicked one gold and black ear.

"You seem to have an affinity for gold. How about Midas? He was a king who turned everything he touched to gold."

The coyote wrinkled his nose.

"Pyrite? Fool's Gold?"

He looked away.

"Goldie?"

He didn't deign to react.

"Sigurd? Sigurd recovered gold from the dragon Fafnir in Norse mythology."

The coyote looked back at her.

"Sig?"

The coyote licked his chops. Petra took that as a sign of assent.

"Sig, it is."

Sig chewed between his toes. He stretched, stood, and began to investigate the other bags that Petra had brought with her from town, the bags from the pawn shop.

"Hey, no chewing. Bad Sig."

Sig ignored her, as if to make the point that he wasn't a dog. Petra shooed him from the bags. He skulked away and threw himself on the futon. He curled up and stuck his nose under his fluffy tail, but watched her with open eyes.

Petra took her clothes out of the bags, folded them, and tucked them away in built-in drawers in the wall of the Airstream. As agreeable as Sig seemed, he could still chew the hell out of that nice leather coat she'd just bought.

She opened the moldering case that contained the guns. She sneezed and left them out on the kitchen counter. That case needed to be pitched; she didn't care how old it was. In the bottom of the gun case, Stan had packed the brooch that had fascinated her.

Petra turned it over in her palm. There was something that chewed at her about this piece. She stared at the shadows in the photos. She didn't have an intuitive bone in her body, but she recognized that something wasn't right about it.

Petra reached for the bottle of rubbing alcohol she'd picked up from the hardware store. She dampened the edge of some cotton with the alcohol and rubbed at the old tintypes. She was certain that an archivist or preservationist would kick her ass for attempting to clean an antique in this way, but she was too curious not to try.

She gently rubbed at the image of the woman. She was pretty, blond, and delicate-seeming. She was dressed in a high-collared dress and had light eyes that seemed to be smiling at something off frame.

Petra wiped at the surface with a piece of cotton dampened in water. The alcohol was already weakening the photo; she didn't know if the solution would destroy it, but it had given her a moment's clarity. This mourning brooch wasn't for the woman in the picture; the hair was too dark to belong to her. Had she carried this, instead? Held it for a lost lover or husband, to have some part of him close to her?

A lump rose in Petra's throat, remembering Des. His casket had been black and glossy and closed. For a while, she'd tried to convince herself that he really wasn't in there, that he'd walked away from the whole thing and was sunning himself on a beach in the Bahamas.

The alternative was too horrible to bear. Petra didn't believe in life after death. She didn't believe in anything that couldn't be sensed or quantified. And when Des had drawn his last breath, she had to believe that all trace of him had been erased from Earth. Hours after the interment, after all the cars of mourners and even the backhoe and gravediggers had left,

Petra remained before Des's tombstone. His parents had the tombstone carved, not her. It said, simply:

Desmond Ainsley
He walks with God now.
1975–2014

Petra stood before the stone, hands balled into fists that bruised the stems of the flowers in her grip. Even though she knew he wasn't there, she told him, "I'm sorry."

But it didn't matter. Because he couldn't hear her.

Petra stared at the locket. She wondered if the woman in the picture thought that her lost love could still hear her. Petra's fingers wound around her own pendant. She could understand keeping tokens of those who had disappeared—after all, she still had this necklace. All she had left of her father, a lion pendant. She used to fantasize that he might recognize her in a crowd someday by its molten glint. She hoped that she'd recognize him too, but her memory had rendered him a bit fuzzy and indistinct over time.

She forced her attention back to the mourning brooch before her. She daubed alcohol onto the other side, wiping at the tintype. A face came into view beneath the grime, one she thought she recognized. The aquiline nose, the set jaw, the dark hair. He was wearing a stiff-looking hat and coat.

It looked like Gabriel. She scrubbed at the photo with water to stop the alcohol's action. It was a dead ringer for him. Uncanny. Maybe a great-grandfather? A great-great-grandfather?

Her rational mind spun and stalled, and her vision strayed to the bag of softly fluorescing clothes on the floor. Maybe. She felt as if there was something going on here that was beyond her ability to grasp. Some puzzle that she was on the verge of unraveling.

"This is one screwed-up place, Sig." She wished the coyote could talk, answer the many questions that curdled in her brain.

Sig snorted from the bed and closed his eyes.

Petra heard the crunch of gravel outside and peered through the door window. Mike Hollander's Jeep was rolling to a stop beside the Bronco. Mike hopped out, wearing not his uniform, but street clothes: a T-shirt and jeans. He paused to appraise the Bronco, circling it.

Petra opened the door. "You gonna kick the tires?"

Mike grinned at her. "This dinosaur's your new ride?"

"Hey. That dinosaur runs."

Mike nodded something that looked like approval. "If it's run for this long, it'll run awhile more."

"I figured it would be good for winter."

Petra was conscious of a pressure at her calf. She looked down to see Sig leaning against her leg. He stared at Mike, ears pressed forward. When she opened the screen door, Sig slipped out and ran down the steps.

Mike's eyes narrowed, and he automatically reached for his sidearm. "Coyote—"

Petra's heart lurched into her mouth. "Mike, no! He's mine."

Mike paused. The coyote trotted past him, stopped, looked him up and down.

"Petra, hon, I hate to tell you, but that's not a dog. It's a coyote." He was using a slow, patronizing tone of voice that must be the one he used when telling tourists that baby bears always have pissed-off mama bears nearby.

"I know he's a coyote," she snapped. "His name is Sig."

Sig slinked away, watching Mike. He trotted over to Mike's Jeep and pissed on the tire.

"Hey!" Mike shouted, rushing toward the coyote. Sig ran away, a jaunty jerk to his tail.

"Ignore him. He's just territorial. He baptized the Bronco, too." She decided that the coyote was a better judge of people than she was.

Mike rubbed at his stubble, laughed. "I can't believe it. You have a coyote for a pet."

Petra crossed her arms. "Is there something you came by for? Other than mocking my taste in companions?"

Mike's grin faded and he stuffed his hands into his pockets. "Yeah. I heard about the trouble with the tweakers. Wanted to make sure that you were all right."

"I'm fine. But you were right about needing to have a gun out here," she admitted.

Mike frowned. "Do you want to make a police report? We can call the county sheriff. He hasn't made it out to Temperance for years, but . . ."

Petra shook her head. "No point in poking the snake." She was hoping it was a one-off, that the tweakers' holey brains would lose memory of her after a while. "But I should give you your gun back."

Mike shook his head. "If you need to keep it for a while, go ahead."

"I bought a couple of guns." She held the door open. "Come see."

Mike stepped up into the trailer. "You haven't done any decorating, yet." His eyes fell on the guns on the kitchen table. "Well, well, well. Are these your new guns?"

"Yup. From Stan's Dungeon."

Mike picked up one of them, whistled softly. "These look like the real thing. You paid some nice coin for them."

"More than I wanted. But I figured that, like the Bronco, if they lasted this long, they'd last awhile longer." She smirked.

Mike opened the barrel, spun it. "You haven't shot these yet?"

"Nope."

There was a gleam in his eye. "Want to?"

Petra grinned. Boys and their toys. "I was going to." She lifted a brick of ammunition. "You game?"

"You bet. I haven't shot anything this old since . . . since ever."

Mike gathered the guns, and Petra picked up the ammunition and a fistful of cotton balls. Mike bounded down the steps to the Jeep, rooted around.

He returned with a plastic pop bottle. "This'll do for target practice." He walked out ten yards and balanced the bottle on the top of a rock.

Petra nodded. She wadded up some of the cotton and stuffed it into her ears. She didn't have proper hearing protection, but she doubted that shooting out in the open like this would cause any permanent damage. She plucked bullets from the box of ammunition, opened the revolver, and began filling the six chambers with bullets.

"You said you'd shot before?"

"Yeah," Petra said. "Mom was a little paranoid. She kept an arsenal in the spice cabinet."

Mike loaded the other gun. His fingers brushed hers for a moment while he fished bullets from the brick. Petra unconsciously drew away. "What'd your dad have to say about that?"

Petra's mouth thinned. "Dad wasn't around. At least, not after I was a teenager." She clicked the gun closed, mindful to point it downrange.

"I'm sorry to hear that."

She shrugged, weighing how much to tell him. She sensed that she could trust him . . . up to the point where the alpha-male bull kicked in. Besides, Sig had anointed him. "He was a chemist. Mom called him 'obsessed.' He said she 'lacked vision.' They argued a lot. Eventually, he left in the middle of the night."

Petra aimed for the bottle, closing one eye and sighting in. "He sent letters for a while. He wandered all over . . . New Orleans, the Everglades, San Jacinto.

As soon as Mom got ahold of the letters, she destroyed them. She still won't talk about him."

"What did they say?"

"Nonsense, mostly. Existential musings. Ramblings about dragons and phoenixes. But my mom let me keep the medallion he sent. That, she said, was worth something."

Petra squeezed off a shot. The gun bucked upward. It had some kick. The shot went wide, vanishing into the brush.

"The last letter he wrote me was postmarked from here. From Temperance. It was a postcard of Old Faithful. All it said was: 'I think I've found it.' And then they stopped."

She pulled the trigger again. The gun bucked and the plastic bottle toppled, rolling onto the dirt. It was somehow easier to talk about this without looking someone directly in the eye.

She squeezed off another shot that sent the bottle spinning away.

"So you came back here to find him?" Mike's voice was hard to hear over the receding roar of the shots.

"It's one of the reasons." She wasn't willing to tell him the rest. The pistol hung heavy in her right hand.

Mike walked out to the bottle, set it back up again. He returned to where she stood. He aimed his gun and fired six shots in rapid succession, barely stopping to resight. In his hands, the gun didn't bob and weave. As the thunder receded, the shredded pop bottle rolled along the ground.

"Nice," she said.

"Let me show you something." Mike stepped beside her. "Fold your hands around the grips of the gun, like this." He showed her the butt of the gun.

Petra backed up her grip on the gun.

"No." He shook his head. "Let me." He set his gun down, stepped behind her. Petra could feel his breath in her ear. "Press the heels of your hands together on the back of it. That will absorb the shock of the shot." He molded her hands around the grips and stepped back. "Try that."

Petra sighted the gun, pulled the trigger. The gun didn't pop up as far in her grip as before. Instead of feeling the shock in her fingers, it was absorbed by her palms.

"Much better," she said. "Thanks."

"Anytime."

Petra and Mike finished off half a box of ammo, stopping only when the plastic pop bottle was reduced to a flattened shred of ribbon. Mike picked it up. "Looks like a jellyfish."

She grinned and looked down at the gun. It felt comfortable in her hands. Just as comfortable as when she'd drawn down on Frankie without even thinking twice. Her smile faded.

"Look, about your dad . . ."

Petra blinked. "I didn't mean to run off at the mouth like that—" But she'd known it might come out eventually, why she had really taken a USGS job in the middle of nowhere. And for the first time, she had been able to speak of her father without tears, which gave her courage.

"I could do some checking. See if there were any missing persons reports or disturbances in the park's files. What year?"

Petra swallowed. "It was 1995."

"No problem. It may take some time, but I'll see if I can dig up anything."

"Thanks. That means a lot to me."

"Sure."

An awkward silence stretched. Mike collected the gun paraphernalia while Petra stared at her toes. "So . . . I'd offer you a drink. But all I have is tap water and ice cubes."

The corner of Mike's mouth turned up. "Let's go into town. I'm the welcome wagon—we can get pizza."

Petra paused, weighing. It wasn't a date. It was, as he said, the welcome wagon. And she could use this opportunity to collect more information about the weirdness that was Temperance.

"Okay. But no more shooting."

Mike shook his head. "Where there are guns, there's always shooting."

"That sounds like a cowboyism," she muttered. But she wondered if there was some truth to it, if the very idea of walking around like a gunslinger in a B-movie invited trouble all on its own.

CHAPTER SEVEN

THE COMPOSTELA

Stroud stood in the field, hands in his pockets, staring at the Airstream trailer. Cal fidgeted beside him, kicking at pebbles on the ground. Stroud watched and waited, still as a fucking snake, until the moon had risen and the crickets sang, well after the ranger and the woman had left the trailer. Moisture condensed from the air on his skin, steaming on his breath.

"This is sacred land," Stroud said.

"Huh?" Cal paused in midkick, causing a stone to slide under his boot. He stumbled a bit, then recovered.

"This was where Lascaris's house stood."

"Lascaris? The old alchemist?"

Stroud smiled. "Yes. The older alchemist."

Cal's cheeks burned red. "The guy that was the founder of the town. I remember from school."

Stroud turned around in a loose circle, as if surveying his domain. "I've spent some time mapping where its exact foundations must lie. There are ley lines, here . . . sluggish beneath the earth. If you close your eyes, you can feel them."

Cal waited for Stroud to close his eyes, then did the same. He thought that he imagined a dim thrumming beneath the scrub brush and gravel. But that could just have been an Elixir hangover. Hard to tell. His head was fuzzy, his joints ached, and he was pretty sure that he wouldn't be able to sense an earthquake at the moment.

"I've found bits of glass here, bits of broken slate from shingles. Nothing of significance, in all these years, walking Lascaris's footsteps like a prospector. Lascaris has hidden his secrets well."

Cal imagined Stroud creeping about with a shovel, muttering to himself, searching for . . . for what? "What secrets?"

"What all alchemists seek . . . the enigma that turns base metal into gold."

"You think he could really do that?"

"I know he did. Temperance flourished with no mines and no miners. Old newspapers described how Lascaris would strike out on 'constitutionals' in the mountains, only to return with sacks of gold nuggets the size of his fists he said he'd gleaned from the streams. No one else ever found gold."

"Wow. He . . . conjured it? Like magic?"

"Some magic, some science. But his secret may have died with him, in the fire that destroyed his home. I know . . ." Stroud trailed off.

Cal stayed silent but opened his eyes, wary.

Stroud knelt to sketch some symbols in the dirt around the circle made by his footprints. Stroud always got chatty when he worked, and Carl suspected that the stringy alchemist was doing more than doodling. "I used to wonder if the townspeople had enough of his experiments, if they burned him out, like Frankenstein's monster. Or maybe it was simply a ruse, designed to allow Lascaris to fake his death and escape. But I found his journals and his old letters, read them until the ink bled into my fingertips. And I learned the truth of it . . . that the Rutherfords killed him. They killed him and seized his creations."

"His creations?" Cal echoed.

"Lascaris made sketches of many fearsome things—objects and creatures that could be the keys to transmuting base metals to gold, of creating eternal life. They're drawn as leaves on a mighty Alchemical Tree—a creation that must exist beyond paper, a thing the Rutherfords now possess.

"Then . . . what's here?"

"Some of his other secrets have to be left behind. Here, in his land."

"Why not just . . . buy the property? It sure doesn't

look like it would cost much." Cal knew Stroud had money. Lots of it. He owned the Compostela, and more cash crossed the bar counter than anywhere else in town.

"I tried. Many times. But the owner would never sell it to me."

"Why not?" Cal blurted.

"I don't know. The bastard is shielded by a legal trust and won't answer me, whoever he is. The land, by all rights, should be mine. I can trace my lineage back to Lascaris and a prostitute who had settled in the original town."

"Oh." Cal wanted to say "congratulations," but wisely zipped his lips before it escaped.

Stroud gazed at the circle and his squiggly doodles. "But if I can't have the land, I'll have Lascaris's power. If that woman tripped over a piece of the legacy that belongs to me, I'll have another piece of his knowledge. Something I can use to create a new golden era for alchemy in Temperance."

"An era? Like the sixties?"

Stroud chuckled. "No. Like times past, in Temperance's heyday. An era that would not just be wealth. If Lascaris had unraveled the secret to turning the miserable dust of this place to gold, then he might just have discovered the key to something even more precious: the elixir of eternal life. Immortality. Gold and immortality are the twin goals of the alchemist. If one is possible, so is the other."

"Not the Elixir you make?"

"The Elixir I make is a pale shadow of the true work."

Cal swallowed. Stroud radiated ambition. And bat-shit crazy. He changed the subject. "Um. So, what's the circle for?"

Stroud sat back on his heels. "It's the Seal of Solomon. For power."

"Power for what?"

"To mark this place as mine. Follow me."

Stroud rose and approached the trailer. Cal was thankful that he wasn't pissing on things to claim them, at least. No lights burned within the Airstream. As Stroud trailed his fingers along the peeling hood of the Bronco, Cal scurried in his wake.

"Are we gonna break in?"

"Not exactly. We could break the front door easily, but I'd prefer to be unnoticed."

Unnoticed would be better. Unnoticed would cause less trouble. Cal circled around the back of the trailer, glimpsing a window that was propped open. He hissed for Stroud. "There's a way in."

Stroud nodded at him, stared up at the window.

"Are we looking for something in particular?" Cal said.

Stroud's nostrils flared. "Magic. There's magic in there. Perhaps the artifact I'm looking for . . . maybe more." Stroud reached up to the windowsill to hoist himself in.

A deep growl emanated from the darkness inside the trailer. Golden eyes glowed. Cal caught a momentary whiff of fetid salami, then there was a blur of fur and flashing teeth.

Stroud gasped and let go, falling on his ass in the dirt. He hissed and stared at a gash on the top of his hand that was filling with blood. Gleaming eyes watched through the window.

Stroud's eyes narrowed. "Not what I expected."

"The guard dog?" Cal squeaked as he scrambled to pick Stroud up off the ground.

"The woman. She's like many of the seekers who've come here over the years, drawn to the remnants of Lascaris's power. An alchemist, a magic worker." Stroud's lips pulled back from his teeth.

"Like you?" Cal's brow wrinkled. The lady seemed fairly normal to him. As in . . . existing in the here and now and not high as a kite.

"Yes. Like me. It takes something to control a wild animal like that. To bend it to guard duty." Stroud turned around, back the way they'd come.

Cal followed. "What now?"

"We'll come back. And be better prepared when we do. But for now . . ." Stroud turned to the circle he'd made. Wind twisted in his hair. "For now, I leave a message that I was here."

Cal resisted the urge to roll his eyes at the Alchemist's desire to piss on his territory.

Stroud knelt, pressing his hands to the dirt. It seemed as if something dark and viscous poured from his mouth, into the grooves he'd etched into the dirt. Something shiny and curling that poured forth, moving of its own volition. It reached for Cal, licking at his shoes, like tongues of metallic fire.

Cal backed away from the darkness that Stroud vomited upon the earth. This was something terrible, something cold and sharp, beyond his understanding. Something that sucked the breath from his lungs and caused his heart to pound in unreasoning fear.

He did what he did best.

He ran.

The Compostela was Temperance's idea of fine dining.

Sort of.

Petra's eyes adjusted to the dimness. Votive candles in red glass holders glowed on scarred tables, creating shifting shadows on the dark wood paneling. Overhead, stained-glass lamps hung on chains—antiques, converted from gaslights, Petra thought. The clack of ivory on a pool table and men's laughter rang in the back. She smelled cheese and pepperoni and stale beer, and her stomach rumbled.

Mike slid into a booth that had formerly been a church pew. All the other booths and tables were full, and this one put them by the former apse, near the bar and the pool table. Mike plucked paper menus from a wire basket that held dried hot peppers and parmesan cheese in glass shakers.

Petra snagged a breadstick from a basket a gaunt waitress in black dropped off. "This is a bizarre little town, isn't it? Sort of stuck in time."

"Yeah. I'm not a native, so it probably seems even odder to me than it really is. Most of the people who live here have been here for generations."

"Where are you from?"

"Arkansas. Wanted to be a park ranger ever since I could remember. I lucked out and drew duty here about ten years ago after I got out of the Army."

"Let me guess—military police?"

"Yes, ma'am." He saluted smartly. "Yellowstone's a sweet gig, but you see some weird shit out here."

Petra leaned forward on her elbows. "Like what?"

The waitress came by to take their order and disappeared. Mike chewed thoughtfully on a breadstick. "Saw a whole camping party killed by poisonous gases from a mudpot."

Petra twisted her mouth in sympathy.

"You're a geologist. You know. Noxious gases bubbled up in muddy water, and the campers were just too close. Probably looking for somewhere warm to camp. It was warm enough near those geothermal gases. I found them after they were missing for a couple of days. It was eerie." Mike's gaze seemed to slide past her as he remembered. "The whole family . . . mom, dad, three kids . . . all in their sleeping bags like they were waiting for Christmas morning." He shook his head, as if to clear it. "That's nice dinner conversation, isn't it?"

Petra rested her chin in her hand. "Anything less gruesomely weird?"

"I saw a raven talk, once."

She remembered the raven that had accompanied Gabriel. "A raven?"

"Yeah. They're smart birds. I read a study from Europe that said they're smart enough to use tools. The ones around here will drop nuts on the roads and wait for cars to drive over them to crack them."

"What did the chatty bird say?"

"I was on winter patrol up on a ridge. It landed on a pine tree next to me. The branch was weak, and it got snow all over its wings. It shook itself off, looked me square in the eye . . . and I swear, it said: 'Fuck.' "

Petra laughed. "No shit?"

"No shit. The bird swore at me. Then it flew off." Mike spread his hands. "I asked one of the reservation elders about it. He said that I'd had a spiritual experience. I told him that I refused to believe that my spirit guide was a swearing raven."

Petra grinned. "I saw a weird raven the other day. It was with this guy, Gabriel, who works for Sal Rutherford."

Mike's gaze darkened. "Yeah, I heard about that. You'd do best to stay out of fights." He took a swig from his beer.

He'd known and hadn't mentioned it, waiting for her to go first, like it was some sort of a test. That irritated Petra. "I hate seeing innocent men get bludgeoned to death."

Mike shook his head. "Sal's men are odd. Always in the company of ravens. Maria Yellowrose's uncle says that they're cursed, but won't say why."

Petra filed that bit of info away to ask Maria about later. "I don't believe in curses."

Mike smiled and took a drink. "You'll believe in swearing ravens before you've been here six months, I promise you."

A commotion sounded from the vicinity of the pool table: a cue slapping down on the felt and balls rolling away. The noise disturbed something flapping in the rafters. Petra looked after it. A roosting dove? The flickering candlelight outlined the shadow of wings in impossibly large and abstract dark shapes overhead.

"I'm telling you, it wasn't natural."

A young man in jeans was arguing with an older man in overalls. Beer glasses and an empty pitcher surrounded the edge of the pool table.

"I think you're drunk." The older man crossed his arms over his cue.

"It was all bent and twisted, like . . . like driftwood. But it was a body."

"Sal Rutherford don't like people talking about what goes on around his property."

"I wasn't the only one who saw it."

Mike's head turned. "Excuse me," he told Petra.

He slid out of the booth, strode to the pool table. "Is there a problem here, gentlemen?" His attitude was congenial, but it seemed as if he wore some authority here. Petra knew that his jurisdiction ended at the border of the state park, but he had the attitude of a cop, whether on or off duty.

"*Nossir.*" The old man shook his head. "The boy here just drinks too much and fancies strange things."

"Do you, now?" Mike turned his attention to the younger man. "I heard you mention a body."

The young man stammered. "I don't want no trouble. The old man's right. I drink too much."

The other young men behind the pool table began to edge away, heading slowly toward the door as if someone had dropped a live, pissed-off snake on the floor. They were looking for escape, but didn't want to draw notice.

Only one person stayed in the corner. A silver ankh dangled from a goth kid's ear, shaded by a shock of dark, razor-cut hair. Petra's eyes narrowed. She knew him. He was in the car of meth heads who had chased her yesterday. And he was way too young to be drinking. The kid scrunched forward on his stool, eyes wide and intently absorbing the conversation. His gaze crossed Petra's, and he glanced away. But he remained, long fingers wrapped around the neck of a beer bottle, watching the scene play out.

"I'm not looking for trouble. I just want to know what you saw. Sounds like it was something bad." Mike kept his voice low and friendly.

"I—" The young man shook his head, then looked past Mike's shoulder. His eyes widened in fear. "I didn't see nothin'."

Petra turned. Four men had walked into the bar. They strode in noiselessly, and that silence followed them as they approached the pool table. They smelled of fresh-turned earth. Petra didn't recognize three of them. But she recognized Gabriel.

Gabriel flicked a glance at Petra. His face was smooth and unmarked . . . not the look of a man who'd had it bashed in with a fence post only a day ago. A raven fluttered down from the rafters to settle on his shoulder.

He tipped his hat at her. "Ma'am." Gabriel turned away to look at the young man. "We heard Jeff had too much to drink. We're here to take him home." His voice was the same rough whisper that she'd heard yesterday.

Mike's eyes narrowed, and Petra saw his fingers twitch toward his sidearm. "Jeff seems pretty sober to me."

Petra watched Jeff's Adam's apple bob as he swallowed. "I, uh, have had a couple of beers . . ."

Gabriel nodded. "And we don't want the boy driving and endangering himself or others. Right, Jeff?"

Mike kept his body between Jeff and Gabriel. "No need to worry. I can take him home."

Gabriel inclined his head, like a bird looking at something shiny. His face was an otherwise impassive mask. "Jeff?"

Jeff edged out from behind Mike and slipped into the knot of men, head bowed. Gabriel turned and followed the men out of the bar, but he glanced back at Petra. Even in the darkness, he looked whole, and that was impossible. Then he turned and walked out, Mike and Petra following a little ways behind.

"Is that the guy Frankie beat up?" Mike asked. He thought like a cop, Petra observed, searching for a flaw in the story.

"Yeah."

"Frankie must be losing his touch."

Gabriel hopped behind the wheel of a pickup truck parked at the curb, and another one of Sal's men rode shotgun. She watched as the remaining two men piled into the back of the truck, Jeff between them. As the pickup started, Petra thought she saw Jeff flinch.

"Will Jeff be all right?" she whispered to Mike.

Mike's hands were clenched into fists. "I hope so. I hope to God that he was just drunk and talking out his ass. Because if he wasn't . . ." One hand reached for his sidearm.

The goth kid had shambled out of the bar, his hands stuffed in his hoodie. He stared at the truck, horror writ on his face as he whispered, "He isn't coming back from there. Not ever."

That was enough. Petra stepped in front of the truck, heart hammering. She couldn't allow anyone to disappear. Not like her father. The headlights blinded her.

"Let him go," she said, but was certain that her voice couldn't be heard over the engine.

The driver's side door opened, and Gabriel stepped out. He turned the lights off. In her dazzled periphery, Petra could see that Mike had drawn down on the men in the back of the pickup truck. Mike and Jeff were having an argument.

Gabriel looked nonplussed. "Get out of the way."

Petra lifted her chin. "What are you going to do with him?"

"We're taking him home."

"I don't believe that."

"I don't really care what you believe." It was said without rancor, only a statement of fact. He stood before her, less than two feet away. His eyes were dilated full and black like the new moon.

"Let him go."

"This isn't up for discussion."

"What *is* up for discussion?" Petra pulled hair out of her mouth that had worked free of her ponytail. "I've got some questions for you. Questions about how you seem very hale and hearty after nearly being beaten to death. Questions about your blood—"

Gabriel's eyes narrowed, and he cut her off. "I'll make a trade. Life for a life. You saved mine. I'll save his."

Petra nodded. That had worked better than expected. He wasn't totally without honor. "Okay."

"But, no more questions." He reached out, laid his finger across her lips. His skin was cold as frost, and she stifled a shudder.

"I can't promise that." She said it honestly. "I'm a scientist. That's what I do."

Gabriel's hand dropped, and he seemed to consider. A crowd was gathering behind the windows of the bar.

"Then save them for later," he demanded curtly.

She nodded, swallowing. She had enough sense not to ask when or where.

Gabriel gestured to the men in the back of the truck. They brought Jeff to him, frog-marching him as he squirmed. Mike was yelling at them to let him go, but the ranch hands ignored him. It seemed that they didn't much care that Mike was armed. As far as they were concerned, it seemed he could have been threatening them with a water pistol.

Petra grabbed Mike's gun arm. "Wait."

Gabriel leaned very close to Jeff, speaking low enough in his sepulchral voice that Petra and Mike could hear, but the gawkers could not. "Start walking. Walk out of this town. Walk until you can't walk any more, and then keep walking."

Jeff nodded, wide-eyed. He took off at a brisk pace down the road, glancing back at them fearfully as he went.

Gabriel and the other men piled back into the pickup, cranked the engine, and drove off in the opposite direction. Petra noticed that Gabriel had forgotten to turn his lights on, and she wondered how the hell he could see in the dark.

CHAPTER EIGHT

MERCURY

The remainder of dinner was a little tense.

"That was monumentally stupid," Mike told her.

Petra bristled. "Hey, that wasn't—"

"But I like your style."

Petra gave him a dirty look.

"Seriously, though . . ." His gaze darkened. "Stay away from those guys. They're bigger trouble than the meth heads."

Petra glanced around. After the scene on the street, the goth kid had disappeared. He seemed to be able to find as much trouble as Petra did, and she wanted to ask him about it.

"What's the deal with those guys? Why doesn't anyone challenge them? Well, except Frankie. Frankie wants to cave Gabriel's head in." And his caved-in head seemed to heal awfully damn fast.

Mike stared down at the tablecloth. "They're Sal Rutherford's men. Sal owns the largest ranch around here, it's been in his family for generations. Those men are his goon squad. They pretty much enforce his will, without question."

"What do the cops have to say about it?"

"The sheriff's deputies around here are pretty damn useless. The sheriff is Sal's cousin. They let Sal run the county as he wants. For all intents and purposes, Sal's men *are* the cops. Which is why you should leave them alone."

"I'm not specifically going out and looking for trouble. I feel like I should point that out."

"Yeah, well, it seems to find you. You should consider moving to the lodge at the Park."

Petra shook her head. "No."

Mike blew out his breath in exasperation. "At least there's law enforcement in the park. Anything that happens there is a federal crime."

"Even if this is the Wild West, I can take care of myself," Petra said.

"Keep those pistols close. You'd be surprised at how wild it can really get."

They played rock-paper-scissors for the tab. Mike

won, but she snatched the bill from the waitress before he could draw his wallet. Mike threw up his hands in mock surrender while she paid, then led her outside and struck off to find his Jeep and pull it around. Petra stood in the buzzing halo of a gaslight, swatting at mosquitoes while she waited for him to return.

"The bugs attack harder when you struggle."

Petra turned, seeing the goth kid leaning up against the wall, smoking a cigarette. "Oh, yeah?"

"Yeah. The mosquitoes sense the carbon dioxide. If you keep still, they ignore you more." He blew menthol smoke into the dark. "Or, you could just take up smoking."

"Nah. I like my lungs."

The goth kid shrugged. "I never seen anybody stand up to Sal's men like that." Shy admiration lit in his voice.

Petra extended her hand. "I'm Petra. I'm new."

"I'm Cal. I'm not." He shook her hand, ducked his head. "Look, about yesterday, I'm sorry about that. Justin can be a total asshat. It's best to steer clear of him."

"Yeah. I gathered that." Petra tried not to look at the purple bruise on Cal's face. Cal turned away into shadow, self-conscious.

Petra let it drop, gestured with her chin back to the bar. "You believe that guy's story? About the body on the ranch?"

Cal's lips thinned. With the black makeup he wore, it made it seem as though his mouth were drawn on unevenly by a Sharpie marker. "Yeah. I believe him. And I think some friends of mine may have gone missing out near Rutherford's place."

"Have you called the cops?"

Cal shook his head and ground out the ember of his cigarette butt out in the gravel. "Cops aren't real fond of taking tips from people like me." The corner of his cartoon mouth quirked up. Petra decided that he was different from the other meth heads. Maybe a guppy in a tank of piranhas, pretending to be a piranha with drawn-on teeth.

Petra stared up at the stars. "Seems like people go missing here a lot."

Cal paused in tapping out another cigarette. "Yeah." He watched her through thickly lashed eyes. "You missing someone?"

"My dad. Twenty years ago. He came here, but never left. At least, that's as much as I can determine." She bit her lip. She knew that if she was ever to uncover any information about her father, she'd have to begin asking for help. Asking everyone.

Cal kicked the gravel. "My dad was never around, either."

Cal glanced up from beneath a fringe of bangs to look at a dog-eared photograph she dug out of her wallet and showed him. The photo captured her father in happier times—sitting on the bumper of his prize T-Bird, arms folded, wearing a dress shirt and necktie. His brown eyes were crinkled in humor, his dark, thinning hair gleaming in the flash.

"I'll ask around about your dad, see if anybody remembers him."

"Thanks, Cal. I mean it." Petra's heart warmed toward the boy. "His name was Joseph. Joseph Dee. He'd be about sixty-five now."

Cal ducked his head. "Just let me know if you hear any more about any bodies being found on the Rutherford property. Two kids, about my age. Adam has blond hair, and Diana has a tattoo of a blue dragon on her arm. They're inseparable."

"I will," she said sincerely. "But with everything I'm hearing about Rutherford's ranch, why would anyone go there?"

Cal fiddled with his cigarette nervously. "The Alchemist sent 'em. The Alchemist doesn't like Sal." His eyes were large and dilated, but with worry, not drugs.

"Who's the Alchemist?" Petra's eyebrow quirked up.

"He's . . . Stroud is . . ." Cal seemed to struggle to find the right label. " . . . like my boss."

Stroud. She'd heard that name at the pawn shop. That was the guy that Stan had called about her compass. Fuck. She decided to be bold. "Stroud. So he cooks the meth?"

Headlights washed over the sidewalk, and Cal retreated into the shadows. "I talk too much."

Mike bounded down to open Petra's door. He followed her gaze into the darkness. "Something wrong?"

"Nah. Nothing." She wondered where the poor kid slept, if he had anyone to look out for him. Not this man he called "the Alchemist."

"Is there any way of looking for that body that Jeff mentioned?"

Mike shook his head. "On Sal's land? Probably not. Remember, the sheriff's department is basically Sal's family. If deputies came out there, they would only find a scarecrow, if they found anything at all."

"Sounds like a nice little political fiefdom he's got set up."

He changed the subject then, to the safe topic of park security, perhaps hoping to lure her to the lodge. Petra listened politely, but made no commitment.

Mike drove her home and watched carefully to make sure she'd gotten inside. She waved at him through the door before he took off.

Petra watched his taillights recede into the night. She was convinced that Mike meant well, but she chafed at the notion that she was a little girl who needed looking after. She hadn't had a father since she was a teenager. She didn't need one now.

Sig was home. He was pacing up and down on the ugly patterned linoleum, toenails clicking.

"Do you have to pee?" Petra eyed the open window. She assumed that he could get out the same way he'd let himself in. But maybe he wanted to play civilized and insist on her opening the door for him.

She opened the door, made shooing gestures.

Sig sat down on his rump.

Petra shut the door and locked it. She filled a bowl with water and left it on the floor for him. He slurped greedily from it and continued to pace.

Whatever his problem was, Sig was keyed up. Petra brushed her teeth, washed her face, and crawled into bed. She felt antsy, too. She briefly considered breaking out Maria's dreamcatcher and taking a long drink. She didn't look forward to troubling dreams, but she expected sleep would be long in coming otherwise.

She fussed with the blankets, reached up to turn out the light . . .

. . . and saw a stain on the aluminum window ledge above her bed.

Petra squinted at it. It looked like blood. Not Gabriel's phosphorescent blood, but plain red blood. It smeared down the edge of the glass. She leaned out the window, saw no one.

But there was a smudged bloody handprint on the outside of the Airstream's metallic skin.

Petra lurched back into the trailer and slammed the window shut. Sig whimpered, hopped up to the bed, and put his paws on the sill.

Petra turned off the lights. She let her eyes adjust so that she could see into the darkness without being seen.

"Was there something . . . someone out there, Sig?"

Sig hopped down from the bed and continued to pace. Petra understood. He was on patrol, thinking that there was something out there, in the complete and inky blackness of Temperance.

"Good boy," she said.

Uneasily, she pulled the blanket up to her chin. Maybe Mike had been right. Maybe she'd sleep better at the lodge. But for tonight, she'd best get used to the idea of trying to sleep with the metronomic sound of Sig's toenails clicking on the floor.

"**W**ell. That's interesting."

Petra peered out of the Airstream the next morning at the burned-out hole at the edge of the property. It looked like a black stain on the earth. She turned quickly inside to stuff all her valuables in her jacket pockets and stash her tools, guns, and ammo in the back of the Bronco. If someone was trying to get into the Airstream, she wasn't going to leave anything behind in it of more value than the homemade spectrometer. Let the meth heads try to smoke some crystal out of *that* contraption.

Sig trotted out of the Airstream, and she locked the door behind her. He yawned, stretched, and headed toward the sagebrush, where smoke rose in a faint tendril. Petra assumed that he had a den somewhere around here, and that he'd be napping for much of the day. But he paused in the brush, sniffing around the edge.

Petra followed him. The scrub grasses had burned away, and it looked as if there was something silvery embedded in odd squiggles in the ground. This wasn't a meteor crater. This was something man-made. And intricately so. Maybe something occultish. Scratches and shapes curved around in a circle, though she had no idea what they meant.

She picked up a stick and poked at the edge of the symbol, expecting the glint of metal she saw to be some kind of forgotten steel tool or litter.

But it wasn't. It moved and wriggled away from the stick, like living water.

Petra picked up the stick and squinted at a droplet on it. "Mercury."

Mercury was poison. And removing it was gonna be a bitch. She wondered if she should contact the property owner or a bomb squad for hazmat removal. She didn't have a phone number for her landlord, just a P.O. box. She fished her cell phone out of her pocket and took a picture of the scene. She hesitated about calling Mike. She knew he'd be down here in an instant, cordoning it off, clucking over it like a good cop. But this wasn't parkland, it wasn't his jurisdiction, and Petra had no desire to be his damsel in distress.

She prodded at the mercury again with the stick. It rolled away, seeming to squirm into the ground.

"Weird," she grumbled, trying to figure out if there was some gap in the ground it was seeking, and hoping it wasn't going to find its way into the water table as it drained away.

Sig walked to the edge of the circle, lifted his leg, and pissed on it.

"Thank you, Sig."

He wagged his tail.

She walked to the Bronco, Sig at her heels. He clambered into the Bronco after her, sitting in the front seat like he owned it.

"Is that how these things work? You pee on them, and then they're yours?"

Sig looked patiently out the window, as if that was a monumentally stupid question and he was expecting her to hurry up and drive.

Petra cranked the Bronco's ignition. She half expected the sound of the engine to scare the coyote away, but Sig hung his head out the passenger window as she began to drive slowly down the gravel road. Maybe he had some domestic dog in him, some ancestral memory of letting his ears flap in an automotive-generated breeze. He seemed happy as the scenery flashed past, his eyes half-closed, the breeze skimming through his fur.

Petra consulted a map Maria had left for her in the glove box. The county sheriff's office was about thirty miles west.

She could report this thing with the burned mercury on her property. And maybe someone there would also know something about her missing father.

She'd see if they were as useless as Mike suggested.

The drive took her east, on two-lane roads sparsely traveled by traffic. The dusty ribbon of road stretched into the glare of morning. Bugs hung over from the night splattered on the windshield, smeared around by the old windshield wipers to become iridescent tracks.

The county seat was in a larger town with a railroad passing through it. Petra wound her way through a ridiculous warren of one-way streets until she found the county jail. It was a small, nondescript two-story building of 1960s vintage, surrounded by a chain-link fence with patrol cars parked behind it. The patrol cars were shiny and clean, as if they were rarely driven. Petra parked the Bronco on the street at a parking meter. She left the windows halfway open for Sig and climbed the steps to an entrance marked LOBBY.

The lobby was little more than a hallway with vending machines and a few plastic chairs. The place smelled like stale coffee. Along the walls hung portraits of the previous county sheriffs. All of them, including the current one, had the last name "Rutherford." Below her, where Petra imagined the jail cells were, the sounds of shouting emanated. Petra approached a window covered with clear Plexiglas and rang a grimy plastic button for service.

A dispatcher came to the window. "Yes?"

"Hi. I was hoping that you could help me. I had someone trespass on the property I'm renting last night. And they burned something close to my trailer." Petra showed the dispatcher the photo on her phone.

The dispatcher squinted at it. "Looks like a fire pit."

"I guess. But there's mercury in it."

The dispatcher blinked. "Mercury?"

"Yeah. It's hazardous material, poisonous. I, uh, dunno if the bomb squad handles that or . . ." Petra trailed off.

The dispatcher just stared. "Well, I guess you could rinse it off with a garden hose or something."

"Um, that would be bad. Is there . . . like a local EPA office or something?"

The dispatcher popped her gum and pulled a phone book from under the counter. "It's about two hours away. Here's their number." She turned the phone book around and pointed to it.

Petra recorded the number in her phone. "Uh, thanks. Is there a report or something I can file on this?"

"Yeah." The dispatcher gave her a form to fill out. Petra filled it out as completely as she could, categorizing the offense as "vandalism" and "hazardous material spill." She was pretty sure that the cops should be filling this part out, and there were several sections that she left blank.

"Okay," the dispatcher said, taking the form. "We'll send somebody out to take a look. They'll call you."

Petra nodded, but stayed standing at the counter.

The dispatcher chewed her gum slowly. It was pink and smelled like peppermint. "Is there something else you needed?"

"I'm trying to find a missing person."

"Wow. You sure have a lot of stuff going on. Do you want to file a missing persons report?" She cracked her gum.

"Well, the person I'm looking for went missing in 1995. Joseph Dee. This was the last place I heard from him." Petra fished her photo of her father from her wallet and slid it under the window.

The dispatcher didn't touch the photo. "Did you file a missing persons report in 1995?"

"I didn't. But maybe someone else did? If he had friends here?"

The dispatcher rolled her eyes. "Just a minute." She turned around and yelled to the office behind her. "Hey, are one of you guys free for a public records request?"

A deputy in a black uniform lumbered to the desk, holding his coffee. "How can I help you, ma'am?"

"I'm looking for my father. He disappeared in Temperance in 1995. I'm hoping that you can help me find him."

The deputy took a deep swig of his coffee, stared at the photo. "Ma'am, do you have a date of disappearance?"

"Not exactly. But I think it was in June."

"Do you have a last known address?"

"No. I was hoping that you could search your records, see if there were any bodies found around that time that match his description."

The deputy frowned. "Ma'am, records retention law only requires us to keep paper records back five years. Anything that old has likely been destroyed or sent to long-term storage off-site."

Petra's heart fell. It sure didn't sound like he was offering to look. "Do you keep anything on microfiche, or electronic records?"

The deputy stared over his coffee at her. "Do you want to file a missing persons report? That's about all we can do for you."

"Yeah. Yeah, I do." Petra was certain that it wouldn't do any good, but was determined to cause them an iota of extra work. Even if it meant them opening a file cabinet or feeding the paper to the shredder.

"Let me get you the form."

Petra spent fifteen minutes filling out the form on a clipboard in the lobby. In that time, two people who asked for records checks for apartment rental applications were arrested on outstanding warrants and taken downstairs to the jail. One of them had a child with her, who was promptly handed off to the dispatcher. The dispatcher dragged a box of toys out from under a table and began trying to calm the crying child with a teddy bear while she juggled the phone to call children's services.

Mike was right; there were no answers to be found here. She'd have to try elsewhere.

Petra slid the form under the window and walked out, punching the number for the local EPA office into her cell phone. At least they'd know what to do about the mercury. The call rang through to voice mail, and she got about thirty seconds of a message recorded before getting cut off.

CHAPTER NINE

FLIGHT

Sal Rutherford was not happy with Gabe.

In Sal's world, "not happy" often translated to petty brutality or reckless stupidity. Some days were better than others, but Sal was particularly pissed today.

"I told you to take care of that problem with the contract hand. You didn't."

"I sent him away." Gabe threw a bale of hay to the floor of the barn loft. Dust puffed up in a cloud that caused Sal to cough and wipe his nose on his sleeve. The watering whites of his eyes were nearly as yellow as the dust.

"I wanted him buried. Gone. Not running his yap to anyone who would listen about there being bodies on the property."

"You wanted me to kill him and leave another body lying around to be found?"

"I expect you to be discreet about where you bury bodies."

When Sal got angry, there was no reasoning with him, no half measures or calculated plans. Everything was black or white, dead or alive. And the boss man felt better when things were dead, especially things with mouths.

Gabe reached for another bale. "It's done."

"No, it ain't. I wanted a body buried." Sal started toward him, but tripped on a floorboard. He stumbled, swearing, face reddening.

"Careful, boss." Gabe lifted the bale to stack it on top of the others.

Sal reached down, tearing the offending half-rotted board up from the floor with a splintering sound. He swung it at Gabe. The plank slammed into Gabe's back in a bright arc of pain. He fell to the floor, gasping.

"Smart-ass sumbitch," Sal huffed. "You ain't gonna forget who's in charge of you."

The board cracked into Gabe's shoulder, his face, his ribs. When his lung collapsed, it brought a gasp of blood to his lips. A trickle of blood bubbled in the back of his throat with a roar in his ears that drowned out the sounds of Sal's swearing and the thudding of the board against his flesh and bones.

The pain was one of the clearest sensations Gabe could remember in a long time. The years had dimmed a great deal of feeling, for him and for all of his men. Many were little more than automatons, now. They slipped through their days in silence, each day the same as the last and the same as tomorrow. There were different masters, over time—the Rutherfords had both kind and cruel descendants. All had labored under the illusion of control, the belief that the Hanged Men were simply part of their inherited furniture.

Sal was the worst so far. Generations of wealth and entitlement had trickled down into a spoiled child that Gabe had been wary of since he'd been old enough to crawl. As a kid, Sal had been known to try to skin snakes alive and set fire to the tails of squirrels. His enthusiasm for cruelty had not waned over time.

Gabe rolled in the straw, thrusting his hand beneath the hay. From under his sleeve, a mass of black feathers rocketed away from his flesh and landed behind the bales. He hoped Sal took that as a flinch, a reflexive urge to protect his head from the assault, and that he had not seen that little bit of mass split away and flutter into the shadows.

Sal stepped back, mopping his brow. This was more exercise than the rancher had seen in months. Gabe idly wished for a heart attack. But he had no idea who the property would fall to if Sal died, and what would be worse—Sal, or an invisible developer who would bulldoze the Lunaria to build vacation condominiums?

Gabe glanced up at the ceiling. A raven paced silently on a beam, watching. He let go, releasing the lion's share of his conscious mind into the bird. He often partitioned his awareness among these black fragments of himself, allowing him to see and be in many places at once—even returning to the Lunaria to help him regenerate. But with concentration, he could force nearly all of his consciousness into one tiny, light vessel.

Now he perched on the beam, watching Sal advance on his own body. He wasn't sure what Sal thought had happened—if he thought that Gabe had passed out, died, or was simply ignoring him. Either way, it didn't seem to matter.

Sal kicked Gabe's body over the edge of the hayloft and it fell as limply as a dishrag off the edge of a sink, down twenty feet to the wooden floor of the barn. It lay motionless, a dribble of blood sliding from the body's lips to the floor. Shadows scuttled into the dark corners of the barn, shrugging out of Gabe's boots and from under the collar of his shirt—bits of his memory and limbs splintering away for survival.

Gabe rustled his feathers and flew, sailing out the window in his fragile new body and into the outdoors. The air whistled through his feathers, pulling him on an air current away from the barn.

For now, he was free.

He hoped that he'd have a body to return to when he got back.

"Hey, thanks for seeing me."

Petra stood awkwardly on Maria Yellowrose's doorstep with Pearl winding around her ankles. Maria opened the screen door.

"It's good to see you. C'mon in. You're just in time for lunch."

A yip sounded from the Bronco, and Petra rolled her eyes. Sig pressed his snout through the half-opened window. His tongue lolled over the edge of the glass, and he made as if he was suffocating. Pearl padded over to the truck to watch the spectacle.

"You got a pet?"

"Heh. I think he found me. He's not exactly tame."

Pearl jumped from the ground to the roof of the Bronco. She slapped her paws on the windshield, teasing Sig.

"Did you feed him?"

"Yes."

"Then he's yours. You can let him out."

"Um. Will Pearl mind?"

"Pearl can take care of herself. Trust me."

Pearl was spread-eagled against the windshield, glowering at the coyote. Sig's wet nose pressed against her belly through the glass.

"I don't know if I can trust him."

"If you're feeding him, he won't wander far. And I'm pretty sure you don't want him pissing on your upholstery."

While Sig was still focused on the windshield, Petra reluctantly opened the passenger door. Pearl reached down and slapped at Sig's tail; he reeled and yipped at her.

"Sig!"

Sig bounded out. He weaved through Petra's legs and trotted up to Maria's house, where Maria was dangling a tantalizing piece of chicken before him. He delicately took it from her hand like a gentleman.

"Where did he come from?" Maria reached out to rub his ears, and he made awful faces of delight.

"He just appeared," Petra said helplessly. "And took over."

Maria cracked a smile. "Frankie would say that you've met your spirit guide. Coyote is a trickster. A powerful friend."

"I don't believe in spirit guides," Petra blurted.

"Yeah, well, you may not believe in spirit guides, but all that's important is that the animal does. That's what Frankie says, anyway."

Sig snorted and trotted into the house like he owned the place.

Pearl glowered at Petra from the Bronco.

"I tried," Petra said.

The cat jumped down and stiffly followed the coyote into the cottage, tail twitching.

Maria's house smelled like vegetable soup and fresh-baked bread. Maria ducked into the kitchen and pulled some bread out of the oven. She was wearing jeans and a halter top, her hair braided tightly around her ears.

Petra self-consciously fingered her own out-of-control hair. She'd never figured out how to do that properly. Whenever she tried, she always wound up with a lop-sided, stringy rope.

Petra sat down awkwardly at the kitchen table, nervously winding her feet around the chair rungs. Pearl followed her, perching on a chair opposite with just her green eyes and grey ears peeping over the top of the table. Sig busied himself with licking random spots on Maria's kitchen floor.

"Thanks for lunch."

"Anytime." Maria brought Petra a bowl of delicious-smelling soup and a slice of piping-hot bread, then scooted Pearl out of her chair and set her own bowl down.

"What's on your mind?"

"I'm trying to figure out how things work around here, and . . . it's not going so well." Petra shredded her bread with her fingers.

Maria chased a carrot with her spoon. "Hon, it's the Wild West. It's not like anyplace else."

"So I'm gathering. I went to the sheriff's department this morning."

"Oh yeah?" Maria's brows creased.

"I'm trying to find information about my father. He vanished in Temperance in 1995. I thought that was the logical place to start looking." The soup was hot and delicious on Petra's tongue. "And I also got a gift from a trespasser last night." She showed Maria the photo of the burned-out circle on her cell phone.

"That's weird."

"And full of mercury."

"Even weirder. The cops weren't impressed?"

"No."

Maria grinned. "You got bupkus, didn't you?"

"It was a total waste of time, effort, and gas. So I made a bunch of these up at Bear's deli." Petra reached into her pocket and pulled out a creased flyer that included a grainy copy of her dad's picture. She'd scribbled below it in capital letters with a Sharpie marker:

HAVE YOU SEEN THIS MAN?
JOSEPH DEE—MISSING SINCE 1995
ANY INFORMATION, CALL 555-555-7419

Maria smoothed it out on the table. "I don't know him. But if you've got more of these, I'd be happy to put them up at the family center and around the reservation."

"Thanks. I appreciate it. I've already papered most of Temperance—the post office, Bear's deli, and the back wall of the ladies' room in the Compostela." She hadn't yet worked up the nerve to duck into the men's room, but maybe she could put Mike up to it.

"Maybe somebody knows something."

"Hopefully, more than the cops."

"Yeah. They aren't really the law around here. Sal Rutherford is."

"So I hear. But why is that?"

Maria soaked up some of her vegetable soup with

the bread. Her fingernails were painted with a warm coral polish. Petra stared down at her own short, rough nails.

"The Rutherfords run things. Always have, at least since the time the town founder disappeared," Maria said.

"The alchemist?"

"Yeah. Lascaris. Lascaris was involved in some creepy shit. And not just creating gold and chasing down the secret to living forever."

"What, then?" Petra leaned forward.

"Monsters." Maria fixed her with a deadpan look. "People have seen all kinds of stuff out here— phoenixes, ghosts, banshees."

"You sound like Frankie," said Petra.

"Frankie isn't always wrong. Even a stopped clock is right twice a day."

The screen door squeaked open.

"Speak of the devil," Maria muttered.

Frankie stumbled inside and flung himself into a chair at the table. "I smelled something good," he slurred.

Maria rolled her eyes, but she stood to ladle out some vegetable soup.

Frankie stared at Petra, rocking on the back legs of his chair.

"Hi, Frankie."

He didn't greet her, just kept rocking. Petra stared into her bowl.

Pearl climbed up on the table and swatted Petra's

cell phone with her paws. Maria removed the cat from the table with an exasperated grunt. "Show the symbol to Frankie. It might shake something out of his meta-physically pickled head."

Petra punched the button to show Frankie the picture, and he took the phone from her and stared at it. "You got a visit from an alchemist, did you?"

Petra's gaze flicked up at him. "What do you mean?"

He turned his mouth up and down, as if working around heavy words. "That's one of their symbols. Somebody wanted you to know he was there." He put the phone down, and a white paw reached up from the edge of the table for it. Petra tucked the phone safely in her pocket.

"Great." Seen enemies, unseen enemies—what did it matter? Petra turned her attention back to her soup.

"Did you find your daddy, yet?"

Petra looked up at him, nearly dropped her spoon. "What?"

"Your daddy's been looking for you." Frankie stared up at the ceiling, began to hum.

Petra slid out from behind the table, knelt before Frankie. "Where is he, Frankie?"

Frankie looked at her with glazed eyes. "In the white space of heaven."

"Frankie," Maria barked.

Petra swallowed. "You don't think he's alive."

"He's here." Frankie's eyes glistened, and his lined hands framed his face. "Alive. In the serenity of his own head. Suspended. But his spirit is elsewhere."

"Jesus, Frankie," Maria said.

Frankie raised his hands as if in surrender, then got up from the table to go outside. The screen door slammed behind him, and Petra watched him slump into the porch swing, head lolling to one side.

Maria shook her head, and her cheeks flamed. "I'm so sorry. He's just—"

"He's family. It's all right." Petra stared after him. "Do you think . . . do you think he's right?"

Maria bit her lip. "I don't know."

Petra kept her mouth shut. She couldn't believe in anything she couldn't see, touch, and measure. But she was seeing, touching, and measuring some very weird shit.

She helped Maria wash the dishes. Pearl supervised Sig licking the floor and the dishwashing from her perch on top of the refrigerator. Sig eventually tired of cleaning the floor and nosed the screen door open to go out. Maria told her about the best grocery store to go to and which mechanics to avoid. She told her about the chuckwagon lunches on weekends set up at the foot of the mountains and when the farmer's market was on the reservation. This felt normal, and Petra began to feel more grounded. The soap on the dishes and the dishrag in her hand felt real. Ordinary. Comforting.

"And, if you haven't noticed, there are a lot more men than women in town, if you're looking to date men," Maria said. "There are also some available women, too."

"I like men," Petra said. "But I don't want to date."

"Understood." Maria seemed to make a conscious effort not to look at the scar on Petra's arm, exposed by her rolled-up sleeves. "There's a whole lot of macho posturing that seems to happen around here. All the men think they're cowboys."

"I'm getting that feeling." Petra groaned. "Mike Hollander has been hanging around. I think he can't decide if I'm a damsel in distress or not."

Maria chortled. "Mike and I used to date."

"Oh. Erf. Is this awkward?"

"Not at all. Mike is a nice guy. He's just a bit too much for me in that whole caretaking role. He really wants to settle down and have a bunch of kids and take them all to Boy Scout camp. You can trust him, though, if you decided to go out with him."

"Eh. I'm not really in the market for the white picket fence right now."

"Just be clear when you friendzone him. He'll take it fine."

"I would like for Mike to be in the friendzone." Petra scrubbed at a bowl vigorously. "How did you guys wind up . . . uh . . . not together?"

"A lot of it was his wanting to ride in on the white horse and rescue me from dealing with crazies in my line of work. Wanting me to move off the reservation and to someplace he thought was safer. And he really didn't get the whole woo-woo thing."

"With Frankie?"

"And me, I guess. I think that I'm fairly spiritual, in

my own way. But Mike is definitely a guy who believes only what he sees. He loves nature, and so do I. But he doesn't feel that there's any kind of spiritual force behind that. He thinks that, when he dies, that's the end, and he's gonna be worm food."

"I could see where that might be an issue."

Maria shrugged, slinging the dish towel over her shoulder. "He's a good guy. Sort of uptight. He can't leave it at work, and I hate being told what to do."

Petra grinned. "I get that."

"Which isn't to say that I would object to you guys dating . . ."

"Friendzone, definitely."

Maria laughed. "Make no promises. See how it works out. Like I said, he's not a bad guy."

They finished the kitchen cleanup, and Petra went out to the porch. Frankie was still slumped in the porch swing, his hat covering his face. Sig was sitting in his lap, also asleep.

Petra gingerly sat beside them, trying to figure out a way to ease the coyote from the old man's arms without waking him.

"That's a fine friend you've found."

Petra blinked. Frankie was awake. His hat moved as he talked.

"I think he'll be a good friend, too."

Frankie pushed his hat back and stroked Sig's ears. Petra noticed that his wrinkly fingers were very long and tapered, the nails oval. "He's very loyal. He won't lead you wrong."

"Lead me where?"

"Anywhere. This world, the spirit world. Have you ever gone on a spirit journey?"

"Ah, no. I have my hands full with this world."

Frankie reached into his shirt for a pipe, tapping some tobacco into it and lighting it. The smoke smelled like sweetgrass, and reminded Petra of her father, for a moment. Frankie shook his head, smiling.

"What's so funny?"

"The spirit world has much to teach you." Frankie shifted Sig from his lap and stood, cracking the bones in his spine as he stretched. "Come for a walk with me. I want to show you something." Frankie ambled down the steps and away from the house.

Petra hesitated. She had, after all, seen Frankie go off and nearly beat a guy to death on the street. But Sig sleepily waddled after Frankie, so Petra did the same. She caught up with him, puffing away, in a field of gold grass and tiny limestone pebbles that shifted underfoot. Sig zipped ahead, just his tail visible over the tassels of the grass. The sun felt warm on her face, and the smell of Frankie's smoke floated over her. She felt peaceful. If she was honest with herself, this was probably the first time she had since she'd come to Temperance.

Frankie followed a worn path out of the grass to a clearing, then sat down on a sandstone slab worn concave by what had to be centuries of asses sitting on it. The slab was the size of a toppled refrigerator, one of six ranged in an oval.

"Oh, wow," she said.

Inside the rough-hewn benches, water gathered in a swallet about the size of a small swimming pool, ringed by a bank of flat stones. The water moved and seethed, likely fed by an underground spring. It was a brilliant blue, more powerfully blue than the sky. Sig paced along the edge and stared at his reflection.

"This is beautiful," Petra said. She knelt at the edge of the water, bracing her hands on the stone. The one she perched on was the size of a doorstep, the sandstone grains hot to the touch.

"It's an old spring. Been here for centuries."

Petra could imagine it—the rocks worn smooth from centuries of gossip and laundry. She scooped her hand in the water. It felt soft and warm, a little cloudy. Sig splashed in and dog-paddled around the edge.

"It's a sacred place. The locals call it a name that means 'The Eye of the Spirit.' "

"I can see why." The outline of the pool was vaguely eye-shaped.

Frankie scooped his hands in the water and took a drink. "It's considered a sign of respect to drink from the spring. Offering the mouth of your spirit to the Spirit of All."

Petra squinted at the water. The Technicolor blue was likely the result of some kind of funky bacteria or algae breeding beneath the surface. She glanced at Frankie, feeling the heaviness of his gaze upon her.

She sighed and cupped her hands. It was likely that there was nothing in it that couldn't be fixed by a round of antibiotics. She pulled the warm blue water to her lips and drank.

She expected it to taste like iron, salt, or some other mineral, but it had no such harsh taste. Instead, it was sweet. Almost like tea. Petra let it slide down the back of her throat, reached in for more. It seemed to quench some thirst she hadn't been aware that she'd had, a longing.

"The sweetwater," Frankie said. He stretched out on his rock and pushed his hat back over his eyes, as if he intended to take a nap. "The sweetwater brings you to Spirit."

Petra wiped her lips with the back of her hand. Her mouth buzzed, humming as if she were playing a harmonica. She leaned over the rock to peer into the water. Her reflection gazed up at her, looking fuzzy and pensive, hair dipping into the surface of the water. She felt suddenly dizzy. Her fingers clutched the sandstone edge, and her vision blurred. Her limbs felt leaden, full of sunshine. She tried to summon a feeling of alarm, but a blue buzz suffused her brain.

"The sweetwater," Frankie said from what sounded like a great distance. "The sweetwater will bring you home."

Petra pitched forward, into the waiting warm blue water.

CHAPTER TEN

ALTERED STATES

Flying.

Air slid through the raven's feathers like fingers through water. His pinfeathers grasped the edge of a hot air current, turning him west. He felt weightless, like paper pushed on the downdrafts of the mountains, insubstantial and free.

Apart.

Away.

This high, this apart, there was no pain, only the push of wind against his chest and the scrape of it trickling down his throat. He climbed as high as he could, leaving the ranch behind like a speck of dust, a tiny scar on the land.

He moved away, instinctively chasing the sun. Nothing could hold him. No duty, no curses, no dusty oaths—not even gravity. The bird imagined what it would be like to stay in this form, with all those years upon years of consciousness poured into a single weightless body. A body that could be undone in seconds by a hawk or an eagle or even an unlucky downdraft. In raven form, he was just as vulnerable as any other bird. For that time, being apart, being suspended between earth and sky . . . perhaps it would be worth it.

The wind pushed up from the south, lifting him higher. At this height, the drafts shredded into his wings. Below him, the smaller scattered sparrows were only dots. A vulture circled in an ever-tightening spiral around something dead.

The raven let the air push him north, flattening his wings wide to a knifelike edge. He sailed like a kite, his shadow passing over ribbons of road and roofs of houses. When he'd split from the body, he'd given no thought to where he was going.

His eyes roamed over fields, pausing on the gem-like blue of a tiny body of water. It was the most color in the landscape, like spilled antifreeze on a baked street. Seductive. He angled his head down, cupping his wings against the pull of the current.

Shiny.

As he swung down, he remembered it had been a

long time since he'd been here. Even then, he'd come on wings. Never on two feet. This was not his territory.

A woman lay motionless in the pool, facedown. An old man gripped her shoulders while a coyote tried to slog out of the water, unable to get his hind legs over the stone ledge circling it. The coyote barked and snarled at the man, in the attitude of a dog defending a pup from a predator.

The man seemed dimly familiar. Trying to remember brought a twinge of pain to the raven's side. He knew, in some part of his vast memory jammed into a skull the size of a walnut, that this man had hurt him. But the woman . . .

The raven swooped down to get a closer look. Blond hair spread out in the pool, turning green in the unnatural water. A golden pendant shone at the surface of the water, tethered by a familiar chain around her neck.

Shiny.

He swooped down, into the chaos of the coyote splashing and howling. The old man, focused on the woman, tried to fight off the coyote.

The raven charged the man. Yelling, the old man swung at the raven, but the bird was too fast for him. He clawed at his enemy's face, drawing blood and curses. The raven fluttered away and reached toward the woman's throat. He'd forgotten his physical limitations; she was too heavy to lift when he was in this form. He pinwheeled back from the struggle with only the snapped chain of the pendant in his talons.

"Damn bird! Get away!"

Thinking that the old man was going to drown her, he dove again. But the man anticipated the attack and slapped at the raven, catching him midair. The blow was heavy against his chest, ringing through him like the time he'd struck a window in a storm. He landed in the dust, beak parted, panting, one wing outstretched.

The old man turned to the woman, reaching down for her.

The raven shrieked.

Grunting with effort, the old man pulled her to the lip of the pool. The woman lay on the sandstone with rivulets of turquoise water dripping from her body. The coyote managed to haul himself over the rock lip of the pool and stumble toward her before falling over, motionless.

The old man stood over the woman and began to unbutton his shirt. He threw his shirt to the ground, began to unzip his pants. His skin was as pale as a salt lick, mottled with the stripes of a sunburn where his sleeves ended.

The raven squawked at the top of his lungs, but was ignored. Gathering his energy for another strafing run, he took two hops in toward the old man, talons scraping in the dirt.

The old man finished stripping off his clothes, glanced down at the woman, then dove into the water.

The raven peered through the dust at him, uncomprehending.

Swift as an eel, the naked figure paddled several circuits in the water. He began to sing, off-key and unintelligibly, splashing like a child to see the sun glitter on the droplets of water.

With trepidation, the raven picked up the shiny pendant and walked to the edge of the pool. The coyote remained where he'd fallen, tongue protruding from his mouth. The raven fluttered to the woman, lying on her back with her eyes closed. He pecked at the shirt button at her wrist, got no reaction. Summoning his courage, he hopped up to her chest, turned his head right and left to peer at her. The shiny necklace swung like a pendulum in his beak. As his talons clutched her collar, she made no move to shoo him away.

His beak held fast to the shiny. He wanted it, not just in the way birds love aluminum foil, gum wrappers, and bits of glass. This was beautiful, yet it was so much more than beautiful. The partitioned bits of his consciousness screamed that it was important.

He opened his beak and dropped the charm on the hollow of her throat. She didn't even flinch. Not then and not even when the old man rose out of the water and splashed at the raven.

The raven shrieked and scuttled off. He fluttered several yards away, to the bough of a contorted pine tree.

From his perch, he could do nothing but watch.

Falling.

Petra braced herself for impact, feeling her gut

tense and her hands splayed and thrusting out before her. The water engulfed her body with a muffled sucking sound. She clawed her way to the surface . . .

But the water was much deeper and darker than it appeared. She couldn't distinguish up from down; air bubbles floated in all directions, giving no hint as to where the surface lay. Diffuse blue light shimmered from both above and below.

She thrashed, lungs burning. She struck out first in one direction, then another. Forcing herself to pause, she tried to float and have faith that the remaining air in her lungs would pull her to the surface. But she simply hung in space, unmoving, suspended. Her necklace drifted, glinting, before her.

This is a stupid way to die, Petra thought. She was a strong swimmer, and had spent years out in the middle of a treacherous ocean. And now a puny spring threatened to be her undoing.

And it was not as if she didn't deserve to be undone. For all that had happened to poor Des, to die by fire in the ocean . . . this was no less than she truly deserved. That knowledge lay at the bottom of her chest like a stone.

Below, she spied a flicker of movement, a pale blur in the depths. She made out the shapes of what looked like paws swimming. The underside of a dog. Sig.

But that way felt like *down*. Like certain death.

She dove down, down. She reached for Sig, for the paws silently churning the water. Teeth claimed her sleeve, trying to drag her further under.

And she let it happen, let Sig haul her to the bottom . . . where she came back up with a gasp that scorched her lungs.

Sound came roaring back, foam and spray hissing at her. She struggled against Sig's teeth and toenails, kicking and fighting to reach land.

Petra crashed up against a rock, hauled herself up on the shore. Sig disentangled himself from her sleeves and flopped, dripping, beside her.

Her breath was a thin whistle as she surveyed her surroundings. She'd been thoroughly prepared to grab Frankie by his collar and shake him for pushing her in.

But Frankie was gone. And this was not the land she'd left, the Eye of the Spirit with the scrub desert spreading around her.

Water lapped against her body in shallow waves. Her fingers dug into silt, recognizing bits of milk quartz and obsidian in a detached way. She'd washed up on some riverbank shore, far from where she'd fallen in. The mountains loomed closer, blotting out part of the blue sky, while sea oats conspired, whispering, in the distance. She could make out a cerulean line of ocean beyond.

Impossible. An impossible landscape. She had never been here, though bits and pieces of it seemed as familiar as a dream, one that mashed up fragments of memory, pressing them impossibly close together.

She dragged herself beyond the rocks, her clothes hanging heavy on her shoulders. Sig trotted behind her. She tugged off her boots to empty them, wincing at a pain in her arm. This place sure *felt* real.

She looked at her right arm, turning it over, expecting to find a scrape from the rocks across the handprint scar on her flesh. But the scar was missing. She ran her fingers over where it should be. There was only a fresh scratch from the rocks. Beneath it, her skin was smooth and pale, as if nothing had ever happened.

Sig lowered his head to the edge of the water to drink. Petra touched her fingers to her lips, remembering. She'd drunk the water from the pool, the water full of that filthy blue algae. And it had probably made her sick. This was likely a dream, a hallucination brought on by some noxious microbes.

That was the best-case scenario. The worst-case scenario was that she'd gotten sick, fallen in the pool, and what she was experiencing now were the last dismal firings of her neurons as her body drowned.

"Damn it, Frankie." Her hands balled into fists around her shoelaces.

Sig yipped beside her, chewing at a toenail.

"You're not real," she told him. "You're just a projection of my oxygen-starved brain cells. Or some kind of psychological hiccup."

Sig wasn't impressed. He finished gnawing his dewclaw, stood up, and shook water all over her.

Petra swore. But she had to admit, her brain was pretty good at rendering the details. It felt like muddy water and smelled exactly like wet dog.

She considered her options. "I could sit here and wait for the hallucination to fade," she told Sig. Really, it was like talking to herself, so what did it matter?

Sig cocked his head attentively, like a good super-ego should.

"Death or the effect of the hallucinogenic algae wearing off. One or the other." Petra squinted at the sky. Funny. It was daylight, but she couldn't see the sun. So much for conventional navigation. "Though, I suppose that if I were dying, it would be over with quickly."

Sig huffed.

"Don't snort at me. I don't believe in an afterlife."

The coyote yawned.

"Great. Now, I'm arguing with myself." Petra pinched the bridge of her nose. "This is giving me a helluva headache."

Sig shook himself one more time, then took off, trotting down the muddy beach.

She gave him a dirty look he didn't bother to turn around and see. "Now you're leaving me?"

Sig flicked a speckled ear.

She gazed after him, at the staccato tracks he made in the silt.

But his were not the only tracks. There were footprints—large footprints from a man's shoes—tracking before him. Sig trotted along in their wake, smudging the edges.

Damn. She wasn't alone. Or maybe she was, and

this was another psychological projection. She pulled on her waterlogged boots and clomped after Sig, kicking up thick clods of mud.

She followed him along the water's edge. The river churned beside her, a surreal turquoise that must have come from the spring somehow. Her boots smacked in the muck, and she struggled to keep up with Sig. His light paws seemed to float on the mud, leaving small indentations rather than the deep ruts she left.

Up ahead, she could make out the silhouette of a man, walking toward the seashore.

"Hey!" Petra yelled.

He seemed not to hear her, or if he did, he didn't acknowledge her. The man was dressed in a black coat, with grey hair tied over his shoulder. He followed the path of the river as it spilled out into the sea.

Petra followed, but she couldn't catch up. She slogged along the edge of the river, where sea oats began to take root in paler sand. Sig slunk behind the oats and growled at the man.

"Where are we?" she yelled. "Who are you?"

The man didn't turn. He walked down to the beach, where the river connected with the transparent water of a familiar ocean. Petra shaded her eyes. A plume of black smoke blossomed in the distance. The whitecaps were stained black with oil.

She finally reached the man, lungs burning from the exertion. Catching his sleeve, she forcibly turned him around. He looked at her, unblinking. His face was as deeply lined as a leaf, with brown eyes staring out at her.

She knew him.

She reached up to grasp his shoulders, shook him hard. A pendant identical to her own, the green lion devouring the sun, spilled from his open shirt collar.

"Dad," she shouted over the din of the oily waves. "Dad, what are you doing here?"

She stared into his gold-flecked eyes, gripping his arms as if her hands were claws. As she watched, those gold flecks expanded, took over. His irises shone gold, and spidery legs of gold leaf crept into his skin, like a contagion.

"Dad! It's me, Petra."

But his gaze was vacant. The gold wound into his hair, twisted into his coat. It was hot, hot as molten metal. Petra tried to hold on to him, but the heat was too much. She released him and backed away as gold twitched through him. It crackled and buzzed like lightning.

Soon her father was completely rendered in gold. Like Midas, she thought, reaching out.

Where her fingers brushed his hand, a fissure formed. The crack splintered up his arm, like an earthquake.

"No . . ." she breathed, but was helpless to do anything but watch as the cracks ratcheted through the statue of her father, ripping into the gold flesh and gold bones. A finger, then an ear, fell to the sand.

She reached down to try to collect them. Perhaps she could gather the pieces, find some way help him . . .

But the image of her father shattered and exploded into gold splinters. Petra flinched, shielding her eyes with her arm.

He was gone. All that remained was a fine metallic dust and bits of weightless gold leaf on the sand, already scattered by waves and wind. She dug her fingers into it, choking back a sob.

"It's not real," she reminded herself, rocking back on her heels. Her hands were covered in glittering dust. She scraped her shaking hand through her hair. This was her imagination. It could not be real. Could not . . .

But if this was all in her head, what other terrible things could be here?

As if in answer, a hot wave enveloped her foot. She looked down to see something churning in the grease and the gold specks. Something living.

She reached down, trying to free herself. But something held her fast—a blackened hand.

She cried out, stumbling backward, trying to haul herself back along the sparkling beach. But the hand would not let go—it was hot and oily, and it singed the leather of her boot. She tried to pull it apart in the hissing seawater.

Another hand grasped her wrist, burning her. Petra cried out, feeling that familiar heat around her forearm, that smell of sizzling flesh.

A face emerged from the water. Charred black lips

pulled back around white teeth, a shock of blond hair crowning raw flesh and sinew.

Petra stumbled forward, slamming to her elbow and one knee in the surf. For an instant, she thought that she might willingly go under, into the oily silence. And she felt she understood this place. That maybe there was a hell. An afterlife, and she was in it.

But she fought. The desire to live surged in her belly, and she struggled, shouting.

A shadow passed over her with a harsh caw. Black feathers flickered in her vision. And she realized that a raven had flown between her and the grasping oil. Not just one—more. Dozens. They swarmed in a cacophony, like black smoke, howling, forcing her and the creature that was and wasn't Des apart.

She felt the grip on her wrist slacken, and she struggled with all her might. She pulled free, scrambled back on the beach, crab-like, away from the seething mass of black. Gratitude rose in her throat. The birds had saved her. The birds . . .

They plucked at the oil creature, devouring him, piece by piece. The only sound that came from the ruined lips was a soft hiss as it sank beneath the waves.

CHAPTER ELEVEN

THE SACRED ANDROGYNE

Petra felt warmth on her face.

Not the stinging heat of oil and fire, but a soft warmth, like sunshine.

She opened her eyes to see blue sky above her. The scar on her wrist was old and white and didn't ache. Something shifted beside her, and she glanced down. Sig lay at her hip, kicking at her in his sleep.

She turned her head, spying the rocky edge of the pool. Her clothes were dry, and her face felt sunburned. Her head throbbed, like a bad hangover. She wondered how long she'd lain here; the sun was descending toward the mountains, kissing just the edge of them.

Struggling up to a sitting position, she howled, *"Frankie!"* The motion made her queasy. Something shiny dropped from her chest down into her lap—her lion charm. She clutched it, fingering the broken chain.

Frankie perched at the edge of the pool, crouching. His skin glistened, and he was naked. He poured water into one hand from the other, seemingly transfixed by the play of the tinted liquid as it spilled from palm to fingers.

Only . . . Frankie was a woman. Frankie's breasts hung low over his chest, and he had an old woman's hips. Even his face seemed softer as Petra saw Frankie for who he was.

"Frankie." Petra stabbed her thumb at the pain in her temple, trying to rub it away. "What the hell?"

Frankie's eyes were distant. "You went on a spirit journey."

"Damn it. I don't believe in that stuff." She tried to sound certain. Something prickly was caught in her hair. She ran her fingers through the crusty dried mess and came up with a glossy black raven feather.

"Doesn't matter if you believe. You went."

"You didn't tell me." She felt confused and betrayed, but also a little awestruck. She turned the feather over in her hands.

Frankie shrugged. "You needed to go. And you weren't alone."

Sig rolled over, displaying his belly. His eyes were

slightly crossed, and Petra worried about the effects of hallucinogenic algae on canines.

Frankie took another drink of the water. He didn't fall over. He remained rooted in place like a tree that had grown at the edge of the spring for decades.

"To paraphrase Maria: Frankie, you're drunk."

Frankie snorted. "I've built up a tolerance to the water."

"You're naked, perched on the edge of the pool." Petra wanted to say the obvious: And you're a woman. But she restrained herself.

Frankie looked down at his arms, plucking at the liver-marked flesh like it was a suit with a stain on it. "Huh."

"You gonna put some clothes on so we can go back to the house?"

"In a minute." Frankie took another deep sip. Water trickled down his chin, between his breasts.

"It's hungry," he gurgled.

"Huh?"

Frankie rocked forward and backward on his heels. His gaze fell into the water, unfocused. "It's hungry. The hungry ghost. Devouring."

A figure stalked across the field. Maria. Her back was ramrod-straight in rage, and her hair flew about her like a dark miasma. "Frankie!"

Frankie pretended not to hear her. Or maybe he really didn't. He stared into the pool, at the blue algal bloom churning under the surface. "It's hungry."

Maria stomped up and snatched Frankie's shirt from the rocks. "What happened?"

Petra instinctively scuttled back, away from Maria's wrath. "I'm not sure. I drank out of the spring and . . . I don't know."

"Jesus. Look, I'm sorry. He does this sometimes. Thinks he's a proper shaman. Even though he's white as vinegar."

"And a woman?"

Maria winced. "Yeah. That, too. He started out as Francine, married to one of my uncles. And then, when my uncle died, it's like he took on his identity, literally stepped into his shoes. Something about needing to be a man to be a proper shaman."

"The sacred androgyne," Frankie mumbled. "Male and female. The alchemical marriage."

Petra started at the mention of alchemy, but Maria had already reached him and was wrapping his shirt around his shoulders. He shrugged against her, pushing the shirt away like a two-year-old who didn't want to be dressed.

"Frankie, damn it, where did you get the booze?" She turned to Petra in frustration. "I did a sweep of the house earlier today, thought I'd hit all of Frankie's usual hiding places: the toilet tank, under the workbench in the basement, behind the oil cans in the garage, even the fucking mailbox, for Christ's sake."

"It's not the alcohol. It's the water," Petra said. Sig

leaned up close against her, just as wary of Maria's anger as she was.

"Yeah. He says that. But I've drunk the water, and not a damn thing has happened." Maria went in search of Frankie's boots, tried to jam them on his feet.

Frankie stared at Petra, stared through her. In spite of herself, it made her shudder. Maybe in an earlier time he would have been a shaman. Today, he was just a drunk old man.

"The spirit of the bones is moving. Like the White Buffalo Woman." His eyes glistened with tears. "Do you remember her?"

Maria grunted, tying his shoelaces.

"Do you remember?" He gripped Maria's sleeve fiercely.

Maria's brow furrowed, as if sorting through the old stories that a younger, more sober Frankie had told her as a child. "She was the woman who turned all her suitors to skeletons."

"All alone. Incomplete."

Maria squatted before him and brushed the hair from his eyes. She kissed his forehead. "It's okay, Frankie." She put his arms through the shirtsleeves and began buttoning him up.

"It's not okay. It's killing. It will keep killing. They want it, what she has. That peace."

Maria clasped the old man's shaking hands. "It's okay, Frankie. Nothing will hurt you."

"Forgotten . . ." Frankie mumbled. His eyes swept the horizon outside. "That timeless peace . . . immortal."

Petra looked away, to the water. She had the sense of intruding upon a terribly intimate scene. She was a stranger, and this was not her family.

A blue, smokelike shadow swirled in the water. She tried to focus on it, imagining that it was some after-effect of the hallucinogen. The shadow curved and curled, and took the shape of a form with claws and teeth, growing more solid and grey.

Sig hid behind Petra's thigh and growled, the fur on his back standing up. It wasn't just her imagination; Sig sensed it, too.

"Go away," Frankie hissed, while Maria struggled with his pants. He, too, stared into the blue depths. He threw a rock at the smoke creature, and the splash and ripples caused the shape to dissipate.

Sig gazed up at her. The fur along his back had calmed, but the coyote still was tense as a spring, tail twitching. Petra wished that she could see what the coyote had seen, to know if it wasn't just Frankie who was hallucinating. Just her and Frankie.

"Something is coming," Frankie announced. "Something hungry."

Petra shivered. Whatever it was that she'd seen, she didn't want to have anything to do with feeding it.

Cal was striking out today. Big time.

Stroud had taken Cal and Justin and a couple other tweakers to run an "errand." After he'd run like a little girl from Stroud the other night, he was surprised the stringy old dude had dragged him along this time. Cal had scrunched up in the backseat of the Monte Carlo, wishing that there was some way that the torn upholstery could reach out and devour him. He didn't like it when Stroud got that cold, metallic glint in his eye that changed color from blue to grey. And Stroud was wearing gloves and a coat in the late summer swelter. That never boded well.

The others didn't seem to notice. Promised all the Elixir they could smoke for taking out Stroud's garbage, they were now taking turns trying to see how many bullets could be crammed into handgun ammo clips before the springs gave out.

"What's the mission, boss?" Cal croaked from the backseat. "Are we gonna go look for Adam and Diana?"

Stroud looked back at him with eyes the color of mercury. Fucking creepy. A bead of sweat formed on the old man's upper lip. "I already sent someone to look for Adam and Diana. We're going to search the trailer on Lascaris's old land, for an artifact. It's gold. About the size of your fist. Looks like a compass."

Cal sunk down in his seat. Great. Back there, again.

One of the tweakers, Kyle, asked, "Anybody living there?"

Stroud's metallic gaze flicked back at him. "A woman. Her name's Petra Dee. A geologist."

Justin looked up from thumbing bullets into the magazine. He lost count, swore, had to empty the clip and start over. "Hey. That's the new bitch. The snotty one we saw on the road the other day."

Curiosity lit in Stroud's voice. "You met her? You didn't mention that."

"Yeah." Justin punched Cal in the arm. "Would've gotten a decent piece of ass if Cal hadn't fucked it up." Bullets spilled on the floorboards and rolled under the seats. "Damn it."

Stroud looked back at Cal more intently, and he squirmed. "Was there anything . . . special about her?"

Cal blinked. "Special? She's kind of cute. In a MILFy way." He decided against telling Stroud about what he'd seen at the Compostela last night. Petra was special in terms of that ballsy standing up to Rutherford's men, sure, but . . . he was pretty sure that wasn't what Stroud was asking about.

"No. I mean . . . magical." A cataract of silver licked up over Stroud's right eye, momentarily obliterating the white and iris.

Cal shook his head. "No. Nuh-uh. Not like you."

"Did she have that coyote with her?"

Cal shook his head. "She was alone."

Stroud frowned.

He didn't say anything more until they pulled up in front of the trailer. Cal hoped to God that Petra had enough sense or luck to be gone. He sighed with relief when he didn't see any cars around.

The men piled out of the Monte Carlo. Justin and the two others were armed. Cal brought up the rear, nervously examining the blade of the tactical knife he'd never used for anything but cleaning gravel out of his boots. Only Stroud appeared unarmed beneath his black coat.

But Cal knew better.

Stroud opened the screen door, tried the doorknob. "Check the windows. See if the back one's open."

Justin always liked to go first. He sprinted to the back of the trailer with the other two young men in tow. Cal moved to follow.

"Not you." Stroud's hand clapped down on Cal's shoulder. Cal obeyed, though he squirmed at the hot, churning feeling in the palm of Stroud's glove. He could feel it through the cotton of his T-shirt, and he tried not to shudder. "Wait."

Justin sprinted back around the corner. "Locked. Looks like no one's home."

"We'll see."

Stroud climbed up the steps and kicked in the door, then motioned for the armed men to go ahead first. Justin and the other two tweakers tumbled all over themselves to get inside. Stroud stepped back. He stripped off his glove, and mercury slid over his knuckles, as if anticipating something.

Cal fought a queasy feeling. Why this regular chick, who ran from them like a freaked-out rabbit on the road? What did she have that Stroud wanted? What could she do that made her powerful enough to both defy Rutherford's men and piss Stroud off?

"No one's here," Justin called from inside.

But Stroud was still careful. He walked into the trailer as though it might be booby-trapped, mindful not to so much as brush the doorframe. He looked at the shabby surroundings, nodding to them. "Take it apart."

And they did. Cal and the young men ripped through Petra's bags, tore the racks out of the oven, even peeled the paneling from the walls. And found nothing more thrilling than women's underwear, a cardboard box with a razor blade jammed in it, and a note.

Cal found the note. It mentioned that some equipment was waiting for Petra at the ranger station. He balled it up and chucked it among the litter on the floor without telling anyone, filing that information away for later. Maybe he could use it, warn her somehow that one seriously pissed-off alchemist was after her.

They left empty-handed. Stroud wasn't happy, but dispensed enough Elixir to each one of them to make the evening pass quickly.

Cal had gratefully accepted his share. Instead of building a bonfire with the others at the Garden, he slipped away. Confident that no one would miss him, he dragged his old dirt bike out of the shed and walked it down the road until he was sure that no one could hear the engine start. It took three tries to get it going, and it buzzed loud as a lawn mower in his ears until he picked up speed.

Night wind and miles slid past him.

Adam and Diana were still gone.

He knew that they wouldn't have just run off, not without him. They were like his family, protecting him against Justin and the rest of the morons. Cal had run away from his last foster home two years ago, and his friends were all he had. He had to find them.

They wouldn't leave him at the Garden, not all alone. They had to know that they were the only reason he stayed . . . didn't they? His vision blurred.

The hired hand at the bar had said a body had been found on Rutherford's land. Hope and fear churned in Cal's stomach as he turned down the dark dirt roads to Rutherford's ranch. He switched off his headlight, bouncing over ruts and rills that shook his teeth until he was nearly out of gas.

He walked his bike along the edge of a freshly mown field that smelled of hay and dew. A few half-finished bales lay scattered about. This had to be where the field hands stopped work, the spot he'd heard about at the Compostela. He propped his bike up against a fence post and clambered over the barbed wire fence. He paced along the edge of it, fear gnawing his chest. He saw no sign of upturned earth that he could identify as a grave. But it was dark, and Rutherford's land was vast. Going alone into enemy territory was fucking stupid.

He rubbed his eyes with the heels of his hands. *Think.* How did the detectives on crime shows find bodies? Not the lame-ass pogues around here that belonged to Rutherford, but the good guys with badges that existed on the other side of the television glass.

They looked for disturbed earth. Right. He'd tried that. But if there was a body on Rutherford's land, his men would surely have found a good place to bury it . . .

Cops would bring in dogs. Yeah, dogs. But Cal didn't have a corpse-sniffing dog. He remembered some guys on a television show looking for Jimmy Hoffa's body under Giants Stadium with some kind of sonar equipment that looked like a lawn mower . . .

Petra. The geologist. She knew dirt. She might know how to find a body . . .

Lights glinted in the distance. Cal squinted. Not flashlights. Something weirder. Like eyes. Lots of eyes, glowing like fluorescent coals that swam noiselessly over the landscape.

Cal didn't know what the fuck they were, but he knew to run.

He raced through the field, grasses whipping at the legs of his cargo pants in a *zip-zip-zip* noise that slashed in counterpoint to his heart. He ran until he thought his lungs would burst, until he reached the fence. Throwing himself on his bike, he cranked the starter, wrenched the clutch, and stomped on the accelerator.

Nothing happened.

"Jesus fucking Christ," he whimpered, struggling to start the bike. The glowing eyes were advancing, and he could see that they had roughly the shapes of men, advancing across the pale field in the wan moonlight.

The engine finally engaged as he let out the clutch with agonizing slowness, and he floored the gas. The little bike growled to life, and he retreated down the road in a cloud of dust that obscured the shining eyes behind him.

The drive home was quiet, with no other cars on the road. Petra's head hurt under the weight of her questions and the remains of her hallucination.

She switched on the radio, fiddled with the dial. A hint of country music bristled through the static, then slipped away. She spun past it, finding nothing but static bouncing off the mountains.

"*. . . the green lion . . .*"

A voice emanated clearly from the speaker, over the roar of the engine and the crackle of the static. A familiar voice—one that sounded like her father's. Impossibly just like him.

Her fingers stilled on the knob. She slammed on the brakes, causing Sig to slide off the seat and onto the floorboards. She cranked the wheel to guide the Bronco to the shoulder and shut off the engine. Sig grumbled and scrambled back into the seat.

"Hush," she ordered.

White noise filtered through the speakers. She worked the knob a fraction of an inch back and forth. Broken words seemed to slip through, warped by distance, spoken in that familiar voice:

"*Go back . . . go back to the sea . . .*"

The fine hair on the back of her neck lifted. It couldn't be him. Couldn't be. She cranked the volume all the way up, pressed her fingers to the plastic housing of the radio, as if she could crawl inside. Yet the voice on the radio sounded exactly as she remembered.

"Dad?"

" . . . *nothing for you here . . . lion . . . gold and dust . . . go . . .*"

The voice slipped away to soft static that filled the truck. Petra sat in silence, straining to hear it again, yearning.

Then sound roared back into the truck, a jolting wall of music that caused Sig to yowl and Petra to lunge for the volume.

"Somewhere, beyond the sea . . . somewhere, waiting for me . . ."

"Bobby Darin," she breathed. She hadn't heard that song since she was a child. The song seemed to crackle out of the speakers with a life of its own, Bobby's voice clear as a bell, as if she were in the parking lot of a radio station.

When the song ended, she waited with white-knuckled hands to hear the soothing pitter-patter of a deejay's voice—a voice that she'd be able to rationalize belonged to a whole other man, that the coincidence of radio reception had dredged up something deep in her memory.

But the song ended, and there was simply silence. No pop and hiss, no jangly advertisements for car dealers or strip joints. Just the whoosh of air across some unfathomable distance.

It was a full fifteen minutes before she cranked the ignition and started toward home.

She swore to herself that she would not cry, no matter the terrible tricks her mind was playing on her, whether they were of her own doing or the lingering effects of Frankie's sweetwater.

She pulled up to the trailer, shut off the engine, and rested her head on the steering wheel. Sig jumped out and immediately began to find someplace to pee, nose to the ground.

After a long moment, she got out, slung her gun belt over her shoulder, and grabbed the Tupperware container of leftovers Maria had sent home with her. She trudged up the steps to the trailer and discovered that the door had a nice dent in the bottom. She pulled one of the pistols out of its holster and nudged the door with the barrel of the gun. The door swung open easily.

"Damn it," she said. Heart hammering, she flipped on the light.

The trailer had been tossed. Well, as tossed as the meager shelter could be. The futon had been over-turned, and the refrigerator stood open. Her spec-trometer had been torn apart, and the paneling had been peeled from the walls. Even the stupid note that Mike had left for her about the equipment was wadded up on the floor. She kicked it.

"Fucking tweakers." She was gonna lose her de-posit, for sure.

She jammed the door back in its frame as best she

could, tearing out a damaged piece of weather stripping. With that out of the way, the lockset still worked, for all the good it did. She locked the door behind her and set the kitchen table up against it. If it moved during the night, she'd hear it. She righted the futon, rearranged the blankets, and opened the windows for some air. Petra figured that the food in the fridge was a loss, but shut the door anyway to save power.

She hung her gun belt up on one end of the futon, turned off the light, and stretched out. She was too tired to drive to the lodge in Yellowstone; she'd stay here tonight. Just for a few hours. Tears of anger and exhaustion dribbled down her nose. She balled her fists against her eyes and gave in to a good cry.

Something scraped the skin of the trailer outside. Petra peered out the window, reaching for her guns, but it was only Sig. He hoisted himself up through the window and lay down beside her with his head in her lap. When she'd been reduced to hiccups, she gingerly stroked his rough fur.

"This place fucking sucks, Sig."

She wondered what her father saw in it, what he'd found to make him think otherwise.

CHAPTER TWELVE

DIGGING IN THE PETRIFIED FOREST

Petra dragged herself out of bed at dawn and lured Sig out of the trailer with a slice of lunch meat. He was irritated when she shut and locked the door behind him, thrashing his tail in the dirt.

"Look, you're just gonna have to find somewhere else to sleep today," she said. "It's not safe for you in there."

Sig sulked and skulked beneath the trailer.

"Come out of there," she insisted. "You are not on guard duty."

She feared what might happen to him if the meth

heads came back. Maybe Sig could hold his own, or at least would have enough sense to run.

She plodded sourly over to the Bronco. She'd slept like shit, and was considering taking a detour into town to pick up some coffee at Bear's before she showed up at the ranger station for work. The Bronco had no cup-holders, but she'd figure something out.

She opened the door, threw her gun belt on the seat, and checked her bag of geology equipment in the back. The compass and her remaining cash were tucked safely in with her tools. She'd no sooner hopped up on the running board than a tawny mass of fur wriggled past her into the truck.

"Sig! Get the fuck out of there!"

The coyote plunked his ass on the passenger seat and stared at her. His lips parted in a canine grin, and his tongue snaked out from behind his teeth.

"Sig, honey, I have to go to work. It's a few miles away. If you get lost, you might not be able to find your way back home."

Sig turned away from her and looked out the window.

Petra crossed to the passenger side, opened the door. She returned to the driver's side and tried to push Sig out. The coyote growled at her, and she backed off.

"So, you're coming." It was a statement, not a question.

Sig slapped his tail on the pleather seats.

"You have to stay with the truck, okay? All day."

Sig looked down his long nose at her. As he panted, it seemed that he was laughing.

"Damn it," Petra muttered. She shut the doors and jammed the key into the ignition.

She decided to nix Bear's in favor of getting to work early. First day, and all. The territory roughened as she drove, and forest began to reach green fingers into the landscape, grass fields giving way to aspen with yellow leaves quaking in the breeze. Petra followed the road signs to the northeast park entrance. Craggy mountain peaks rose around the road with lodgepole pine trees clustering at their feet. Some stood upright, while others had fallen victim to forest fires from years ago, charred and broken and still not decomposed.

She turned on the radio, hoping to hear some snippet of the voice she'd heard the night before, but she only caught fragments of weather reports and country music. A pang of disappointment lanced through her chest, but she left the music on, hoping.

The Bronco's engine growled as the altitude increased. The Lamar River wound up and around the road, alternating from the right to left side as she crossed bridges. Moose waded in the cool water up to their necks. Bison wandered in fields burned golden by summer's heat and spangled with purple lupin flowers. She could imagine that this place had truly been untouched for centuries, that it had shaken off all efforts at human habitation.

She followed the road signs to the Tower Yellowstone cluster of buildings. She passed the lodge that

Mike had spoken of, a charming log and stone building with a gravel lot half-full of vehicles. For a moment, she thought longingly of a full-sized bathtub and bed linens that didn't smell like stale tobacco, but she was certain that coyotes were not allowed. And it did have the distinct disadvantage of being located across the road from the Tower Ranger Station. She pulled into the parking lot beside Mike's Jeep and rolled the windows of the Bronco halfway up.

"Stay here," she told Sig. She had visions of getting charged with poaching by some less friendly ranger than Mike.

Sig lay down on the seat and yawned. It seemed that he might behave. Maybe.

Mike was waiting for her at the door, with two cups of coffee in hand. He handed one to Petra. "Good morning, sunshine. Just saw you roll up."

"Thank you." Petra slurped the coffee greedily.

"Sleep well?"

"Not so much."

"I saw your handiwork around town. Nice wallpapering job with those flyers, but that's not a good way to attract attention. Now every nut job in the county has your phone number."

"Yeah, well. That's the least of my problems." She made a face. She didn't want to tell him, but she had to. "Some idiots broke into my trailer yesterday while I was gone."

Mike's brows shot up. "What happened? Why didn't you call? What did you see?"

She took a deep breath and told him what she knew. Mike listened with narrowed eyes, one hand hooked in his gun belt as she described the damage.

"Nothing was taken," she said. "I think it's gotta be those tweaker kids. Hopefully, since they didn't get anything, they won't be back."

"Maybe. But they seem awfully fixated on you. I'll call the sheriff this morning to get some paper on this. I don't think they'll do much. However . . ."

Petra suppressed the urge to roll her eyes. Here it came.

" . . . You should stay at the lodge," he said.

"The lodge doesn't take coyotes." She wasn't going to abandon Sig for the sake of convenience.

"You can stay with me."

"I appreciate it, but I can't." She couldn't, for a whole helluva lot of reasons.

"Look, you're lucky, but luck's only gonna get you so far around here."

"I'll call Maria, okay?"

Mike's chin lifted. "That would be an acceptable compromise."

Petra nodded.

"C'mon. I'll show you what the USGS sent for you." He gestured for her to follow him inside the station. "They shipped you a whole load of stuff."

A long counter held informational pamphlets and forms for fishing and camping permits. The building smelled the way most old buildings did to Petra: like earth and dust. Mike led her to a back room filled with radios and weather monitoring equipment. Tucked in the corner were two large wooden crates with Petra's name on the manifest.

"Presents from Uncle Sam." Mike sipped the dregs of his coffee. "Want a crowbar?"

"Please."

Petra worked the lid of the first box open. Inside, she found a file folder with instructions. Nothing exciting. Her assignment was to take soil samples from Specimen Ridge and the surrounding areas. The majority of the contents of the box were plastic vials and forms to attach to them, plus return postage cardboard boxes and packing materials. But USGS had seen fit to give her a few additional tools: maps, a bucket augur, a GPS-based Azimuth pointing device to record exact information about the soil samples, sample bags, a compass, rock pick, altimeter, a soil sampling equipment kit in a case, microscope, binoculars, hand lenses, and a stereoscope. She'd brought many of her own tools with her, including the lenses, picks, rock climbing gear, and compass. But the USGS items were shiny new, and she looked forward to playing with them.

The second box was filled with packing peanuts. Petra scooped as many of them aside as she could, but static electricity stuck them to her shirt. She dug until Mike turned the box over on its side, spilling the peanuts out on the floor. She dragged out a red metal device with wheels and a handle.

"What's that? Looks like a lawn mower."

Petra grinned. "It's a ground penetrating radar

device. It allows me to study bedrock without disturbing soils or rock layers." She paged through the instruction manual that came with it, showing him fuzzy pictures of stripes. "This stuff is used from everything to finding lost utility lines to land mine detection and archaeology."

"Cool." Mike squinted at the striped drawing. "How deep does it go?"

"Depends on the soil composition, clay properties, and conductivity. Could be as little as one meter for really opaque soils to more than five thousand for clear ice. The average is about thirty meters under normal conditions, though." Petra grinned. She couldn't wait to use the new gadget; she hadn't handled one since grad school.

"You can leave as much stuff as you want here," Mike said. "I can't imagine that you're gonna take all of that with you up the mountain."

"Thanks. I appreciate the storage space."

After cleaning up the staticky packing peanuts, she sat down on the floor and started dividing up what she'd need for the day. Mike went to answer the ringing phone, and she arranged the equipment and forms into the backpack she'd bought at Stan's Dungeon. She tucked the rest into the crate and shoved it back out of the way.

With her gear slung over her shoulder and pushing the GPR cart before her, she met Mike in the main room.

"I'd be happy to give you the nickel tour," he said, leaning on the counter.

"I don't want to take you away from your work."

He shrugged. "I'm the only one at the station right now, but I can give you the tour after work."

"Okay. I'll come by when I'm done." Maybe she was being too suspicious, but most men who'd showed any interest in her wanted something. Maybe Mike only wanted someone to talk to, and was just clumsy about it.

"Take a radio," he said. He plucked a walkie-talkie out of a charger and shoved it across the counter to her. "Just in case you need anything. Which way you headed?"

"Thanks. My instructions are for Specimen Ridge."

"Trailhead's two miles down the road, leading from the parking lot. Take one of those." He pointed at a display on the counter of what looked like tiny fire extinguishers.

She picked one up and read the label. "Bear spray?"

"Better than mace. Stay upwind of it, and be careful."

"Will do." She gave Mike a smart salute that made him smirk.

Petra clomped out to the parking lot with her gear, scraping the wheels of the GPR unit in the gravel. Sig scrambled up off the seat of the Bronco and pressed his nose to the window as she loaded her gear. All the windows were already smeared with snot marks.

As she pulled the Bronco out of the parking lot onto the main road, she wondered if he'd ever been in the park before.

At the trailhead, she parked the Bronco and popped open her door. Sig clambered over her lap and bounded to the pavement of the empty parking lot, wagging his tail. She reached for him, and he ducked away.

"Don't let anybody see you," she grumbled, grabbing her gun belt. When she put it on, the guns were concealed neatly beneath her jacket. She didn't expect to be charged with carrying a concealed weapon—even though, from what she'd seen, the only law enforcement around here was Mike.

Consulting her map, she set off toward Specimen Ridge.

It felt good to be working again.

The thinness of breath that Petra had felt when she first arrived in Temperance was diminishing. She found that she could fill her lungs without struggling, and she pushed forward, hiking through a sea of wild grasses and sage dotted with elk. The trail dropped away where a creek met the river, splashing a cool mist of water against her face. She even stopped to strip off her boots and socks and soak her feet in the tempting shallows. The river was bracingly cold, coming down from the mountain. Completely unlike the warm, sluggish springwater from yesterday. The sun was warming overhead, and she closed her eyes, listening to the gurgle of the current.

This far out in the wild, she felt safe. Not like she did in Temperance, with the people with their guns and odd blood and strange history.

Sig followed her dutifully throughout the morning, though he was irritated by the squeak and clattering sounds that the GPR cart made as she pushed it along before them. He was doing a good job of pretending to be a dog; the few tourists that she encountered didn't look twice at him. Once, he tore off after a rabbit, and Petra feared that she'd lost him. But he returned a few minutes later with the rabbit clutched in his jaws. Petra figured that it was simply good manners to take a break and allow him to eat his prize.

She continued south and east to Specimen Ridge, the slopes covered in tall grass and yellow mustard. She climbed the ridge slowly. This was higher than she'd ever gone, and she was determined to pace herself. She'd read that this was a place where amethyst and opal were often found. Volcanic ash had insinuated itself into trees, petrifying them. They stood at the summit, broken stubs among the rubble of yellow rock and pine, pale as bones. This layer was one of dozens of fossilized forests that lay beneath the ridge. Each successive forest had grown atop the one before, to be subjected to the same fossilization process.

She powered up her handheld GPS device, wrestled the clipboard out of her backpack, and logged her position. Switching on the power of the GPR cart, she was rewarded by the glow of the readout screen between the handlebars as it booted up. In an environment as fragile as Specimen Ridge, she'd only be able to take soil samples at a limited depth. The GPR would allow her to see beneath the surface, to see what had lain in darkness for thousands of years.

She pushed the cart along the surface of the ridge, watching how the radar waves created a striated picture of the world below. She could see striations that suggested levels of porous volcanic rock, thick streaks of basalt, and dark black shadows that could be obsidian. She saw drifts of buried ash and the sketchy shapes of petrified tree roots, deeper layers of the buried forest. The surface levels were squiggled, indicating uneven erosion as the petrified trees resisted and the minerals around them washed away. It was a ghostly image, sketching out a past that no living person had ever seen with their own eyes, a history of fire and silence sealed up in the earth. She watched, riveted, as the hidden forest revealed itself to her.

Petra ran the GPR cart until the battery indicator ran low, then turned to take the soil samples designated in her instructions. She should have allowed the cart to charge thoroughly overnight, but she couldn't resist taking it out for a test run.

The soil samples were boring, entry-level work: augur out a sample at a fixed depth, place the sample in a jar, record the exact location, label the jar. Wash, rinse, repeat. But Petra was grateful not to have work that was critically important. She never wanted the responsibility of life and death ever again. She'd be happy to be a drone for the rest of her life.

Petra set her augur to the ground while Sig busied himself with marking his territory. No respect for history. She carefully chiseled samples of the petrified trees into her bottles. She ran her fingers over the spider tendrils of roots. They were gorgeous in their asymmetry, a once-fragile living thing transformed to eternal stone. The wood itself wasn't part of her USGS work, but the samples might make for a fascinating paper. She could imagine the roots of these dead trees winding down into the primordial darkness she'd glimpsed before. She was one of the few to see the entirety of such an ancient tree. She imagined how she could assemble the data in a descriptive portrait. Show the world what a strange and eternal place this was.

She worked her assignment until the sun lowered on the horizon, and hefted her full pack of sample bottles. Bored, Sig was making a pest of himself by attempting to chew the wheels on the GPR cart. Petra wrested the cart away from him. She'd have to come back tomorrow with a full battery and more bottles. She descended the ridge from the northwest, to come directly back to the parking lot. The path was little-used, barely more than a footpath.

Light slanted through the pines as she descended. Squirrels flung pinecones from the trees at Sig, and he growled and snapped at them. They squeaked and chattered furiously in the trees.

Petra hurried through the assault, covering her head with one arm and thrusting the squeaking cart ahead of her with the other. She tripped over a rut in the trail and fell sprawling to the pine needle-covered ground. She swore, hoping that none of the plastic sample containers had broken. She sat up, grumbling at her skinned palms. Sig was beside her, casting a dirty look at the originators of the air raid behind them.

Petra's back pocket rang. She rolled over and dug her phone out of her pocket. Leave it to Mike to not trust her on a stroll through the woods.

"Yeah." She cradled the phone in the crook of her neck. "This is Petra."

A thin hiss echoed from her phone.

"Hello?"

She glanced at the caller ID: UNKNOWN NUMBER. Her grip tightened on the phone. Maybe someone had seen her flyer and had some information about her father. She was terrified to scare the caller away.

A voice echoed from what seemed to be a very far distance:

"*Get away. Now, while you can.*"

"Dad?" She sucked in her breath. God, it sounded like him. Just like him. It—

A dial tone echoed in her ear.

"Dad, don't . . ."

It was him. It had to be. With shaking fingers that smeared sap all over the keypad, she scrolled for the last incoming call and hit the CALL button. It rang exactly twice and went dead.

"Damn it." Yet hope flared within her. She'd heard her father's voice, she was certain of it. He'd called her, and that meant he *had* to be alive, somewhere. Maybe she could get Mike to trace the number.

"Huh."

She paused in climbing to her feet, squinting at something pale and splintered below the pines. Her GPR cart had rolled away into the soft bed of pine needles. The shape beyond it looked like a piece of the petrified forest. Had the ridge eroded on this slope enough to reveal another, older incarnation of the forest?

Her curiosity piqued, Petra crawled forward on her hands and knees. Pinesap stuck dried needles to her palms.

Sig growled. Petra looked back at him. His fur bristled, and he crouched close to the ground.

"You need to get over the squirrels. Really."

But Sig wasn't looking up. He was looking past her, at the petrified specimen. His nose flared and shivered.

Petra reached into her pack for a pick. Was Sig sensing a snake . . . or . . . God forbid, a larger predator? A bear?

A thin, reedy moan echoed from the foot of the pine.

Petra scrambled back, heart hammering. She dropped the pick and reached for the bear spray.

The moan sounded again. It didn't sound like a bear. It sounded . . . *human*.

Petra crept toward the sound, expecting to find an injured hiker. The pine needles were soft underfoot, muffling her steps. Sig slunk before her. But he didn't go beyond the tree. He stopped at the jagged piece of petrified wood, whimpered, circled it.

Petra peered at what she'd assumed to be a centuries-old tree. Something dead and silent. She pressed her hand to her mouth. "Oh, my God . . ."

It wasn't a tree. This thing was horribly, horribly alive. Bones were warped and twisted, calcified around what was unmistakably a human face. She saw no evidence of eyes in the sockets, but she did see teeth in a jagged, frozen jaw. A thin, wordless keening flexed the ribs.

Her hands scrabbled in the pine needles for her pick. "Hang on. I'll get you out of there." She swung awkwardly with the pick, splintering away pieces of petrified material and summoning blood to the jagged surface. The thing shrieked.

Petra recoiled. This wasn't someone encased in a prison of petrified wood—the prison was the person. A prison of bone.

She dug through her pack for her walkie-talkie.

"Mike, this is Petra. Are you out there?"

Static crackled. *"Hey, Petra. See the sights?"*

"I need paramedics, now."

"What's your twenty?"

"Huh?"

"Where are you?"

"Back side of Specimen Ridge." She read her GPS coordinates off her handheld device. She dropped it twice before she gave him a complete reading.

"Sending out help now." There was a burst of silence,

as she could imagine Mike working the radio panel at the ranger station. *"What happened?"*

Petra stared stupidly at the warped figure before her, wound around the roots of the pine tree. "I don't know," she whispered. "Just get here."

Mike sent the complete cavalry. Within fifteen minutes, a helicopter was in the sky above her, scaring the squirrels from their perches. A rescue ranger dropped down a line with a basket. There wasn't enough room to land in this cover. Sig disappeared into the underbrush, terrified of the noise.

"Ma'am," the ranger shouted over the sound of the blades overhead. "Where are you hurt?"

Petra pointed to the shape under the tree. The man wriggled out of his harness, clomped toward the bent figure. He knelt before it, and Petra could see him pale under his helmet visor. He spoke into his radio for what seemed to be a long time.

The helicopter sound receded, and Sig glided out of the underbrush to lean against Petra's leg.

"What the hell is going on?" Petra shouted to the ranger.

He held up his hand. "Stay back, ma'am."

Petra obliged. She retreated down the track along with Sig, away from the tree. Soon, the sound of engines could be heard. Mike and a phalanx of other rangers appeared on four-wheelers. She breathed a sigh of relief at seeing him.

"What's going on?" he asked, brow creased. "They said you found a body."

Petra shook her head. "It's not a body. I don't know what it is. But it's alive." She looked back at the pine tree, where medics had erected an oxygen tent.

"Barely." A female medic stood up and approached them. "I could hear a breath, but I lost it. And I don't know how to do CPR on . . . on that."

"What the hell happened to him . . . her? Is this a hazmat or biohazard situation?"

"I don't know. I . . . I've got nothing on this."

"Time to move up the food chain, then." Mike keyed his radio. "Get me the Department of the Interior. Tell them we have a situation."

The adrenaline didn't fade gracefully.

Petra stewed in her own adrenaline juices for hours. After hiking down the ridge on shaking legs, she stowed Sig, her guns, and the gear in the Bronco. Following Mike's stern instructions to wait at the ranger station, she busied herself with scrubbing the skin on her hands raw and plugging in her GPS cart to charge. She'd made it to her third cup of coffee before the National Guard showed up.

They'd questioned her for two hours before letting her go. Petra kept having to go to the bathroom, and she was sure that they thought that she was on drugs. But, damn it, she had to pee. And the coffee wasn't helping.

They kept wanting to know if the victim had said anything. Petra couldn't tell them anything that made any sense, and they eventually seemed to decide that she was an idiot. At least since there wasn't any immediate evidence of radiological or biological threat, there was no need to be stripped and hosed down in the parking lot as she'd feared. But they gave no information whatsoever about what they thought was happening.

The Guard cleared out after midnight, trucks rumbling away in the night. Petra wondered if one of them held the body. She hadn't seen an ambulance pass the windows.

Mike leaned tiredly on the front counter when she came out of the ladies' room. "Trouble follows you."

"Yeah, I know." Petra rubbed her eyes. "What happened? Did they take it—him, her—to a hospital?"

"They tried to dig it up, but it didn't survive. At least, that's what they tell me. The Guard took it with them to have it analyzed at the state lab."

"Do we know who it was?"

Mike frowned. "There was a hiker who went missing. His family called and said that he hadn't checked in for several days. Some guy who showed up in spring and was determined to hike the whole area before winter. They're gonna do a DNA test. I'm hoping that it wasn't him, but your guess is as good as mine. And . . . I wonder if there's any connection to what Jeff said he saw before he recanted and got driven off into the night."

"On Rutherford's property?"

"Yeah. I've asked the Feds to put an APB out for Jeff, see if they can find him. I want to talk to that guy without the goon squad looming over him." Mike drummed his fingers on the countertop, his gaze unfocused.

"Um. Not to add to your workload, but . . . I was wondering if you could do me a favor?"

"Favor?" he echoed.

"I got a call on my cell right before I called you. Came up as an unknown number. I wonder if it would be possible to trace it."

"It would probably be possible." His eyes narrowed. "Are you getting prank calls from those flyers you put up?

"Gah. I don't think so . . . I don't know. It sounded a lot like my dad. He told me to get away, while I still could."

"Sounds like good paternal advice." Mike stared at the ceiling, as if thinking. "We have a guy. We could justify the trace as part of an ongoing investigation—either as part of your dad's disappearance, or potentially associated with that body you found. But it might take some time."

"Thank you. I really appreciate all you're doing to help me. Really." Petra sighed. "I'm going to go get some sleep. I'll touch base with you in the morning?" It came out as a question, not a statement. She really wanted to leave, and didn't want to have to wrest permission from the Guard.

"Yeah. Just don't leave the area. Not that you were planning on running off, since you're having a slumber party with Maria, but I'm required to tell you that."

"Sure," Petra said. But she didn't know if she meant it.

She kicked gravel across the parking lot to the Bronco. Her jeans squeaked on the pleather seat as she got inside and slammed the door. She fished her cell phone out to dial Maria's number and announce that she was inviting herself over. Fog had formed on the inside of the glass, frosting the interior in the dim light of the ranger station. Coyote nose smears decorated the glass.

"Sig?"

She expected to find him snoring on the floor-boards, but nothing furry moved in the darkness. She looked over her shoulder into the backseat.

"Sig, you'd better not be chewing on my shit . . ." If he'd torn up the USGS equipment, she'd be fucked.

A low growl emanated from behind the backseat. It sounded like something truly feral, not the semi-tame dog that the coyote had been pretending to be.

"Sig? Are you okay?"

She saw a pair of ears silhouetted against the back window and the glint of Sig's golden glare. Something shuffled and squeaked in the back, kicking against metal. Petra reached up for the dome light and craned to view the backseat. Her other hand hovered above the Bronco's horn. A whole nest of rangers would come running if she leaned on it.

The yellow light illuminated Sig perched on a dark heap of limbs. Holy fuck—it was a person. Sig's teeth were wound in a black hooded sweatshirt, and lanky cargo pants-covered legs bent at an odd angle.

"It's me. Cal." A frightened eye peeped up over an elbow. Sig snarled and nipped at his earring.

"Cal. What the hell are you doing here?"

"I rode my motorbike."

"No . . . what are you doing here, in my truck?"

Sig chewed on his hoodie cord, and Cal whimpered. "I was gonna ask for your help. I saw the note that said you were gonna be at the station."

"You broke into my trailer. And my truck. And you want my help with *what*, exactly?" Petra's eyes narrowed.

"Look, that wasn't my idea. That was the Alchemist—uh, Stroud. I was just along for the ride."

"What the hell were you doing in my trailer? Looking for money?"

"No. He wants some antique you have. Says it looks like a compass. Gold. Must be worth a lot of money."

Petra's gaze flicked outside the fogged window. "You know that there are park rangers out there? I could have you arrested."

"Please." Cal looked at her with traumatized eyes. "Arrest me. Just get your coyote off me. He's standing on my bladder, and I really have to pee."

Petra nodded at Sig. "Good dog."

Sig bared his teeth.

"So you came back to search my truck, is that it?"

"No. Like I said, I came to ask for your help."

Petra stared at him. "People don't normally grant favors to burglars."

"I'm sorry. Really. I didn't have much choice in that."

"What do you want? Money for meth?"

"No. I need your help looking for the body that the guy in the bar was talking about. On Rutherford's ranch." Cal's mouth thinned. "I think . . . I think it might belong to one of my friends."

"Why do you think that I can help you?"

"I saw this thing on TV about geologists looking for Hoffa's body under Giants Stadium." Cal's Adam's apple bobbed. "You can—you can do that, right?"

Petra lifted an eyebrow. "Maybe. But you're gonna owe me."

CHAPTER THIRTEEN

BODY COUNT

"Do you see anything yet?"

Cal drifted along in Petra's wake, staring at the glowing light on the display of the ground penetrating radar cart. It was already beginning to dim under the half charge she'd given it at the ranger station. The cart bounced over ruts and bent grasses at the edge of one of Rutherford's fields. There was no sign of Rutherford's ranch hands in the waxing moonlight, but the shadows and movements of the breeze made Petra jump. The light was enough to see by on this clear night. Enough to be seen.

"Nothing yet," Petra hissed. "You're supposed to be keeping watch."

"Your coyote seems to have that under control."

Sig walked ahead of them, sniffing in the breeze. His ears stood straight and alert as he scanned the darkness.

"Look, I don't want to get your hopes up," Petra said. They'd been out here for hours, pacing behind the cart and looking over their shoulders. "This could take days, under even the best of conditions. We have no idea where Jeff found that body."

"We've gotta try," Cal insisted.

Petra was inclined to agree, if only for curiosity's sake. She'd come partly because Cal had asked her, and partly because she wondered if the body he'd seen really resembled the one she'd found on the ridge. One body in such a bizarre state was a fluke, but more?

She frowned as she stared at the readout monitor. The striations of the ground were odd here. The layers of soil scanned more opaque than most, but she thought she saw more black areas than she should.

"What is it?" Cal bounced on the toes of his boots.

"I dunno. This land is weird." She pointed to the voids in the scan. "It looks like tunnels."

"Prairie dogs?" Cal suggested helpfully.

"No. Bigger than that. Almost like a cave system. They're all over here." She chewed on her lip. "Almost looks like a mine, but less regular. More organic." She wished that she had permission to be here, to ask questions. This might be an interesting geological feature to map.

"Hey. Your coyote is freaking out."

Petra looked up from the fading monitor. Yards ahead, Sig was clawing at the ground, tossing clods of earth.

She shrugged. "Well, we could try looking *there*."

She dragged the cart to where Sig was excavating. He whimpered and gave ground to the cart, but paced in a circle as Petra scanned the earth. She squinted at the readout. A spot had formed a few feet below on the scan, the readout showing broken sediment and disturbed earth.

"Huh."

"What is it?"

"There might be something there."

"How do we tell for sure?"

Petra looked at Cal with enduring patience. "We dig. Go get the shovels out of the truck."

Cal skittered away to the dim hulk of the Bronco. Petra fingered the keys in her pocket. She liked the kid, but she didn't trust him enough to leave the keys in the ignition. So far, he hadn't done much to earn it.

Sig didn't wait for Cal. He tore into the ground as if someone had buried his favorite lunch meat. Petra picked up a clump of earth. It felt loose and granular, not hard and packed down like the rest of the soil here. It had been moved recently, since the last time it had rained. Water hadn't had the opportunity to seal the clay together and drive the oxygen out. It made for easy digging, and Petra became more convinced that there was something below.

By the time Cal had brought the shovels back from the truck, Sig had sunk up to his shoulders in his hole. Petra whistled for him to come out, and he clambered up in a spray of dirt. She wrinkled her nose, vowing to wash him.

Cal clumsily set his shovel into the ground. He and Petra worked in silence for a few minutes, until her shovel blade struck a tree root.

But there were no trees in this part of the field.

Petra knelt, brushed the dirt away from a pale shape that gleamed in the moonlight. She sucked in her breath.

"What is it?" Cal croaked.

Petra stood back, so that her shadow didn't interrupt the meager light. The claw of a hand reached upward in the soil, frozen in the dirt. But it wasn't simply a hand. Bone grew over a watch and curled in a delicate lattice between the last fingers, a webbing that had been shattered by the shovel blade.

Petra held her breath. She could still hear the watch ticking. Or maybe it was her heart. She glanced sidelong at Cal.

Cal sat on his ass on the ground. He was shaking.

"That's human?" he whispered.

"It looks like it. Sort of."

He let out a quavering breath, sweat glistening on his forehead. Petra sat back on her heels beside him.

"There's a watch," Petra said. She didn't have much

interest in poking and prodding the body, but it was clear that Cal needed her to be in charge, here.

"A watch," he echoed.

"Yeah." Petra squinted at it. "It looks like a man's watch. Silver with a black dial." She leaned forward, rubbed at the broken crystal. "Has a Jolly Roger on the face."

Cal swallowed. "Adam never wore a watch. Some Taoist shit about being in the moment. It's not him."

"That's good, right?"

Cal shook his head. "Not really. That Jolly Roger watch belongs to one of Stroud's other guys. There's gonna be hell to pay."

Petra reached for her cell phone.

"What are you doing?"

"I'm going to take a picture, for evidence. And then I'm calling for help."

Cal blinked at the flash. "You can't do that."

Petra stared at him. "There's a body. We have to report it."

"The county sheriff's office won't touch it. This is Rutherford's land." He looked at her incredulously, as if she was just plain stupid.

"Yeah, well. I think I know some people who will be interested in a calcinated body." Petra dialed Mike's cell phone number. It rang five times before a muzzy voice picked up.

"Yell-ow." Stubble scraped the receiver.

"Mike, this is Petra. I, uh, have a problem."

"Why am I not surprised?" Petra heard bedsprings creak, and she imagined that he was sitting up and looking at his clock. "It's three in the morning. And you're supposed to be bunking with Maria."

"You know that body that Jeff was talking about at the Compostela?"

"Yeah. Do I really want to know where you're going with this?"

"The Feds might. Cal and I just—"

"Who's Cal?"

"A kid from town. His friends were missing. Long story. But Cal and I are looking at a calcinated body at the edge of one of the fields. Like the one from Specimen Ridge. I'll write down the GPS coordinates, but I want to know what you want us to do—should we cover it up or leave it be or . . ." Petra realized that she was babbling.

Mike cut her off. His voice was suddenly steely and alert. "Are you at Rutherford's ranch?"

"Yeah."

"I'll talk to the Feds about getting a warrant. Get the hell out of there, now."

"But—"

"Leave it and get out, now. It's not safe."

"I—"

"Now."

"Uh, okay." Petra shut the phone off and stood, grabbing the shovels. There was something in Mike's voice that chilled her. As much as she resented being told what to do, she had to defer to his authority in law enforcement issues. And this was the second body she'd found in a day. Not a good start.

"What happened?" Cal asked.

"Get the gear and get into the truck. We're leaving."

She gazed out at the moonlight horizon, blowing out her breath in frustration. No matter what rational thought demanded, none of the rules seemed to apply here.

Fuck the rules.

Today was going to be different. No more stone-walling, no more ignored questions. No one was giving Petra any answers, so she would damn well dig up her own.

She'd risen early, before light crept into the window. She hadn't slept, anyway, and figured that there was no point in lying in bed, stewing, for another couple of hours. Nor had there been a point in knocking on Maria's door in the middle of the night, so she went back home after she and Cal unearthed the body. She'd spoken to Mike when she'd returned to the trailer, for-warding the smeary shot she'd taken in the field that looked like a scarecrow Halloween decoration. Sort of. It was blurry and dark, and she had to convince herself really hard to see the likeness of a body. He'd promised to contact the Feds, who could then get a warrant. But he couldn't say exactly how long that would take.

By dawn, she was on the road to Yellowstone,

coffee from Bear's deli in hand. Sig rode shotgun, looking pissed. The coyote had spent most of the night scratching and chewing his skin, and Petra had found her legs covered with dozens of tiny round red flea bites in the morning. Fortunately, Bear's convenience store stocked flea collars. Petra had gone three rounds with Sig in the front seat of the Bronco before she'd managed to get the damn thing on him. She'd finally distracted him with a piece of donut and wrestled it around his neck. She didn't know how long it would stay, since he kept trying to bite at it and slide his paws under the buckle to get it off.

"Sig, quit being a drama queen. If you're going to act like a domesticated animal, you have to take the bad with the good. And, yeah, you're getting a bath when we get back."

Sig cast her a dirty look with half-slitted golden eyes, as if to say: *I am not a domestic animal.*

Petra didn't see Mike's Jeep as she passed the ranger station, which was a good thing. Maybe he was doing something useful, like getting a judge out of bed. Besides which, she didn't want him giving her grief about going back up on Specimen Ridge.

This early in the morning, there was no sign of tourists. The trail to the ridge had been obstructed with an orange blockade and sign that said CLOSED FOR MAINTENANCE. She sidestepped it and retraced her footsteps from yesterday.

She knew that there had to be a rational explanation for what had happened to that body. Was there something about the ground, some toxin or chemical stew in a mudpot that could cause petrification at an accelerated rate? Was this simply a victim of some odd medical illness? Petra remembered reading an article in a magazine about a biological mutation that caused excess skeletal bone growth. She couldn't remember the name of it, but it was worth looking up. Mike had to have an Internet connection at the ranger station.

And more data would yield her answer.

She climbed up the ridge, chiseled away some more samples from the petrified trees for comparison. They came away in her hands as thin and brittle as mica. Hopefully, the bones of the trees could tell her about the bones of the body. She worked until she had dozens of samples from as many different trees as she could find. Sig slunk behind her, as if embarrassed that any other wildlife might spot him sporting a flea collar.

She expected to need to use her GPS to identify the exact location of the body, but the National Guard had left behind enough markers. Tracks had made a muddy mess of the trail. Yellow caution tape surrounded the pine tree, cordoning off a hole about three feet deep.

Petra began collecting soil samples from the perimeter. She didn't see any evidence of a mudpot that could be stewing toxins, but that wasn't to say that none existed. Mudpots were vents of geothermal pressure and gas that superheated water and earth around them, giving the effect of a witch's bubbling cauldron. Yellowstone was most famous for the Artist Paint Pot and the Fountain Paint Pots. But mudpots, like water-falls, were too numerous to be completely cataloged in a park measuring nearly three thousand five hundred square miles.

She approached the hole cautiously, stepping in be-tween the pine tree roots to get a better look. Curios-ity had overwhelmed any sense of fear. People scared Petra—they were volatile, unpredictable. But the natu-ral world could always be explained. It behaved accord-ing to established laws that didn't change. Petra could play by those rules.

She poked around the bottom of the hole, filling her vials. The Guard must have been here for a good while with their shovels. Her eyes glittered in delight when she saw something white and shiny at the bottom of the hole—a fragment of bone. She tucked it away in a sample bottle and climbed out, exhilarated. She'd make sense of this, one way or another.

With a cranky coyote in tow, she clomped back down the ridge. Cranking the ignition on the Bronco, she drove back toward the ranger station. By this civi-lized hour, cars were in the parking lot—including Mike's Jeep. He was standing outside the station, talk-ing into his cell phone, when Petra saw him.

Mike clicked off his cell phone. "Been trying to reach you."

Petra shrugged. "Reception must be spotty."

He frowned at her. "Look, I'm not trying to be an asshole, here. But there are rules, and we've got to follow procedures."

Petra spread her hands, incredulous. "Mike. We found a *body*."

"Yeah, and if we want that body to stick to Sal Rutherford, we have to dot all our I's and cross our T's." He put his hands on his gun belt, exasperated. "You don't get it. This is like trying to take down Jesus Christ."

Petra shook her head, and she could feel heat rising behind her freckles. "You're right. I don't get it. I don't get how meth heads and cattle barons run the Wild West. I don't get how the local sheriff's office doesn't get their hands or their cars dirty. I don't get how people just disappear. *I don't get it.*"

"Hey. I'm on your side. Honest," Mike said quietly.

She looked up at him, and there was such sincerity and hurt in his expression that she felt a pang of regret.

She cast her eyes down. "I'm sorry. I know that this isn't your fault. You've done nothing but try to help me."

"It's okay. Really." He awkwardly patted her shoulder, and his hand lingered an instant too long. "How about some coffee?"

"Okay. But can I have some water for Sig?" The coyote leaned against her leg. Probably doing his damnedest to transmit the escaping plague of fleas onto her jeans, she thought sourly.

A grin split Mike's face as he looked at Sig. "Is that coyote wearing a flea collar?"

"Yeah. And he's not too happy 'bout it."

"You know, there are places we could get you a real dog."

Sig gave him a dirty look.

"I'm happy with Sig, *thankyouverymuch*." Petra opened the tailgate to the Bronco, and the coyote scrambled in for a nap.

"You been out collecting samples?"

"Yeah. Couldn't sleep." She didn't tell him *where* she'd been collecting samples.

Worry creased his tanned face. At least, it looked like worry and not suspicion. "You shouldn't be out here by yourself. Especially with your knack for finding dead bodies."

"I have Sig. And the bear spray," she said, then changed the subject. "Any news on the body on the ridge?"

Mike frowned. "Not much. The working assumption is that it's the body of the missing hiker. They apparently found a backpack somewhere in that mess that contained a wallet, a whole lotta money, and some drug paraphernalia."

"Money?"

"Yeah. Like several thousand dollars. Who the hell knows what for."

"Do you have Internet in there?" Petra gestured with her chin at the ranger station.

"Yup. This way." Mike led her to a back office with a surprisingly new computer and laser printer. A screen saver of classic Pac-Man chased pastel ghosts around the darkened monitor.

"Nice. Very retro screen saver for a shiny new box."

"I think that was leftover money from a Homeland

Security grant." He grinned. "Gotta keep on top of things in the outside world." He typed in his password, interrupting Pac-Man's hunt, and turned the chair over to Petra.

Petra settled in and searched for "bone overgrowth disease," which led her to the name of a specific syndrome.

"Fibrodysplasia ossificans progressiva, also called FOP," she muttered. "Hey, look at this." She pointed to the screen. "This disease causes body tissues to ossify when injured."

"Wow." Mike gave a low whistle when she called up a picture of a badly distorted skeleton covered in uneven sheets of bone and cartilidge. "That's sorta like what we saw."

Petra nodded in satisfaction. "Can you find out if the hiker had this disorder?"

"I can make some calls." Mike disappeared to the radio room, leaving Petra to her own devices.

She rummaged through her box of goodies from USGS and set up her microscope. She found a few slide images on the Internet of FOP bone cross sections. She eagerly began to chip down the bone fragment she found to make a decent slide. After she'd clumsily made a thin enough slice, she slipped it on a prepared slide with an aqueous solution. Adjusting the magnification, she peered at the sample.

She could see the same clumps and voids in bone cells in her sample as the one on the virtual slide on the Internet. She was no biologist, but this seemed to be leading her in the right direction. Except . . .

She rested her chin in her hand. FOP was a congenital disorder. People began experiencing symptoms as children. She'd encountered a grossly progressive case. How had someone that ill gotten up on the ridge in the first place? Bone growth in FOP patients was fast, but could it be that debilitatingly fast? A scan of the articles she'd searched suggested that wasn't possible. Severely malformed bones like this took years to develop. There was no way that this guy was well enough to hike around Yellowstone for months while turning into a skeleton. And the odds of having two cases in a week . . . it defied rational explanation. She hated that.

Mike returned to the small office. "I spoke with the hiker's sister. He was twenty-two, reportedly in good health, and no known medical conditions other than an appendectomy when he was twelve."

Petra leaned back in the chair. "So much for that idea."

"I also heard back from my friend about your unknown caller."

"Oh yeah?" At least that seemed to be moving quickly. "Did he get an address?"

"You know anybody with an address in the middle of the Bermuda Triangle?"

She stared up at him. "What?"

"As near as he can determine, it bounced off a land-bound cell tower and two satellites. And the signal came from the middle of the ocean. Which is just not possible."

Petra stared at the wall. "I don't . . ." Could it be someone she used to work with, out on a boat or a drilling platform? But she knew of no drilling going on in that part of the world.

"Could be a data error. This kind of shit happens. But I'm curious as hell to see if you get any more calls." Mike took a swig of his coffee and looked at her microscope. "Whatcha looking at?"

She didn't want to tell him she'd been poking around the scene. "I'm getting started on the soil samples from yesterday."

"I'll let you know if I hear anything else about that body." Mike shook his head. "I hope they keep us in the loop."

"Yeah." But Petra knew enough about bureaucracies to know that was highly unlikely.

Mike handed her a yellow legal pad. "And humor my bureaucratic tendencies. When you get a minute, write out your statement from last night. Also any contact information you have for this Cal guy."

Which was nothing. She didn't even have a last name. She scribbled down her recollection of the night's events, along with the GPS coordinates for the body at the ranch. She felt as if maybe she should draw them a map with stick figures, too. As she wrote, she felt her writing grow angrier and less legible. She ripped the pages off the legal pad, signed them, and set them aside, blowing out her breath.

Enough of bureaucracy. Time for science.

She organized her soil samples and began to prepare and examine slides. She found bits of ash and the heavy metals that she'd anticipate in geothermic soils, even a fragment of amethyst in one of the samples. Then she switched gears and started to run slides of the petrified forest wood. The pattern of the wood looked as she expected it to—bits of silicon and white quartz and carbonized organic compounds in shades of brown. She'd managed to get a bit of a calcified microfossil on one chip. The structure was strongly reminiscent of the bone cells in her sample.

She drummed her fingers in frustration. Without the equipment here to do any kind of specialized analysis, she was at a dead end—on this mystery, anyway. Petra rummaged through her sample sack for a bottle she'd prepared at the trailer. It contained a neatly cutout piece of the shirt she'd worn when Gabriel bled all over her the other day, a sample of the phosphorescent blood that contained gold.

She moistened a swab in distilled water, pulled some of the stain off the fabric, and smeared a new slide. Slipping a slide cover into place, she peered through the microscope.

Interesting.

Petra remembered examining her own blood in biology class in college, large roundish blood cells interspersed with small fuzzy platelets. This looked nothing like that. The red blood cells she saw weren't round—they were spiky. Like viruses. But viruses were too small to be seen under a standard microscope. These were huge. And they showed no signs of degradation, as she'd expect plain blood cells to demonstrate.

Petra shivered. Whatever it was, she hoped it wasn't contagious. It sure as hell didn't seem normal. She shut off the microscope, swept her slides into a box, and grabbed her jacket.

It was time to see if Gabriel had some answers.

CHAPTER FOURTEEN

OLD SCARS

The Rutherford ranch appeared less fearsome by daylight.

Bucolic, even.

Cattle meandered behind barbed wire fences in tall grass at the foot of the mountains. Petra guessed that they were Angus, nice walking steaks. They crowded into shady spots beneath lonely trees, thickening the shadow. A few interlopers had wandered into the fields; a couple of pronghorn had jumped the fence and were grazing greedily with the cattle. Petra saw no evidence of human caretaking for miles, just black specks of cows against the green and gold of the fields.

Nor did she see any evidence of federal agents descending upon the farm and digging for bodies. She passed the area she and Cal had excavated the night before. It appeared undisturbed from her vantage point at the road: no crime scene tape, no guards.

Sig hung his head out the window, barking at birds in the sky. The ravens cawed back to him.

"You can't catch birds," Petra told him.

He turned and fixed her with a bemused look.

She thought for a moment. Gabriel always seemed to be in the company of ravens. She looked skyward and followed the birds.

She wound around dirt roads for miles until she spied a structure in the distance. Her binoculars showed her a sprawling ranch house. It looked as if it had been rooted in the ground for many decades—timber and stone, with a metal roof oxidized green from the rain. It reminded her of the lodge. Some distance away from it stood a barn that dwarfed the house, a ramshackle structure of rotting wood.

Petra rolled up to the barn, parking the Bronco beside a beat-up truck. She recognized it—the pickup that Gabe had driven from the Compostela. She hopped down and Sig followed her, ears flattened. The shadow of the barn pressed cool against her skin.

She screwed up her courage, walking into the barn with Sig at her side. Her heart hammered, remembering Mike's warning.

"Hello?" Her voice sounded cockier than she felt, though.

Straw dust motes were suspended in thin ribbons of sunshine from the cracks in the walls and ceiling. The smells of rust and dust and manure had sunk deep into the structure. Farm equipment that she couldn't identify was stacked in corners, parked within the structure, making a labyrinth of metal. Eerie silence hung here, interrupted only by the scrabbling of birds and mice in the hayloft. Behind the shafts of light lay darkness.

"Hello?" she called.

She spied a raven perched on the hood of a 1940s vintage tractor. Her skin prickled. The bird paced back and forth agitatedly, ruffling its feathers.

Gabriel and his ravens. He had to be here.

Behind the tractor, she spied a dim glow. Not the clear yellow gleam of sunshine nor the silvery blue hues of fluorescent light. This was a seething and familiar glow—the glow of Gabriel's blood. She followed it, walking behind the tractor.

She gasped.

A body lay sprawled, unmoving on the floor. Softly shining blood soaked the man's flannel shirt. His elbows and knees were turned at unnatural angles.

Petra knelt beside the body. Brushing aside straw, she stared at a battered but familiar face.

"Gabriel?"

His eyes were swollen nearly shut, and golden blood leaked from his lower lip and ears. She pressed her fingers to his throat. She felt a slow hum, like static on a radio. He was still alive. Alive-ish.

She reached under his arms and hefted him up to a sitting position. Seeing the front of his shirt, she felt instantly queasy. Through prickles of straw, she could make out the lumps of contusions and broken bones. And—*oh, fuck*—he was missing a hand. She stared at his empty sleeve, where his arm just . . . ended.

She struggled to her feet, hauling him with her. She was mindful not to try to touch his ribs, but there was no way to avoid manhandling his injuries. Oddly, he felt lighter than she thought he should, like he was a drained shell of a man.

She half-carried, half-dragged him toward the barn door. His boots trailed in the straw. Ravens fluttered after them, casting flickering shadows.

"I've got to get you out of here," she huffed. He slid out of her arms when she reached the Bronco. She wrestled the door open, shoved him in the passenger seat. Sig leapt into the backseat, affronted by the stickiness and loss of his territory on the front seat.

Petra scrambled over to the driver's side, cranked the engine. The Bronco started up with a snort and growl, and she backed out onto the dirt road. A squad of noisy ravens followed like tin cans strung behind a bride and groom's getaway car.

Mike had been right. The ranch was more dangerous than she'd imagined. Her sticky fingers clutched the steering wheel.

A shot cracked into the back of the Bronco, shattering a taillight. A raven splintered off from the rest of the flock with a shriek, spiraling toward the blue sky.

"Sig, get down."

Petra scrunched down in the seat and floored the gas. She looked back in the rearview mirror at a portly middle-aged man holding a gun. He made no move to pursue her, just stood and watched her retreat. Something about the smile on his face chilled her in the afternoon heat, even after he vanished in a haze of dust.

The lone raven was a dot in the sky to the north, dissolving into the blue.

The raven careened dizzily into the sky. Clouds and ground whirled around him. One wing's primary feathers had been shredded at the edges by birdshot. He struggled to right himself, clawing the air with his talons and feathers.

Dimly, he knew that he'd lost the other ravens, the other, smaller fragments of his consciousness. But there was nothing for that, now. He snagged an air current sliding down from the mountains that swept him north. Panting, he followed it, letting it push his body forward in the blue.

A familiar landscape unfolded below him: the sparkling blue eye of the spring and the fringe of golden fields swaying beyond. The air current began to peter out, the raven swept his uninjured wing low to turn into a spiral. He landed gracelessly on the roof of a small house, hopping twice before skidding to a teetering stop at the edge of a gutter.

The raven bowed his head, beak parted. He shoved his wing forward, examining it, then pulled the feathers through his beak to seal the damage and knit the feathers as whole as he could make them.

On the ground below, a cat sat and stared up a him, her eyes dilated and black.

The raven cawed shortly at her, and she meowed. Stiffly, she stalked around the edge of the garden, having agreed to grant him a few moments' sanctuary.

Human voices emanated below him.

"Old ghosts are catching up with us."

A bronze woman with long black hair set her briefcase down on the porch floor. The raven crept forward and peered over the gutter. An old man sat in a porch swing, muttering to himself. His eyes were closed, and he seemed to be asleep. The raven recognized him— the old man from the well.

The woman paused to kiss the top of his head.

The old man's eyes fluttered open. "They're coming for your friend."

"Huh?"

The old man blinked at her. "Wha?"

"Never mind," she said. "I'll make spaghetti for dinner."

"Yup. Gotta do something with that bumper crop

of tomatoes." The old man rubbed his creased forehead. "How long have I been asleep?"

"Dunno. I just got home. When did you start hitting the bottle today?"

"I haven't." The man stuck out his lower lip like a petulant child.

The woman opened her mouth to argue, but her attention was captured by the rattle of a truck coming down the road. The shiny pickup stopped in front of the house.

The raven knew that truck, and he screamed a warning.

The woman and the old man ignored the bird, staring at the pickup. But the cat heard him. She wriggled under the porch.

The back of the pickup was full of Sal Rutherford's men. And Sal himself was behind the wheel.

"Get inside, Frankie," the woman growled.

"I ain't going nowhere," he said.

Sal slid out of the truck and ambled up to the porch. "Afternoon, Miss Yellowrose." Though his words were civil, they dripped with sarcasm.

Miss Yellowrose crossed her arms in front of her. "What do you want, Sal?"

His cold smile faded. "You were at my ranch today. I've come to get back what you stole."

The woman's chin lifted. "What the hell are you talking about?" She hefted her battered briefcase. "I've been at work all day."

Frankie climbed to his feet, swaying. "Maria's no thief."

Sal wasn't convinced. "I saw your Bronco leaving my barn. Nobody else has a piece of shit quite like that one."

"I sold it. Couple of days ago."

Sal's mouth twisted. "What've you been driving to work, then?"

She pointed. "Frankie's Explorer." She pointed to the green SUV in the drive, now effectively blocked in by Sal's truck.

Sal walked over to the Explorer and slapped his palm on the hood. He winced, so it still must have been hot.

"Who'd you sell it to?" His eyes narrowed in suspicion.

"Some tourist whose car broke down. I felt sorry for her."

"She got a name?"

"No. She paid cash. She took the title with her."

Sal rubbed his stubbly chin. "You don't mind if we take a look around, do you?"

"Yeah, I mind. You aren't the cops. This is tribal land. So get off it."

Frankie reached into his back waistband. A pistol shook in his grip. "You heard my niece. Leave."

Sal backed off, hands open. "Take it easy, Frankie. I'm just trying to get back what's mine."

The line of silent ranch hands behind him didn't retreat. They folded around Sal, approached the porch.

Frankie fired. The raven couldn't see if he hit anyone; the three men rushed him in a wall of flannel. Before Maria could shout, Frankie was on his belly with a knee in his back, swearing a blue streak. The gun was in the dirt. The two remaining ranch hands stormed into the house. Inside, the raven could hear the thump of furniture being tossed.

"You can't do this," said Maria. "You aren't a law unto yourself."

Sal lit a cigarette, shrugged nonchalantly. "You keep tellin' yourself that, Miss Yellowrose."

"What the hell are you looking for?" she demanded as glass broke indoors.

"Just a misplaced piece of property," Sal said, blowing smoke into her face. "Something that I wasn't quite finished with."

His throat under the heel of a ranch hand, Frankie croaked, "You just keep burying those bodies, Sal. Sooner or later, they're gonna rise up against you."

"What did you say?" Sal leaned down and jerked Frankie's head back by his hair.

"He's drunk," Maria pleaded, trying to force herself between Sal and Frankie. "Leave him alone!"

"Them corpses are gonna be the end of you," Frankie growled.

"Get him up," Sal said.

Maria hurled herself at Sal and slugged him across the jaw.

Sal recoiled, rubbing his face. And returned the favor. The blow flung Maria across the porch, cracking the back of her head on the mailbox. She was unconscious before she hit the ground.

Sal gestured at the ranch hands. "Leave her here. The old man comes with us."

He glanced up then, as if he sensed he was being watched. The raven scuttled back on the roof, clinging to the curled shingles. He did not budge until he heard the sound of an engine and saw the truck leaving down the gravel road.

"Sig, you're gonna have to surrender your flea-infested bed to our guest."

The coyote growled.

"Look, I'm not in the habit of hauling strange men home, but you're gonna have to deal."

Petra dragged Gabriel's limp body out of the truck into the Airstream. It was like wrestling with a rag doll—awkward, floppy, and expressionless. She didn't know where else to take him. She couldn't take him to a hospital. What on earth would they make of that glow-in-the-dark blood? And she couldn't leave him at the Rutherford ranch. She had no other choice but to invade Sig's bed. She hoped that Gabe survived. There was no good way to explain the body of a man with glowing blood in her bed. If anybody cared.

Besides, she was curious as hell.

She dumped Gabriel's unconscious form onto the futon. Petra cast about the trailer for materials to use as a first aid kit. She came up with the bottle of alcohol she'd gotten from the hardware store, the aluminum tape she used to create the spectroscope, the X-acto knives, and a couple of fistfuls of cotton.

Good enough.

She grasped Gabe's right arm, pushing the sleeve up. His hand . . . his hand just wasn't there. Below the wrist, a jagged wound seemed to suggest it had been torn off, but there was no blood. Not even seeping. She turned his arm over, examining it. Was this an old wound, somehow? But he had been whole the last time she'd seen him . . . it made no sense. Perhaps he used a very good prosthetic that she hadn't noticed? She still bound it up with a towel from the bathroom, wrapping it tightly with aluminum tape.

Next she unbuttoned Gabe's shirt, exposing wounds in his shoulder and ribs. It looked like someone had struck him with some kind of a blunt object—a baseball bat? Thick swelling and contusions had formed over prickly areas that suggested shattered bone. She gently wrestled Gabriel out of his sleeves, feeling as if she were pouring spaghetti into a drinking straw.

She sat back on her heels. She didn't know how to deal with wounds like these. Gabriel's skin was cold and smooth across his well-muscled chest. In the shade of the trailer, the wounds looked like splatters from a paintball gun, pulsing a shimmering yellow from the edges. It was as if his skin were stretched tight over a great and terrible light, and rends in his skin allowed it to leak out.

But what captured her attention the most was the

scar around his neck. It was white, raised, and as thick as two of her fingers. An old scar. What the hell had happened to him? Had he survived a suicide attempt? Had someone done this to him?

Wherever Gabriel had been, he'd had a long road.

She turned on the light overhead. In the artificial brightness, his blood was red and ordinary. Less disconcerting. She opened the windows to give her more light, cranking open the blinds and letting the thin breeze trickle into the Airstream.

Resolutely, she began to clean the wounds at his shoulder, wiping at them with the cotton and the alcohol. Gabriel's eyelids fluttered, but he didn't so much as hiss as she tried to clean that blood from the holes in his body where the swelling had split flesh. She probed as deeply as she dared before her stomach turned. It seemed as if one of the wounds had just missed what she guessed was his axillary artery.

The next most serious wound was the one that split his ribs. Petra could see the swelling and feel the unevenness of bone. A large chunk seemed to be missing. She pressed an ear to his chest. It seemed the right side of his chest rose evenly, but not the left. When she listened to his breath, it gurgled in his throat. A collapsed lung. Shit.

"Why do this to you?" she murmured. She was certain that Gabriel was not a good, upstanding citizen. Upstanding citizens did not attempt to make loud-mouthed ranch hands disappear. But she thought she saw a glint of something else in him. She couldn't identify what that was.

And she likely would never learn, if he bled out on her bed. With renewed determination, she reached for the aluminum tape. If she could drag him upright, maybe she could tape the ribs so that they didn't move further.

She worked in silence, swallowing her squeamishness. When she removed his boots, she found that one of them was entirely empty, that his foot didn't exist beyond the ankle bone. His body felt curiously hollow, and his face remained slack and unconscious. She knew that she should be wary of him. Every scar and wound on his body screamed a warning that he was dangerous. But there was something about him that piqued her curiosity. He was handsome enough, in a somewhat cold and remote way. He wasn't pretty the way that the ridiculously shaven and airbrushed men in magazines were. He wasn't shiny. He was solid, real. His jaw was strong, nose a bit too large, hands callused—well, the one that remained, anyway. She granted herself the small thrill of physical attraction, the first awakening of that dormant sense since Des had died. It was normal to feel that way around an attractive man, she told herself—purely a physical reaction. Gabe reminded her of stone: flawed and opaque, with scars veining his skin.

And not fragile. Her eyes traced the wounds. Poor Des had been fragile.

She blinked away a sudden blurriness in her vision.

She reached out shakily and laid the flat of her hand on his chest. It was cool under her palm as it rose and fell. She held her hand there until it stopped shaking.

She *should* be afraid of him. Everyone else in this town seemed to be.

But it seemed safe to feel a twinge of fascination for a man who was as close to indestructible as she'd ever encountered. This puzzle.

She leaned over him, a tendril of her hair brushing his chin. She wondered what would happen if she kissed him. He would never know, locked away in his unconsciousness. But she wondered what it would feel like, if his lips would feel like Des's mouth. Or if it would summon that terrible heat of grief again.

Her lips brushed his. His mouth was cool, and tasting him was like tasting frost. The chill prickled against her lips. Something melted. Whether it was his mouth or something in Petra, she couldn't tell.

She drew back, her heart hammering. Des always smiled when she kissed him, even in his sleep. Gabriel was smooth and unyielding. She felt immediately ashamed at what she'd done, knowing that she'd crossed a boundary without permission.

Selfish. It was selfish.

She slid down to sit on the warm linoleum floor and rested her head next to his shoulder to keep watch.

Petra dreamed of sunshine and ravens.

The dream felt like sitting in a car, drenched in late afternoon light, the gold of it pressed against her closed eyelids and warming her face. The shadows of ravens flitted over her, their wings rustling over a low hum. Or it might have been the low hum of an engine.

But it was the hum of blood, of Gabriel's body.

A raven screamed.

Petra jerked awake. She rubbed her warm cheek, pressed against the futon. She reached up to make sure Gabriel was still breathing, but he wasn't in bed. Her fingers clawed empty blankets.

The sound of wings flapping washed over her, some residue from the dream come flaring back. She spun toward the source of the sound. Sig pressed against her hip, growling, his hair standing up.

Gabe stood in the middle of the floor, a black silhouette against the gloaming western light from the windows. He held his arms outstretched, and a battery of wings flowed to him—*into him*. Ravens flew through the open windows, slamming into his body.

Petra scrambled away until her back hit the wall, drawing her knees up to her chest. She wanted to shriek, but her voice was choked off, as if she'd swallowed some of that terrible darkness gathering before her.

CHAPTER FIFTEEN

VENIFICUS LOCUS

The ravens melted into Gabriel, splitting the setting sunlight and dust motes with the knife-edges of their feathers. He turned to face her. His eyes glowed with reflected sunshine. His bare chest and hands and feet were whole, no deep dents or missing limbs.

Petra shrank back from the unnatural shadows and brilliance.

Gabriel stumbled.

Automatically, Petra jumped up to steady him. She lowered him to the futon, blinking her light-dazzled eyes. It seemed he weighed a great deal more now than he had a few hours ago—as if he had changed from aluminum to lead and promptly passed out. She reached for his throat to take his pulse. Her fingers quaked as she struggled to feel something.

Gabriel's hand reached up and grabbed her wrist with his whole right hand, stilling it. His eyes twitched open. "Don't."

"You need treatment of some kind—" She stared at his hand. It was entirely unmarked, smooth and whole.

"*Don't.*"

Anger rose in Petra, and she could feel the heat of it in her face. That, and the metallic fear under her tongue. It was easier to cover the fear with anger. "I don't want a dead man in my house."

Gabriel started to laugh, laughed so hard that the movement summoned a smear of blood to his lips. "Too late."

Petra wrenched her hand free and started daubing at the wound on his ribs. To her amazement, she could feel that the swelling had decreased. The fracture wasn't immediately apparent, and the bleeding had stopped entirely.

She let her hands fall. "What are you?"

Gabriel turned his head to the window, refusing to answer. "Where are we?"

"My trailer."

He closed his eyes. "You shouldn't have taken me from the barn."

"You would have died." She was beginning to think that maybe she should have left him, that she'd allowed something very dangerous across her threshold. And once invited in, it might not be so easily convinced to leave.

"Unlikely. My kind is usually quite . . . hardy."

Petra dug into her jacket pocket for the mourning brooch. "Your kind?" She held the brooch in her fist, shoved it under his nose. Her curiosity warred with terror, and she clutched the brooch hard to keep her hand from shaking. "What the fuck are you?"

"Where did you get that?" he demanded, his voice a low growl.

"So you know what it is."

He turned his head away.

She flipped it open, jammed it into his face. "Is this a relative of yours? Or is that you?" Her heart hammered with the accusation. It was the most irrational thing she'd ever said.

He stared at the mourning brooch and reached up to touch it, but his hand fell. He turned his amber gaze on Petra. It seemed that he was weighing her, how much to tell her.

"Are you some kind of fucking vampire?" The question was ridiculous. Vampires existed only in books for preteen girls. They were about as believable as unicorns and the Tooth Fairy. Her fascination had driven her to the edge of reason. She took a step back, trying to physically reel herself in.

He licked his lips, eyes dilated black in pain. Pain and something else. Amusement?

"No. Not a vampire. A Hanged Man."

Then he turned his face toward the wall and passed out. She poked him, but he gave no response. She slid her fingers up to his neck and traced the raised scar there.

"A Hanged Man," she repeated. That would explain the mark. But no one really survived a hanging . . .

She chewed her lip. Maybe he had survived it, somehow, with the help of these ravens. But what could he have done to invite such an attack? Or did he have a talent for being in the wrong place at the wrong time?

And the ravens—she had no explanation. No explanation for what could cause him to heal and to regrow limbs before her eyes.

Sig pressed his cold nose against her face, and she put her arms around him. He, at least, was real.

Petra awoke to a pounding on the trailer door. She groaned and scrambled to her feet. She'd been sleeping on the floor—not well—and had developed a crick in her neck where Sig had jammed his foot in his sleep.

She peered at Gabriel. Still breathing. Good.

He talked in his sleep. Much of it made no sense. He muttered about Lascaris, about alchemy, trees, and ravens. His meanderings reminded Petra of Frankie's cryptic predictions and her father's old postcards. He'd finally stopped muttering after the moon had set, when it seemed that he slept deeply enough to ward off dreams and allow Petra some sleep of her own. Until now.

Petra padded to the door and peered through the glass. It was Maria Yellowrose, holding a shotgun. And she did not look happy.

Petra opened the door and tried to slide down the steps to talk with her outdoors, but Maria strong-armed her way into the trailer.

"What the fuck did you do?" Maria demanded.

"What are you talking about?" Petra tried to block her view of the rest of the trailer interior. It was still dark, and only dim predawn light filtered through the blinds.

"Sal Rutherford and his men came to my house, looking for you. I spent the night unconscious on my porch," she snarled. Petra noticed that the left side of her face was covered in a brilliant magenta bruise. Her swollen lower lip quivered. "And they took Frankie."

"What?" Petra's hand flew to her mouth. "What happened?"

"Sal saw the Bronco at his ranch. Said you'd taken something of his." Maria brandished the shotgun. "I don't give a shit what it is, but I want it back to trade for Frankie's life."

Sig slithered between the two women, whining piteously at Maria. He was laying the "good dog" routine on thick, trying to make peace.

"Give me back what you stole from Rutherford."

"I didn't steal anything from him. I—" Petra pressed the heel of her hand to her brow. "Shit. You're just gonna have to trust me. I didn't steal from him. I found a body on his property. A fucked-up body that looked like it'd been doctored in a special-effects workshop."

"I don't trust you." Maria shoved the barrel of the shotgun into Petra's shoulder. "If you won't tell me, you're coming with me. And then Sal can get it out of you." Her eyes were wide with fear, and Petra could see that it wasn't a selfish fear, but fear for her uncle.

Something glowed in Petra's periphery, and she saw Maria blanch and point the shotgun past Petra. "What the hell—?"

Gabriel sighed. "It's not her fault. It's mine." He flipped on the kitchen light.

Maria seemed to take in his torn and battered appearance. And his shirtlessness. His chest was smooth and unharmed, but spattered in bits of blood. "What the hell happened to you? You look like you got your ass kicked playing paintball."

"Sal wants me. Petra thought she was rescuing me." Gabe gave her an annoyed sidelong glance.

"I need to get Frankie back." Maria's mouth was pressed into a hard slash. There was no way that she was going to budge.

"We'll do a trade. I'm pretty certain that Sal will let Frankie go once he has me." As if that ended the discussion, Gabriel searched the floor for the remains of his tattered shirt and began to shrug into it.

"But what will he do to you?" Petra asked softly. "Will he turn you into one of those calcinated bodies, like in the back field?"

Gabe looked at her neutrally, as if they were discussing whether to have a ham sandwich or chicken salad for lunch. He sat on the edge of the futon to put his boots on. "That's not your concern."

Maria lowered the shotgun uneasily. "All right." She flicked her gaze at Petra. "I'm sorry, but I'm still pissed at you." It seemed that she said it more to convince herself.

"You have a right to be."

Maria looked down at the coyote. Sig sniffed her shoes, sat back on his haunches. He cocked his head, trying to be cute. Petra rolled her eyes. *Flirt.*

Gabriel stood, his balance wavering from foot to foot. "Let's go get Frankie."

A car crunched down the gravel road and stopped before the trailer. Maria squinted through the blinds. "You expecting company?"

"No."

Petra shouldered up to the window, half-expecting it to be Mike's Jeep. But it was a red Monte Carlo.

"Piss," she muttered.

"Who is it?" Gabriel demanded. "Is it Sal?"

"No. Meth heads." Petra hoped that Cal wasn't in the car. A middle-aged man in a long black coat got out, holding a silver pistol. That must be the one Cal called "the Alchemist." Stroud. A young man clambered out of the passenger seat, brandishing a machine gun. She recognized him: the kid who had tried to chase her along the road, Justin. And out climbed Cal, blinking in the daylight.

"Shit." She sighed.

"You're a popular girl. What do *they* want with you?" Maria peered through the blinds.

"They want an artifact I found."

"Artifact?" Gabriel echoed.

"Yeah. Some kind of compass Sig dug up in the dirt."

Maria ratcheted the shotgun. "We can stick 'em back in the dirt."

"Wait." Gabriel's hand fell on her shoulder. "Stroud's more dangerous than you think."

Maria's lip curled in a snarl. "What the hell do you want us to do, then?"

"Keep the door locked. And wait quietly."

Before Petra could protest, Gabriel was at the far side of the trailer and had slipped noiselessly out the back window. She did as she was told, turning the flimsy lock on the door.

Maria growled. "That motherfucker better not be running. If he is, I promise that I *will* perforate his ass with birdshot."

A knock rattled the front door, the silver gun barrel on the glass. Petra instinctively stepped away, fumbling to reach for her gun belt slung on the kitchen chair. Sig stood before her, teeth bared, head down in a fighting posture.

"Petra Dee. You know what I want." The Alchemist's voice leaked under the door. It sounded like the rustle of dry leaves, a man who had smoked everything on Earth.

Petra swallowed. Cal had apparently spilled his guts.

Maria shook her head, laid a finger to her lips. She lifted the shotgun to chest level. Her intention was clear: If the men came through the door, their asses were grass.

"We can do this the easy way or the hard way," Stroud said.

He tried the door, found it locked. A bullet cracked through the lockset, showering sparks. Then the door burst open, and Stroud barreled in.

Maria pulled the trigger. The shotgun bucked upward in a deafening roar in the small space. Petra's ears rang, but she didn't know if it was from the thunder or the pounding of her heart as she watched Stroud fall backward from the steps onto the ground outside.

Petra squeaked. It burned her throat, but she couldn't hear it.

Maria chucked the next shell into the chamber, advanced on the door. Sig was at her heels, and Petra drew up the rear with a pistol in each hand. She was in awe at the coldness with which Maria moved. No hesitation. No fear. Nothing like the terror that was uncoiling in Petra's stomach.

Stroud lay sprawled on the ground, twitching. The pistol glittered beyond his reach. Maria carefully picked her way down the steps. There was no sign of Justin. Petra followed, guns in her sweat-slick, quavering hands. Maria kicked Stroud over and gasped.

Cal started toward the trailer, but Petra trained one of the guns on him.

"Don't move." Her voice sounded a helluva lot more confident than she felt. Cal slowly raised his hands. He was unarmed.

"Get down," she told him.

Cal obediently got on his knees in the dust, but his gaze was fixed on Stroud.

Stroud's shredded coat was not red with blood. Instead, tiny drops of quicksilver retracted through the holes in the coat, sliding away from view like dozens of tiny fingers. His eyes remained closed. Petra could see the rise and fall of his chest, which seemed to be coated in some kind of liquid armor.

"What the fuck?" Maria murmured. She knelt to take his pulse.

"Drop it, bitches." Justin's voice oozed from the side of the car. He'd popped the driver's side door open as a shield before his body, a gun braced on the open window like a detective on a bad cop show. It was a big gun—an MP-5 submachine gun. Petra hadn't seen one of those outside the hands of military personnel. It looked like an absurd toy in the hands of the young man, like it should have an orange painted safety tip.

Petra was the only one remaining on her feet with guns. She kept one on Cal, who was cringing close to the dirt and aimed the other toward Justin. They were peashooters compared to the MP-5. But she thought that if she was in a cop show, she should bluff. "We've got three guns. You have one. How's your math?"

His pupils were dilated. He was clearly hopped up on something. Awesome.

"I don't think you've got the balls to blow me away, lady."

Petra's jaw twitched. He was right. But maybe he didn't know it.

Sig slowly advanced on Justin. He was between them, skulking low and moving to the car. He emitted a throaty growl that sounded like a terrible engine winding up.

Justin aimed his gun toward Sig. "Call your fucking dog off."

"Sig, come here!" Petra shouted. Panic welled in her voice.

She saw Justin's finger flex on the trigger.

And she fired.

The shot shattered the side mirror, causing Justin to flinch. Satisfaction stung her. She glimpsed a blur moving from the corner of the trailer, rushing up behind Justin—Gabriel. He tackled Justin against the open car door, as Sig slithered under and began to tear into him with gusto.

Something scraped the dirt at her feet. Petra looked down to find that Stroud's eyes were open, and he was pointing his pistol at Maria's face. The shotgun lay two inches from her hand in the dust.

"What the fuck are you?" Petra growled. She'd had

enough of things that didn't bleed right, and she was tired of asking the question.

Stroud ignored her. "Give me the *Veneficus Locus*." He opened his free hand.

"I don't know what the fuck you're talking about." She seemed to be saying that a lot lately, and it made her head hurt.

"Don't be coy. I don't have time for it. You found it here. Give it to me."

Suddenly, the Alchemist was mauled in a furry mass of growling coyote flesh. Sig ripped at his arm and face. Stroud slapped at him, but the coyote had a good grip on his gun hand, chewing like a dog with a rawhide. Maria seized the opportunity to snatch up the shotgun. She stood on Stroud's chest and pressed the barrel to his head.

"I will feed you to the coyote in tiny little pieces if you don't drop it."

Stroud reluctantly released his gun. Maria kicked it away.

Sig released Stroud's sleeve. He started coughing, hacking against the dirt. He spit droplets of what looked like mercury on the ground, pawing at his mouth. The hair on his back stood on end. Petra threw her arms around the canine, rubbed his chest. The droplets rolled away from his spittle, climbed over rocks and rills to slide back under Stroud's sleeve.

"What the fuck did you do to him?" she cried.

Stroud grunted. "Heavy metal poisoning's a bitch."

A gunshot echoed in the vicinity of the Monte Carlo. Justin was on the ground, looking like he'd gotten the shit kicked out of him. He fired at Gabriel, who stood over him, empty-handed.

Petra cried out.

The three-shot burst disturbed the collar on Gabe's shirt, nothing more. Justin fired again, and Petra saw the bullets tear into Gabriel's thigh. Without reacting, he reached down to scoop up Justin, lifted him in one hand. It was like watching Superman on a really pissed-off day. She watched in fascinated horror as Gabe slammed Justin down on the hood of the Monte Carlo. The car's hood caved, and Justin sprawled like a limp fish.

During the whole fight, Cal had stayed on his knees before the car, hands on his head. "Can I move now?" he squeaked.

"No!" Petra yelled. "Absofuckinglutely not."

Cal shrunk closer to the earth, as if he could make himself disappear into it.

Gabriel looked at Petra. "You want me to kill them?" he asked quietly.

"No! They're just kids!"

Gabriel picked up Justin's unconscious body and slung it down against the back tire of the car, as if he weighed nothing. Then he reached into the backseat and came up with a set of jumper cables. He pointed to Cal. "You. Get over here."

"Uh . . . me?" he squeaked.

"Yes. Or I will beat you into unconsciousness like I did your friend. Your call."

Cal scrambled up in a cloud of dust and obediently crawled beside Justin. Gabriel tied them together, back-to-back, with the jumper cables, then crossed the gravel to stare down at Stroud.

"Are you done with the Alchemist?" he asked Petra.

Stroud spit a glob of mercury at Gabriel's face. Without waiting for Petra's response, Gabriel hauled him to the car, reached into the ignition for the keys, and popped the trunk. He threw Stroud into the trunk as if the Alchemist were a bag of mulch.

"Whoa, what are you doing?" Petra squeaked.

Gabriel looked at her levelly. "This guy is dangerous. Trust me, this is the safest place for him."

And he slammed the trunk shut.

Petra raided the tiny grill outside the trailer for a decent-sized charcoal briquette, crushed it up in water, and was forcing Sig to drink the mixture. He made terrible faces, but Petra kept cooing at him and promising him lunch meat.

"What's the charcoal for?" Maria asked. She was impatient to be on the road to rescue Frankie, but her concern for the coyote was evident as she patted his flank.

"It looks like he got a snoutful of mercury. If he ingested it, that could be bad news. I'm trying to do some amateur preemptive chelation therapy by feeding him charcoal." Petra poured some more of the mixture down Sig's throat. Sig shook his head and drooled.

"Will he be okay?"

"I hope so. If he starts acting lethargic or vomiting, I'll know that it didn't work and that he actually swallowed some."

Gabriel came back inside to lean against the kitchen counter. Petra avoided eye contact with him and concentrated on pouring water into Sig's mouth.

Maria shook her head. "I don't know how this is possible. How can a man take that much birdshot to the chest and still be walking around? How can you?" She looked directly at Gabriel, who was conspicuously fine after his run-in with multiple bullets.

Gabriel shrugged, said nothing.

Petra pressed him. "I've heard Stroud called 'the Alchemist.' I assumed that was because he was the local drug lord. But I'm getting the idea that it means something more. That silvery shit on his chest . . . I thought that was armor, but it's mercury. And he bleeds it."

Gabriel flicked a glance toward the car. "He's a half-baked puffer. He can't turn base metals into gold or craft an immortality procedure. Instead, he just spends his time playing with mercury and crank. He's dangerous, but only if you get in his way." Gabriel stared at Petra. "So, what did you do to get in his way?"

"Nothing!" Petra protested.

Maria sat back on her heels. "He said he wanted the *Veneficus Locus*. Said you found it here."

Petra dug into her pocket. "I think he wants this."

She held the compass in the flat of her hand. It just looked like a pretty sundial that needed to be cleaned up. Maria looked at it and shrugged.

Gabriel was across the room in two quick steps. He cocked his head to one side, studying it with his cold amber eyes, but made no move to touch it. "Where did you find this?"

"Out here. Sig was digging and led me to it." She gestured nonspecifically to the field.

"Do you know what it is?"

"My Latin sucks, but a *locus* is a locator, right?"

The corner of Gabriel's mouth turned up. "It's a magic locator. Sort of a dowsing rod for magic. The symbols around it are invocations for purity and direction. The seven rays symbolize the seven alchemical processes of transformation. The scripts indicate their associated planets and metals."

Petra's eyebrow quirked up. "Show me. How does it work?"

"All magic has a cost to use. This thing runs on blood."

"Excuse me?"

"See that groove circumscribing the interior of the compass?"

Petra peered at the smooth circle that ran around the directional points and Latin words. "Yeah?"

"Put a drop of your blood in the groove."

Petra made a face. He was impassive when he said it, but she refused to take this shit seriously. She snatched a piece of paper from the kitchen table, ran it across her fingertip. Wincing, she waited for a fat red drop to well up from the paper cut. She squeezed it into the gold compass, then wrapped her wounded finger in a paper towel. She held the compass in her free hand.

"Okay, now what?"

"Orient it to true north."

Petra turned the compass so that the sundial faced north. The blood swished a bit in the track. She stared at it. "Now what?"

"Give it a minute."

Petra stared at it, resisting the urge to tap her foot. She flicked a glance up at Gabriel. "This is bullshit. It's not doing anything."

"It's over a hundred and fifty years old. Give it a minute."

"Jesus, people. We're wasting time—" Maria began, but her voice stilled.

The blood began to creep along the track, like a slow-motion comet. It seeped along the edge, gathering itself, just as Stroud's mercury had. It rolled along the track like a perfect ruby marble, picking up speed, spiraling faster and faster.

Then it stopped, wobbling near the northeast part of the compass. Petra carefully lifted it to eye level, marveling at the perfect roundness of the drop, wondering how it retained surface tension. She looked over the edge of the drop at Gabriel.

"You gonna tell me why it likes you?"

Gabriel's mouth turned downward. "No."

"Interesting," she said, lifting an eyebrow.

The drop split in two. One drop remained fixed on Gabriel. The other split off and wobbled in the direction of the door, then stopped.

"I don't get—"

"It's Stroud. Stroud's in the trunk of the car," Gabriel said.

Petra's eyebrow quirked. "Are you shitting me?"

The drops broke tension, leaking into the groove, like a damp ring left on a coaster. Before her eyes, the gold seemed to absorb it, leaving only a rusty stain behind. Petra flipped the compass over. "Interesting parlor trick. But . . ."

Maria put her hands on her hips. "Can we stop playing with toys, please, and get started rescuing Frankie?"

"You're taking this really well." Petra said. Better than she was.

"What do you mean?"

"Men with mercury armor. Magic detectors. Bulletproof cowboys."

"I've seen weirder shit than this before. I'll process the hell out of it later. Maybe over some of Frankie's gin. But later."

"What about the the kids Gabriel tied up? And Stroud, roasting his ass off in his trunk?" Petra said, resisting the urge to ask Maria exactly what that "weirder shit" involved. "We gotta figure out what to do with those guys."

"We could call Mike," Maria suggested. "Though . . .

this isn't his jurisdiction. He'd have to call the sheriff, after he got done wigging out."

Gabriel shrugged. "I'm in favor of driving them out of town and dropping them off. They can find their own way home. Or not."

Petra shuddered, thinking of Jeff. "No. We can't just leave them." Stroud might be dangerous, and Justin an asshole, but Cal didn't deserve this.

"Screwing around with them's gonna take too much time. We gotta help Frankie." Maria drummed her fingers on the refrigerator.

"How about I call the sheriff when we leave, okay?" Sweat prickled on Petra's brow. "If the cops are on Rutherford's side, and they hate Stroud, they'll be here ASAP. Right?"

Gabriel gave a small frown, as if she was being hopelessly naïve. "Your decision."

"Then I'm calling the sheriff," Petra said firmly, though she was sure she didn't have a full grasp of the political nuances of the situation.

"Up to you to explain to them, then," Gabriel said.

"Damn it." Petra groaned, digging her cell phone out of her pocket and dialing. She had no idea how she was going to explain this shit to the cops, but at least there wouldn't be blood on her hands.

Maria grabbed the shotgun. "Then let's pay Sal Rutherford a visit."

CHAPTER SIXTEEN

THE HANGED MAN

"Let me try this again."

Petra clutched the Bronco's steering wheel, keeping her eyes on the road. Maria was cruising at a breakneck pace down back roads in Frankie's Explorer, and Petra was determined not to fall behind and lose her. But Gabe could almost see that her brain was whirring just as quickly. She continued to assault him with questions, while he sat serenely on the passenger's side. Sig lay on the bench seat between them, one paw wrapped over his muzzle, as if to ward off any more of Petra's charcoal concoctions.

Gabriel regarded the coyote with amusement and a bit of wariness. Having lived with ravens, he knew something about familiars. They arrived and never left. He wasn't sure what to think about this one. The Locus hadn't recognized him as magic, so maybe he was just an ordinary coyote. Or maybe whatever magic he represented was far beyond the reach of the Locus.

In all, Gabriel was amused by Petra and her companion. It felt good; he hadn't been amused in a very long time. He was also a bit befuddled, if he truly admitted it to himself. She showed no fear of him, had marched right up to Rutherford's doorstep. He was accustomed to people scattering in his wake like dandelion fluff. Not chasing after him like a stubborn nettle.

"You're bulletproof, but Frankie can beat the shit out of you with a fence post. How the hell does that work?"

Gabe stared stoically out the window. "We're not having this conversation."

"But Sal Rutherford can hurt you. That's why I had to scrape you off the floor of the barn."

Gabriel didn't answer her. She might be entertaining, but he wasn't sure how far to trust her. He hadn't wanted to trust her *this* far with the knowledge of what he was. And it needed to stop. There was nothing to be gained by telling her that his situation was actually under control. His healing had been slowed by lying on the wood floor of the barn, but he'd sent parts of his body out to the tree to heal and return. The ravens'd had a devil of a time locating him when he wasn't sprawled under the hayloft.

Petra tried a different avenue. "How do you know so much about this *Veneficus Locus?*"

"Let's just say that I've been around here awhile."

Petra gave up, focused on stomping the gas to pursue Maria's receding taillights. "We can't just surrender you to Sal."

"You don't really have a choice. Besides, Sal won't kill me."

"Why not? Looks like he tried."

"I'm useful to him." He said it simply, without attachment.

"Why tolerate that? You can deflect bullets like fucking Superman," Petra said.

"It's not what it seems," he said laconically.

"You a masochist?" Petra bit her lip. It was a charming gesture. He noticed that she did it when she was nervous.

"No. But I get what I want out of the arrangement."

"You aren't really good with this conversation thing."

"Nobody really talks to me." He said it with the same matter-of-factness, no self-pity.

"They're afraid of you."

"Yes." The corner of his mouth turned upward. He was unused to such directness, and he couldn't help but admire that her thoughts slipped past her lips unfettered.

"I'm not afraid of you." She said it with defiance.

"So I've noticed." He looked at her, hard, lifting an eyebrow. He could *make* her afraid of him. Of that, he had no doubt. If she continued to chase, she would come up against a nightmare that she'd never forget. Better that he stop playing games and get her to abandon the line of inquiry.

Petra squirmed, frowned. "Look, I can circle back and pick you up as soon as we take Frankie . . ."

"You're delaying the inevitable through misguided intentions. Some things haven't changed here since men arrived. And you will never know the reasons why. You'll be forced to accept them." He said it coldly, with as much frost as he could muster. After so many years, that was formidable.

Petra fumed silently. Acceptance clearly wasn't one of her strong points. And Gabriel bet she'd be damned if she'd be improving that aspect of her character anytime soon.

The Rutherford ranch spread around them. Gabe hoped that Maria would pull off the side of the road, allow them to formulate a strategy before they stormed in with guns blazing. But Maria was evidently a fan of charging forward without stopping. She pulled up right before the barn, shut off the engine, and hopped out of the truck with her shotgun in hand, long skirts swirling around her.

"This is gonna go over real well." Petra sighed, climbing out of the Bronco.

Ravens cawed overhead, perching on the edge of the barn. The rest of the ranch hands shambled out of the structure. They said nothing. A few nodded in Gabe's direction.

"Where's the boss?" Gabe asked.

"Here."

Sal Rutherford strode out of the barn at a leisurely pace. He had the irritating attitude of a man in complete command of his surroundings, one hand tucked into the belt loop of his jeans and the other resting on the holster at his side. The whites of his eyes had a jaundiced yellow tint, but the sunburned skin around them crinkled in wicked mirth.

Maria stood her ground, shotgun balanced on her hip. "We've come for Frankie."

Sal grinned. "I'm not sure I'm willing to give him up. He says some very interesting things when he's drunk."

"He's crazy. Crazier when he's drunk. Nothing he says is the truth," Maria said, but the desperation in her voice glittered too brightly.

Gabe stepped forward. "Let him go. I'm back."

Sal rubbed his chin with an exaggerated gesture, pretending to consider. "You can see him," he conceded.

Maria bristled, but Petra put her hand on her arm.

Sal shouted back to the barn, and two of his men dragged Frankie out. Frankie was limp as a dishrag. There was no blood, no sign of a beating. Maria rushed to him, patted his face. Gabe could smell the vodka staining the front of his shirt from where he stood. His head was soaked in it.

Maria turned on Sal. "How much did you give him?"

Sal shrugged. "We gave him all he wanted. And then some."

Gabe's gaze flickered to the interior of the barn. He could see a funnel, some garden hose, and empty bottles in a vomit-filled puddle by the door. They'd force-fed him.

Beside him, Petra's hands balled into fists. "Bastard."

"Let him go," Gabe repeated. "You have what you wanted."

Sal made a show of considering, wallowing in his power. "I think that perhaps you overestimate yourself, Gabe. Your uniqueness."

Gabe cocked his head. "What do you mean?"

"Let's just say, I think that I've figured out how to replace you." A smile played on Sal's lips. He stank of magic, like sulfur and mercury and salt.

Gabe's gaze flickered past the barn, to the tree and the Lunaria beyond.

Something shimmered, and it wasn't just the heat.

He strode past Sal, past the barn and the Hanged Men, into the tall grass. Sweat prickled his brow.

"Gabe!" Petra shouted after him.

He waded into the field, feeling the awful energy of spilled magic swirling around him. It clung to his skin, roaring in his ears like ocean and blood. Overhead, the sky had darkened to a bruised grey, and the wind rattled over the land. Ravens descended upon the Lunaria, cawing, agitated.

He began to run, his breath charring his throat. He could feel the Lunaria's roots reaching into the earth underneath his feet, sense its magic shaken awake. The tree had been asleep for a century, and now . . .

He skidded to a stop, heart in his mouth.

"Sal, what have you done?" he whispered.

The tree reached to the sky with glossy dark branches, wind hissing through the leaves. Ravens fluttered amid them in a deafening cacophony, screaming at this thing that had disturbed their nests.

A body dangled from the lowest scarred branch. It spun lazily in the wind, like a tire swing, hands slack at its sides and feet skimming space.

Gabe rushed to the body, took its weight on his shoulder. There was no telling how long it had been there.

"Oh, my God," he heard Petra breathe behind him.

Being tied up in the hot sun was bad enough.

Being tied to the motionless sack of meat that was Justin, listening to the Alchemist cook in the trunk was worse.

Cal strained to scoot forward in the dust, away from the car, but Justin was dead weight His awkward heft caused Cal to fall to his side on the ground. Frustrated, he kicked at Justin's legs. Justin didn't react. Cal hoped to hell he didn't piss himself in his unconscious state.

Cal looked up at the trunk. It sounded like an overheated radiator, ticking like something was boiling in there. Stroud had stopped screaming and swearing about fifteen minutes ago. He wondered if the Alchemist was dead—or worse.

A finger of mercury dribbled out of the gas tank cover near Cal's head, and he wormed away from it, grunting, trying to haul Justin's limp body. But the mercury slipped and spiraled over the back of his neck with hot, wet fingers. Cal whimpered, pressing his face into the dirt and scrunching his eyes shut.

Gravel crunched in the distance, tires on the road. He felt the mercury hesitate, then retract.

He started yelling. "Hey! Over here! Help!"

He wasn't sure what he was hoping for. In the best-possible reality, Petra had developed a crisis of conscience and had returned to let him go. In the worst, it was the cops she'd called. Whichever, it was better than being killed by Rutherford's man. He was pretty sure that dude had been ready to toss Justin and Cal into the trunk with Stroud like a cozy tweaker family.

The crackle of a radio sounded through an open window. A car door opened, and boots shuffled on the ground.

"Unit six is en route to your location," the radio hissed.

"Roger that, Dispatch," an unfamiliar male voice said.

Cal pressed his forehead to the ground. Shit. The cops. But he reasoned that spending the night in jail would be better than getting fondled by Stroud's mercury. *Gotta look on the bright side.*

The boots stopped before him. Cal looked up. "Hey."

A cop with a buzz cut, mirrored sunglasses, and arms the size of deli hams squatted down before him, one hand on his gun. "You all right?"

"Um, yeah. But this guy's not." Cal wriggled to show him Justin, his head lolling backward against Cal's shoulder.

The cop took Justin's pulse. "Out cold." He keyed the radio at his shoulder. "Base, I need the squad here ASAP."

Cal shrugged his aching shoulders. "Uh, do you think you could untie me?"

The cop looked at him, then the broken door, then back again. "I'll trade you for some cuffs."

"Sure. Anything. I swear I'll be good."

The cop reached for the jumper cables and began to work them loose. Cal's gaze slipped to the trunk. Stroud was still in there. He watched another bead of mercury form on the seam of the trunk lid and slide off.

For a moment, Cal felt powerful. He could zip his lip and say nothing, and maybe the Alchemist would roast in his own shiny juices or bleed out from the dusting of birdshot he'd taken. If Stroud was dead, Cal could get on his bike and get the hell out of Dodge.

But reality set in with a sharp pang in his stomach. He had nowhere to go. And he wasn't sure he could live with having a death on his conscience. Deep down in his gut, he knew he wasn't a badass. Plus, if he left Stroud in the trunk and Stroud somehow survived . . .

Cal shuddered violently. If that happened, he'd be dead. And not just dead in a quick-and-painless, bullet-to-the-back-of-the-head kind of way. He remembered the feel of the mercury on the base of his neck, and was pretty sure that the Alchemist would make him suffer.

"Um," he squeaked at the cop. "There's a guy in the trunk."

The cop's hands stilled. "What did you say?"

Cal rolled his eyes. He'd overheard Petra tell the dispatcher that there was a dude baking in the trunk. Evidently, something got lost in dispatchland. "There's a guy in the trunk of that car," he said again.

The cop stood, his hand on the butt of his gun. Cal squirmed his hands free of the jumper cables but stayed where he was, on the ground, with his hands in his lap. Justin lay beside him, drooling onto the dirt.

The cop went to the driver's side of the car, reached in, and flipped the hood release with an audible *click*. He circled around to the trunk, drawing his weapon.

Cal held his breath as the cop opened the trunk. The cop stood there for a moment, not speaking, his expression unreadable. Cal wondered if he was staring at the dead Alchemist, curled up in the fetal position and cooked like a turkey.

The cop aimed the gun into the trunk. "Hands up."

Cal swallowed. He felt a bit of disappointment, mingled with relief.

"Out of the trunk, nice and slow."

Stroud looked like shit. He climbed out of the trunk

like a cramped-up old man, all tangled up in his black coat, white and sweating. What looked like bits of aluminum foil stuck to his skin, and he wore what seemed to be a crazy-ass silver glove glued to his hand.

The cop lifted his gun. "Keep your hands up."

Stroud complied, though it seemed he could only bring them to shoulder height.

"Where's the woman who called 911?" the cop demanded.

Stroud glared at him with eyes the unnatural color of a storm. "I don't know."

"What were you doing here?"

Stroud spat in the dirt. "Selling fucking Avon."

"Did she put you in there?"

"No. It was one of Sal Rutherford's men. But she sure didn't do anything to stop him."

The cop reached for the radio pinned on his shoulder. "This is Unit Fourteen. Be advised that—"

Something flickered in Cal's vision, flashed in the sun. He realized in an instant that Stroud was lunging toward the cop with that shiny glove. Ribbons of liquid metal extended from the fingers, reaching around the cop's neck. Instinctively, the cop clawed at the liquid metal, but the skin of mercury wrapped tight around his throat, tight as a steel cable. He squawked and turned red as a tomato, then fired his gun randomly, wildly. Cal scrambled to cower behind the fender of the car. The metal fingers around the cop's neck snapped back, away, as if they'd touched something hot. The cop fell to his hands and knees, gasping.

Stroud was doubled over, howling like an aggrieved cat.

"Jesus, you're hit!" Cal climbed to his numb feet and dragged Stroud back to the Monte Carlo. The Alchemist was holding his side, groaning in pain. Cal shoved him in the passenger's side, reached behind the sun visor for Justin's extra set of keys, and jammed them in the ignition. He glanced in the rearview mirror. Justin was still slumped on the ground, and the cop was climbing to his feet, croaking into his radio.

Cal stomped the gas, spinning out.

The cop fired the remainder of his clip at the Monte Carlo's tires as the engine revved. He hit a door panel, but the car spun off, peppering him with gravel.

"Oh, fuck. Oh, fuck." Cal's heart pounded so hard that he thought his chest would explode. He stared in the rearview mirror at the figure stumbling in the drive.

"You did good, boy." Stroud reached for him and patted his cheek with that hot silver hand.

Cal flinched as silver tendrils crept across his face.

"Get the knife on my belt. Cut him down!"

Petra's shaking fingers scrabbled around Gabe's waist, searching for a utility knife. She removed it from its holster, ripped it open.

The limb on which the body was suspended was easily twelve feet above ground. Petra shimmied up the trunk of the tree. Leaves tore in her hair and birds screamed as she scrambled along the branch. She could feel scars here, old wounds in the wood that had formed knots and bulges. Scars from other ropes, from a long time ago.

She sawed at the fresh rope with Gabe's knife. The sharp serrated blade chewed into the fiber, severing it in three strokes. The body fell to Gabe's shoulder.

Petra awkwardly swung herself back down. She landed gracelessly in the grass on her hands and knees beside Gabriel, scraping her hands. She crawled over to the prone form. Maybe the man was still alive, maybe Gabe had been in time to save him . . .

Gabriel hunched over the body, surrounded by ravens. One perched on his shoulder. Another stood on the chest of the body, nibbling at shirt buttons.

Sig circled the body, whining, and backed away.

Petra pressed her fist to her mouth. The neck and head of the body were swollen, eyes bulging, tongue protruding. But the face was recognizable. It was Jeff, the ranch hand from the Compostela. The one who'd found the body on Sal's ranch. The one who'd run his mouth too loudly and too long.

"Is he——?" She bit her lip.

Gabriel shook his head. His amber gaze was furiously cold.

Petra looked up. The other ranch hands circled them in the field with an eerily silent reverence. They held on to their hats, keeping them from tearing away in the wind.

"What the fuck did you do this for?" Petra screamed at them.

The raven who'd been nibbling at his buttons hopped over to Jeff and began plucking at his eye. Gabriel shooed it away.

"They didn't do it." Gabriel's voice was murderous. "*He* did."

Sal strode past the Hanged Men, surveying his work. "I don't think he was ripe, yet."

Petra looked down at the body. In the shade of the tree, a gold fluorescing shimmer dribbled from Jeff's lip, twisting and turning like spider silk. The mottled bruising and abrasions around his throat seemed to pulse with light, as if he'd swallowed a flashlight.

His right arm twitched.

"Jesusmotherfuckingchrist." Petra jumped back, landing on her ass in the dirt. Sig backed away, ears flattened. She couldn't hear him over the racket of the birds, but she could feel his chest vibrating in a growl against her arm.

Jeff's arm seized and jerked. Gabe turned him on his side. The body twitched, and strings of light-vomit dribbled from the broken jaw.

"He can't still be alive. He's—" Petra stared at Gabriel. "He's not like you. Is he?"

Gabe's mouth was set in a thin line. He stared at Sal. "You should not have done this."

Sal shrugged. "Seems to have taken. I considered it an experiment."

Gabe climbed to his feet, stepped over Jeff's seizing form. "You have no idea what you've fucking doing. None. The Hanged Men weren't made this way."

Sal stabbed a finger at the tree. "You all came from that. From the Lunaria."

"The magic isn't what it used to be. It kept collapsing, fading." Gabe pointed to a couple of men at the fringes of the circle. "Hell, they can't even speak. Three of them aren't even passable to take into public. Why did you think you could do any better?"

"I . . ." Sal seemed on the verge of admitting something, but he bit it back. "I couldn't have him running off at the mouth." His gaze was black, blacker than the eyes of the ravens. "He was dead, either way. Might as well have made him useful."

Gabe hauled back and slugged him. Sal collapsed like a ton of bricks. Gabe stood over his boss's body for several seconds, and it seemed to Petra that simple act of violence weighed more heavily on him than she could fathom.

Gabe turned back to Petra, his eyes glowing amber. "Take Maria and Frankie. Get out of here."

Her fingers knotted in the brittle grass. "I'm not going anywhere."

He looked down at her. "If you don't go now, Sal will do to you what he did to Jeff."

She stared at the twitching form, looking like a half-smashed lightning bug. "What the hell's happening to him?"

Gabe shook his head. "He's dying."

Her heart thundered in her throat. "I'm not going anywhere until you give me some answers."

"I can have them put you off the property by force." His mouth pressed into a grim slash.

She lifted her chin. "And I'll come back with cops. For Jeff and for that calcified body in your back forty."

He appeared to weigh something imperceptible. A raven fluttered down onto his shoulder. It seemed to speak conspiratorially to him, leaning close to his ear with feathers brushing his cheek.

He gestured with his chin to the men. The Hanged Men. "Get them all off the property before the boss wakes."

Two of the men came forward and grasped Petra by her forearms. She could feel the cold radiating from their hands through the cotton of her shirt. Sig growled, snapping at the men. Her hands curled into fists.

She could fight. But there would be no point. There were more of them.

She opened her hands and allowed herself to be led away.

"Down, Sig," she told the snarling coyote. He fell sullenly into line behind her.

Looking back over her shoulder, she glowered at Gabe as the wind whipped through her hair. This wasn't over, she vowed, as the Hanged Men marched her back to the barn. She tried to talk to them, to ask them what was going to happen to Jeff. But they just looked through her and beyond, into the leaden sky.

They'd left behind two men at the barn to watch Frankie and Maria. Maria sat on the back tailgate of the Explorer with her arm around her uncle. The old man was blinking, dazed. His head kept dipping forward into unconsciousness, and Maria was trying to keep him from sliding off the tailgate.

"Where are Sal and Gabriel?" Maria demanded.

Petra shook her head. "Gabriel said we can go." She didn't know how to begin to form the words about what had happened to Jeff. But the most important thing was to get help.

"I'm going to take him to the hospital," Maria said firmly. "He's got alcohol poisoning. Bad."

Frankie looked up, fixed Petra with his thousand-yard gaze. "You can stop the hungry ghost."

Petra took a step back. Rain began to spangle the dirt before her. "Frankie, I don't know what—"

"You can," he insisted. "You must."

In the distance, a dust plume lifted and twisted. Petra squinted at the road. The dust resolved into cars, lots of them, with U.S. government plates.

Petra's heart lifted. Mike had come through for her.

"Who's that?" Frankie slurred.

"Cops," Petra said. "Lots and lots of cops." She turned to grin victoriously at the Hanged Men.

But they were gone.

Vanished, as if they had simply dissolved in the warm rain that began to patter down on the dust in a steady dull tapping.

CHAPTER SEVENTEEN

DOWN THE RABBIT HOLE

Petra stood in Rutherford's field, rain thudding on her scalp.

Beside her, Mike kicked at chunks of dirt, watching with his hands in his pockets as federal agents dug through the mud with shovels and a backhoe. A hole ten feet deep yawned behind yellow crime scene tape, runnels of water sliding back into the red soil to make a filthy soup.

"You sure this is the right spot?" he asked neutrally. Again. Rain dribbled down his temple. It could have been sweat.

"Yeah. The GPS said so." Petra's mouth flattened. "It was right here."

A man in mud-streaked coveralls looked up at them, shook his head.

"I swear," Petra insisted. "It was here. Just like the body at Specimen Ridge. I sent you the picture."

Mike rubbed at the moisture on his brow. "Well, it's not here now."

"They must have moved it."

"Probably." Mike seemed to take what she said at face value, for which she was grateful. "But this is the only spot named in the warrant for the Feds to search."

"Did they look at that tree? For Jeff's body." Petra had not told Mike about how Jeff had glowed and twitched. Her credibility was questionable, as it was. But she had asked them to search for him.

"They walked past the tree while looking for Sal. That much, they can get away with. If there's evidence of a crime not named in the warrant out in the open, they can look. But they didn't see anything and are lobbing that ball back to the locals." He rubbed the back of his neck, which Petra knew he'd stuck out for her.

"Why am I not surprised?" Petra stared up at the sky. It was thick and close, like smoke, tendrils reaching toward the ground.

"Maria says she wants to press charges against Sal for kidnapping and assault."

"Did they find Sal, at least?"

"Yeah. But he wasn't in the field near the tree, like you said. He was propped up on the rocker on his front porch when they went to serve him. Unconscious. Had a hell of a shiner."

Petra blew out her breath. "They arrested him, then?"

"They'll turn him over to the locals—tribal police and the sheriff's department—for what he did to Frankie and Maria. When he gets out of the hospital, that is. Unfortunately, he didn't commit a federal crime."

Petra lifted her eyebrow. "And this body's a federal crime?"

"It's a matter of national security, if it's a contagion, or a pattern of serial killings that began on federal property, like a national park."

"Sounds like territorial hairsplitting."

"Yeah, well. If you want to get shit done, sometimes you've gotta get creative."

"At least Sal's gonna be behind bars. Until he posts bond."

Petra kicked ferociously at a clod of mud. Instead of skittering away like a stone in a satisfying fashion, it disintegrated and stuck to her boot like a cow patty. "You need to ask Gabriel. He knows."

"I would if I could. But none of the ranch hands can be found."

"None of them? There are more than a dozen of those guys, roaming around."

"They're gone, now. Maybe they're off having a drink. Or they blew outta town the instant they saw us coming."

The Feds climbed out of the hole, and the backhoe began to fill dirt in.

"That's it?" Petra said, feeling deflated.

"Yeah. Unfortunately." Mike plucked at the yellow tape. "But you should feel good. Sal's going to jail. Maybe not for the reason you wanted him there, but there *is* a happy ending."

"Yeah. Some happy ending."

Petra walked back to the cars with Mike. Sig sat inside the Bronco, his nose pressed to the glass, tongue writhing through the condensation. There was digging going on without him, and he felt left out. Petra opened the door, and he rewarded her with a lick on her chin. She solemnly scratched his ears.

"Hey. You did good. Really," Mike said awkwardly. He chuffed her on the shoulder, but the gesture came out all wrong.

"Right." She gave him a wan smile and slid behind the wheel.

"I heard that you had some more visitors at the Airstream today."

"Little bird told you?" Petra was eager to know that the cops had indeed come for Cal and company.

"Word gets around. One of the deputies they sent out got nearly choked to death and shot at your prisoners. Two of 'em got away."

"Which two?" She hoped that Cal was one of them.

"Sounds like Stroud and a goth-looking kid escaped. One was left behind—a blond kid who was beat to a pulp. He's at the hospital. The sheriff's office wants to talk to you."

"Are they gonna go after Stroud and Cal?"

"Yeah. I expect that they'll do a proper raid once they get their ducks in a row and get some federal backup. Stroud did try to kill one of their own, and that's not a deed they'll let go unanswered."

Petra frowned and stared through the smeary windshield. "Look, I didn't want anybody to get hurt."

"I don't fault you for defending your castle, Petra. You do what you've gotta do when it comes to protecting yourself and your property. But why the hell were they there?"

"Stroud's after an artifact I found on the property." There was no reason to lie. "It's something that I think belonged to Lascaris. And I'm not giving it to him."

Mike shook his head. "Please don't go back there. I mean it." He wasn't ordering her. He was asking. And that carried a lot of weight with Petra.

"I'll stay with Maria. Promise."

"Okay."

She cranked the engine and guided the Bronco out on the muddy road. She headed north toward town, tires splashing through the puddles, waving back at Mike to make sure he saw her.

Once she was out of his line of sight, she turned left and doubled back on one of the many truck ruts that crossed Sal's land. The ancient shocks on the Bronco squealed in protest. Sig complained at the terrain and rolled off the bench seat to the floor.

"Sorry, dude." She wrestled with the wheel as the Bronco bounced over the uneven land. "We aren't done here, yet."

From the floorboards, Sig huffed and snorted. He made a hacking noise that sounded suspiciously like a cat with a hairball.

"Just don't barf. Please."

She reached the barn as the light began to shift. Though the sun wasn't visible behind the low-hanging grey clouds, twilight began to darken their shadows on the pale fields. The contrast was stark, almost like a black and white photograph. Petra parked the Bronco out of sight on the far side of the barn.

When she popped the door, Sig tumbled out. He retched twice in the dirt and looked miserably up at her, snorkeling back a string of drool.

"I'm sorry." Petra squatted and rubbed his back, cooing at him. "I'll make it up to you. I promise."

She hugged the coyote to her chest and looked over the landscape. Sal was gone. The Hanged Men were gone.

The cops might not be able to search for answers, but that didn't mean that she couldn't.

She rooted around in the Bronco for her gun belt and flashlight while Sig cleared his palate by drinking from a mud puddle.

She stared at the barn, where ravens paced along

the eaves. They were quiet, walking slowly, watching her with sober indifference. This was where she'd found Gabriel, where Sal had kept Frankie prisoner. It seemed like as good a place to start as any.

"Where's your master?" she called to them.

One of the ravens cocked his head, but didn't answer. The gesture was very similar to Gabriel's mannerisms, a bit mechanical, like a clock run down over time.

They weren't agitated, not like when she'd found Gabriel passed out on the floor of the barn. Maybe that meant Gabriel and the rest of the Hanged Men were truly gone. But the presence of the ravens might also mean that the Hanged Men were still here, hiding somewhere and biding their time until the ruckus cleared out.

She pulled the Locus from her pocket, oriented the compass to north. She licked her lips and rubbed at the paper cut she'd given herself back at the trailer. She picked at the wound, summoning a reluctant drop of blood that splashed into the groove of the Locus. The blood spiraled lazily around the circle, then stopped due west, directly at the barn.

Petra climbed to her feet, mindful not to spill the blood. She put one foot in front of the other, keeping an eye on the Locus.

Sig make a quizzical noise.

"Yeah, well. I'm not entirely buying this, either." She tried to sound more certain than she felt. "We're going to find Gabriel."

She walked into the cold shadow of the barn, sweeping her flashlight beam before her. The light wrung suggestions of movement from the farm equipment, stretching crazed shadows of cages and metal spines. Broken glass from a shattered liquor bottle crunched underfoot, and she smelled soft straw and sharp gasoline. Sig snuffled along the ground in front of her, snooting vigorously among the tools and bags of fertilizer. Something made him sneeze.

She shined the light on the Locus. The drop of blood wobbled, moved, leading her farther into the barn. The bead led her to a dusty corner, to a pile of scrap wood and metal.

Petra stared at it. It looked like junk: bits of wheels, planks, and broken crates. She swept her light through the mess, scanning through cobwebs. There was something uneven about the floor here, and she blew away sawdust. She could make out the outline of a square shape below. Putting her shoulder to the pile of debris, she scraped it aside with a splintering shriek.

Petra grinned. A trapdoor pierced the floor, with rough and rusty hinges. Maybe it led to a cellar. Maybe it led to something more. She set the Locus down carefully .

Petra tugged at the door handle, and it opened with some effort. She shined her flashlight down into the hole. She could tell that the walls were earth, and she smelled dirt. A tunnel sloped off and to the west.

Sig looked askance at the burrow, one ear folded backward.

Petra pocketed the Locus and dangled her feet into the tunnel.

"You can stay here, if you want," she told him. "But Alice is going down the rabbit hole."

She swung down into darkness. Her feet hit first, but she lost her balance on the uneven surface and pitched forward. The flashlight bounced away.

She felt dirt under her fingers where she'd slid down at an an angle. She could see the glow of her flashlight behind her, and she scrabbled in the dirt for it. She shined the light back and forth, trying to get her bearings.

Sig came down in an avalanche of loose soil, all churning claws and fur. He landed on Petra's chest and knocked her ass over teakettle until she came to rest against an earthen wall, tangled in coyote.

The hatch banged shut above, blotting out the dim square of light from the barn.

"Shit."

Petra scrambled to the top and pushed up on the hatch, but it was too heavy for her to lift from this awkward angle.

"I guess that we're committed," she told Sig.

She swept the flashlight ahead of her in the tunnel, feeling loose dirt, then the stirring of air. She stumbled forward, her breathing echoing in the closed space. Sig pressed his nose to the ground, delighting in the strange odors. Petra supposed that he was accustomed to enclosed dens in his predomesticated life.

Petra had never been claustrophobic, but the knowledge that she was unable to retreat terrified her. She'd always had a way out. She swallowed her fear and kept moving forward over the uneven ground, feeling worms moving in the crumbling clay walls that were still wet from today's rain. She brushed spiderwebs and drizzling water away from her face, tried not to imagine what might be making the squeaking sounds she heard above her. More than once, Sig paused and began to dig in the earth. He'd lag behind, and she would hear crunching sounds.

These tunnels must be what she saw with the ground penetrating radar, this labyrinth underground. She wished that she had more time to explore, to map out this expanse with her GPR device. The Locus was admittedly useful, in its way, but she wanted to apply some technology to that magic. She paused to draw blood from her skinned knees to consult the Locus, which kept urging her west.

She stumbled in the darkness for more than two hours by her watch, feeling her way along the walls and following the clotting bead of blood on the Locus. Eventually, the passageway widened, and she could see light up ahead.

Light. The surface. She breathed deeply, heartened by the sight of the comforting glow. She moved toward it, and realized that it wasn't sunshine after all.

The burrow widened out into a large chamber that pulsed with an unearthly golden luminosity. But it was a glow she recognized—the same fluorescing shine of Gabriel's blood in the dark.

She turned on her heel, staring at the ceiling. Tree roots reached down from the roof of the chamber, glistening with that pulsing light and dripping sparkling water. It was beautiful, alive in a way that she hadn't contemplated plants or minerals being truly alive before. If she believed in a fairy kingdom, this would be the place that Titania and Oberon ruled.

Gingerly, she reached up to touch one of the roots. It felt warm, and the movement of the light throbbed through the wood. She gazed on it in wonder. What would this look like, if she could take it apart and analyze it? Would it contain gold and phosphorus, like Gabriel's blood? Or some strange version of chlorophyll, like plants that grew in caves?

As her vision adjusted, she realized that she wasn't alone.

Shadows surrounded her. She gasped, stepping backward. The shadows didn't move in the pulsing light. She approached one of them, squinting to see as she became aware of a putrid smell, like an unattended compost pile. A flicker of yellow light played over the form, and she stifled a scream with her fist as she shined the flashlight full into the forest of tree roots.

A decomposing body hung suspended, feet not touching the ground. She could make out the glisten of moldering flesh over white teeth, the bottomless black of an eye socket. Something foul and viscous dripped from it to the floor.

And there were more. More than a dozen, dangling like rotting fruit. Bits of intestines protruded from abdominal cavities, rotting limbs attached to torsos only with bits of stretched-out sinew. The remaining flesh was mottled green and black, bloated. Petra's heart hammered in her mouth.

The roots shifted with a rustle, reaching toward the mouth of the chamber, the way that sunflowers turn toward the sun.

Petra shrieked, and Sig growled.

Behind her, Petra heard the scrape and shuffle of footsteps. She backed up against the wall of the chamber and Sig crouched down before her, the hair on his back rising.

It was Gabriel. He strode into the chamber, carrying something. With horror, Petra realized that the bundle he held was a body: Jeff, bent and broken as he had hung from the tree. Gabriel himself looked inhuman: His eyes glowed in the darkness like fireflies.

His voice was soft and resigned, echoing oddly in the chamber. "I see you found the Lunaria."

"What the hell is this?" Petra's voice was barely more than a whisper. It scraped her throat raw to speak around her fear.

"This is the secret of the Hanged Men."

Gabriel lifted the body up to the roots, as if he were making an offering. The roots rustled down, gathered the body to them with what seemed like tenderness, and lifted it into that biomass of teeming light.

Petra struggled to understand. Images of John Wayne Gacy's basement surfaced in her mind. "These bodies . . ."

"Are the Hanged Men. Each one of us was hanged from this tree. The Alchemical Tree, the Lunaria. The marriage of heaven and earth. It's a remnant of one of Lascaris's old experiments. At one time, he worked the land, trying to work the alchemical processes on a larger scale."

"Alchemical processes?" she echoed.

"How do you not know?" he asked her. "You wear the Green Lion devouring the sun." He gestured at her neck.

Petra clutched her pendant. "It was my father's. He disappeared here, many years ago."

"And you came to search for him?" Gabe's voice fairly dripped with skepticism.

"Yes. What does 'the Green Lion devouring the sun' mean?" She tried to focus her mind on the puzzle, not the horror crowding around her.

"It signifies mercury dissolving gold—the dissolution process. There are seven processes that the alchemist must accomplish in order to achieve a perfect transformation: calcination, dissolution, coagulation, sublimation, mortification, separation, and conjunction. This tree is frozen in the mortification stage. We all are." He reached up and touched a root. It curled around his hand like a lover's caress.

"The Hanged Men are a product of a flawed and incomplete process. We cannot be transformed or restored to perfect, eternal life. Or even an imperfect mortal one. We are suspended in the mortification stage, what the old masters called the Black Raven or the Raven King—the black, decaying stage of alchemy. All things that give rise to life must first decompose."

"How long," Petra squeaked. "How long have you been trapped?"

Gabe smiled, and it was a sad smile. "A very long time. I was the first to be hanged from the tree. The others came later."

Petra's nails bit into her palms. "How long?" she demanded. "Is that really your picture in that mourning brooch?"

His eyes cast downward. "Yes. Since the spring of 1862."

"But Sal nearly killed you."

Something dark and murderous flitted across his face. "Wood. He used wood. The tree gives us life, and only a tree can take it away."

"This is it?" she croaked, gesturing to the bodies. "This is the price of living forever?"

His mouth flattened. "Yes. We must return here, to the Lunaria. In its embrace, we decompose and are reborn again. Day after day, night after night. We can't go more than a couple of days without it. We can't wander very far from it. We're bound together, always in its shadow."

"Is that . . . is that what's happening to Jeff?"

Gabe stared up at Jeff's body. The roots were busily winding around it, digging into the skin with a wet, sucking sound. Unbinding him. Remaking him. "The magic has drained out of the tree. Each successive generation of Hanged Men has been less . . . human."

"They don't speak," she said.

"Some can, and choose not to. Some can't. It's been more than a century since anyone dared . . ." Gabe closed his eyes. " . . . since a Hanged Man was made. Sal will have made an even more terrible monster than we are, if Jeff survives."

"Sal's in the hospital. He's going to be arrested," she said numbly.

"I know. But he will be back."

Petra looked down at her hands. She had intruded upon something intimate and sad. The fear drained out of her in the face of trying to understand this terrible curse, to apply some logic to it.

"I'm sorry," she said, simply.

Gabe nodded. "I appreciate that. That sympathy. But you had no hand in it."

She took a deep, quavering breath. What would he do, now that she had seen this? "Will you turn me into one of those ossified skeletons?"

Gabe blinked.

She said it with her chin lifted, steeling herself, standing before a train that was inevitably going to run her over.

"No," he said quietly. "Those were not our doing. And I'm not a reasonless killer."

She squinted at him. "But you moved the body on the ranch. You hid it."

He inclined his head. "We did. Because we didn't want the police crawling around the ranch to find . . ." He sketched the Hanged Men with his hand.

"Oh. But what . . . what are they, then, if you didn't do it?" she asked.

"I'm not certain. I have theories."

"Such as?"

"Initially, I thought it to be a result of one of Lascaris's old experiments. Some part of the calcination process reawakened."

"Calcination," she echoed.

"Calcination is the first alchemical process, the reducing of a material to bone to purify it. Once the material is calcined, it can be dissolved in the next stage. But this step of the process is flawed as I have seen it, in which the bone seems to react with overgrowth." He stared up at the surface in frustration. "We've found three bodies here, on the ranch."

Petra licked her lips. "Three?" She'd seen just the one, with the Jolly Roger watch.

"We found what we thought was a man and a woman together. Then a man."

"Those must have been Cal's friends. Adam and Diana." Her heart ached for the boy. He'd be alone.

"Cal and Adam and Diana are Stroud's people?"

"Yes."

"Spies." Gabriel narrowed his glowing eyes. "I always thought Stroud was a charlatan, incapable of anything substantial in the alchemy department. But I begin to wonder if he might have something to do with this runaway calcination process."

"I found a body on Specimen Ridge," Petra said slowly. "Like the one here. It has microscopic elements similar to petrified wood."

Gabe frowned. "Interesting. Lascaris spent some time working on Specimen Ridge."

"So . . . he used Specimen Ridge because of the calcined petrified remains there?"

Gabe shook his head. "No. His experiments *created* those petrified forests."

Petra stared at him. "I don't believe you."

Gabe laughed, a bitter sound that caused the tree roots to retract and writhe. "After all this, you don't believe me?"

"Let's just say that, even if I believe everything you've told me. About you. About the Hanged Men. About Lascaris. I still have a hard time believing that alchemy can affect geology on a grand scale." She shuddered and looked up at the hanging shadows.

Gabe leaned forward on the balls of his feet. With his hands in his pockets, he looked a bit nervous. Hesitant. "What if I could prove it to you? Show you something truly amazing."

"More amazing than this?" Petra lifted an eyebrow.

"More amazing than this. And beautiful." He glanced up at the rotten fruit. "It smells better, too."

"So . . . you're not going to kill me?"

Gabe shook his head. "No. This is the most conversation I've had in a hundred and fifty years. If I killed you, I'd have to talk to Sal." He grimaced, and there was a dark glint of humor in his gaze.

Petra swallowed, gave a tentative smile. Her curiosity was devouring her fear. "Okay. Show me."

CHAPTER EIGHTEEN

THE MARRIAGE OF HEAVEN
AND EARTH

"**A**lchemy is a strange art. It's horrible and beautiful
at the same time."

Petra followed Gabe down the tunnels that smelled
like earth and metal, trailing her fingers along the
walls. She could make out various layers of sediment.
Parts of the tunnels looked as if they were man-made,
held up by haphazard stones and support beams. Other
parts seemed entirely organic, as if a giant mole had
dug a perfectly round and smooth pathway. Sig seemed
most interested in those areas, sniffing vigorously.

"You seem to know a lot about it. Were you an alchemist?"

Gabe laughed and shook his head. "No. I was a Pinkerton agent."

"No shit? You were . . . as a strikebreaker? Private security?" She blinked, dredging her memory for old history classes.

"Lascaris kept pulling gold out of thin air, and his investors were beginning to wonder how he accomplished it. And whether the secret could be reproduced."

"Lucky you."

"Luck had nothing to do with it. Pinkerton sent me to investigate Lascaris because I'd investigated other occult cases: phony fortune-tellers, spontaneous human combustion, séances. I had an academic knowledge of alchemy and the supernatural, but not a practical one."

"So . . . you were the nineteenth-century version of the *X-Files*?" Petra struggled to frame it in modern terms.

"I don't know what you mean."

"Never mind." Sal probably didn't invite the Hanged Men over to his house to watch television and eat popcorn. "The Pinkerton business . . . Is that . . . is that why you were hanged?"

"I was hanged because Lascaris caught me nosing around his house. The folks in Temperance didn't take kindly to anyone making accusations about their hero." He rolled his glowing eyes.

"Lascaris was a hero?"

"Sure. He was the entire economy for the town."

"Wow." She stared up at the leak in the ceiling of the tunnel, drizzling rainwater. Sig paused to bite at the flow and slurp noisily. "Did Lascaris dig these?"

Gabriel's gleaming eyes bobbed ahead. "I think he made some of them, just to make it look like he was busy hunting for gold. The Hanged Men dug the more useful ones underneath the barn and one under Sal's house. We don't know about the rest. We suspect that the tree made some of them of its own volition."

Petra was itching to get her hands on a sample of that tree, to look at it under the microscope. She was kicking herself for not breaking off a piece when she'd had the chance. "Does Sal know about the tunnels?"

Gabe shook his head. "Not really. He knows that we go to ground. But he has no idea about the extent of them, where they go, and how far they go."

"That's convenient for you guys."

"At times, it's ensured our very survival."

"I imagine that it's difficult to remain in the same place for years on end. Never changing. Someone must have suspected, at some time?"

"Rarely." Gabe shrugged. "The Rutherfords seized the Alchemical Tree from Lascaris's control. They have always had ranch hands, and we have been theirs, since that time. We're sort of like inherited farm equipment. Most people are people."

"What does that mean?"

"Most people don't want to acknowledge any

weirdness in their midst. The natural reaction is to go out of one's way to ignore it. It's a fairly easy reaction to exploit."

"Still . . . no one in town notices that you don't age?"

Gabe glanced sidelong at her. "You were the first. We keep to ourselves, and most people pay no attention to us."

"That must be terrible." She couldn't imagine, living years on end, days without change, with no one acknowledging one's existence. It would be like being invisible.

"Eternity isn't very glamorous," he admitted. "It's a lot of shoveling shit, watching the seasons turn. It's actually pretty boring."

"I can't imagine a hundred and fifty years of cow shit."

He chuckled, and the sound seemed to thaw some of the chill that radiated from him. "It *is* a lot of shit."

"Do you miss it?"

"Do I miss what?"

Petra struggled to put what she wanted to in words. "Do you miss being alive? Do you miss the woman in the locket?"

He paused. "Not as much as I used to. I think that the . . . fervor . . . for life dims over time. Like I said, some of the Hanged Men are little more than automatons."

"The ones that came later?"

"Yes. I doubt that they can do much more than tell the difference between day and night. When to go to ground, and when to wake. I wonder . . ." His amber gaze clouded, and his voice trailed off.

"You wonder?" she prompted.

"I wonder if, when the magic drains completely out of the tree, that's also my future."

"Becoming an automaton?"

"Sometimes, I think that it would be a great relief. To no longer miss the life I once had. To no longer miss Jelena."

"She was your wife?"

He nodded.

"She must have grieved for you." Petra thought about his hair, carefully plaited in the brooch.

"She did. And I let her."

"What do you mean?" Her brow wrinkled in puzzlement.

Petra thought she detected residue of old pain in his voice. "She came looking for me after I was hanged, with Pinkerton's men. But I hid."

"Why?"

Gabe's mouth turned down. "I had no right to ask her to remain married to a corpse, to ask her to sleep alone while I rotted beneath the earth."

"But if she loved you—"

"Jelena was fragile." Abruptly, he turned away. "And my vows were until death. We're not human. Not anymore. There's no use pretending."

Petra stared at his back. "Seems awfully angsty to me."

"You're a scientist." The tunnel opened, and he

paused to look over his shoulder. "But your scientist's mind might enjoy this."

Petra stared into the soft, shining darkness.

"Oh, my God," she breathed. "It's gorgeous."

The tunnel opened into a massive cavern, covered in crystal. Crystal particulates crunched underfoot, growing along the walls and reaching up into the ceiling. The ceiling was pierced with a hole through which moonlight streamed, illuminating a black mirror of water at the bottom. The full moon's reflection shivered on the surface, split and shattered by water that dripped from the skylight above, as if the heavens met the earth here. The crystal picked up the soft glow, reflecting and refracting that light into the darkest corners of the cave. The chamber was mostly in shadow, but she could still make out Gabriel's silhouette amid the sparkle of the rock.

She knelt, picked up a handful of broken crystal on the ground. She studied it in the beam of her flashlight. Quartz in such quantities was geologically improbable for this locale. Still, she expected it to be quartz, but the crystals were shaped all wrong. Frowning, she licked her palm.

"It's potassium nitrate," she said. "Saltpeter. But it's impossible for it to grow in such huge formations."

"Lascaris made it," Gabriel said. "Once upon a time, it was an old well. As near as I can suspect, he was working the conjunction process, trying to separate out elements. He called it his 'star chamber'—his *Camera Stellata*."

Sig wandered to the edge of the water, snuffled at it. Petra skimmed her hand over the surface, and the salt stung her scraped palms.

Sig splashed into the pool, and she recoiled from the spray. He paddled out into the water, leaving slivers of moon reflection in his wake.

"At least I won't have to wash him," she muttered. And the salt would probably kill off most of his fleas.

"The water. It's heavy. You can float on it." Gabriel stood in the half darkness, eyes shining. This was the first thing she'd seen him take genuine pleasure in.

"Like the Dead Sea?" Petra let the soft water run through her fingers. It smelled like the ocean.

"Yes. So much of it's dissolved into the rainwater that it's become heavier than a body."

"I want to try it." She meant it, in a bold and reckless way that sat uneasily with her.

Gabriel grinned, his teeth white in the gloom. "I won't watch."

Petra clicked her flashlight off. Only the moon was visible on the water, and its sparking reflection in the crystal, shifting as the water lapped at the bank.

She chose not to imagine if Gabriel had some kind of preternatural night vision. But she couldn't see the glow of his eyes, and assumed that they were either closed or he had his back turned. Petra had never been shy about nudity in the service of scientific inquiry, anyway.

At least, that's what she told herself.

She slipped out of her clothes and left them in the

fine salt gravel at the edge of the pool. The salt prickled against her toes and stuck to the soles of her feet as she waded in. The black water slipped around her body, feeling luxuriously soft against her skin.

She sighed and leaned back, feeling the water lick her cheek. She floated with darkness all around her.

She'd felt this way sometimes on the rig at night, when she'd stood at the railing with Des, watching the gulls bob sleepily on the surface of the water. She'd failed to realize how fragile that sense of peace was. How fragile Des was.

She closed her eyes and let the water wash over her, rinse the tears from her face. She spread her fingers out and let her body sink up to her chin into the black. The water blotted out light and sound, life and feeling. So tempting. So tempting, to stay here, in the numb dark.

Gabriel's voice seemed to echo from the ceiling. She couldn't fix on his exact position. "It's amazing, isn't it?"

"It's just like the ocean." She tried to clear the memory and the tears from her voice.

"Is that where you came from? You smelled like salt when I first met you."

Petra's brow wrinkled, and she was suddenly self-conscious. "Yes. I used to work on an oil rig."

Sig paddled in a circle around her, splashing in the black. She reached out and grasped his tail. He snorted and swam out of her grip.

"Temperance is a long way from the ocean."

Petra looked up at the moon. "I made a mistake

that blew up an oil rig. Killed three people." Somehow, in the darkness, it seemed easier to confess. "I loved one of them."

She thought she heard a sigh in the black. "Love isn't forever."

Petra stared up at the blurry moon. Of all people, he would understand that much. "No. It isn't."

Gabe led Petra back through the warren of tunnels. She followed in silence, seeming to be mulling over all he'd told her.

And he was still unsure he'd done the right thing in telling her, but it was done.

Maybe he'd been too long underground, and human conversation was too much of a novelty. Maybe he was simply too old and numb and didn't care about keeping secrets anymore.

Or maybe it was the way that her hair smelled like salt as it dried.

Gabe rubbed his eyes. He'd been too long without companionship of any substantive type. Especially women. And he talked too much. As soon as he returned her to the surface, he was certain she'd bring back the federal agents. Sal would come back, burn the Lunaria, and that would be the end of things. A suitable ending, all things considered.

So maybe it didn't really matter much what he did, anyway. He'd had enough time, not done much with it. Maybe he should just let it all go.

He paused before a tunnel that split off in a fork. He pointed to the left. "That's the way back to the barn. I'll send someone to let you out."

"You're not coming?"

He shook his head. "I need to check on Jeff." He closed his eyes. "I need to see if he's going to survive."

She laced her hands behind her back. "I want to come with you."

He blinked at her. Hadn't she seen enough rotting flesh? He'd tried to soften that horror by showing her the Star Chamber, to show her that bit of his own secret wonder. But he had no desire to take her back to the Lunaria. "I don't think—"

"I want to go," she said firmly.

He shook his head. "If I have to put Jeff out of his misery, you don't want to see that."

She swallowed. "Yeah. I do."

She was entirely unlike Jelena. Though he knew better than to think that she felt anything else for him but the fascination of a scientist examining a bug at the end of a pin.

But she stood before him, freckled and disheveled with clothes streaked in mud . . . and utterly luminous. And for a moment, Gabe allowed himself to believe that she perhaps wanted something more from him than answers, than the unraveling of secrets and mysteries. He was more than a hundred and fifty years old. He deserved at least one illusion.

"All right," he said, and turned right down the tunnel, back to the Lunaria.

Light filled the chamber, and Petra shielded her eyes from the glare with her hand. "Why is it so bright? Are they burning?"

"It's dawn. They're waking up."

The golden glow sunk into the bodies, flowing from the roots. He could hear flesh fizzling, bones crackling, and the hiss of air in lungs. The bodies were suffused in cocoons of light that shone bright as a summer's day.

The Hanged Men dropped like angels from the ceiling, one by one, detaching themselves from that light source as delicately as dandelion fluff.

When the glow faded, they stood as whole and perfect as if they'd just been made, except for the terrible scars around their necks. They were nude. Clothes could not have survived that terrible rotting.

Petra looked away, a delicate flush spreading behind her freckles, as the Hanged Men hunted for bundles of clothes tucked away in the tree roots and stashed along the floor. Gabe's gaze roved among the roots, searching for Jeff.

And found him.

The Lunaria hadn't entirely released him. He dangled like a half-split milkweed pod trailing its contents along the floor, leaking strings of light from one arm. His head was bent back at a broken angle. His fingers twitched and jerked in the blackness. Roots reached down to comfort him, to pet him. He made a low keening noise that made Sig back up and growl.

Gabe reached up, took his head in his hands, pried

open the eyelids. Jeff's eyes were unevenly dilated, one iris entirely black in the socket and tearing gold.

"Is he—?" Petra asked.

Gabe's mouth was dry. "The Lunaria isn't strong enough to restore him. Maybe it could have, years ago, but now . . ." It was no use thinking of what could have been.

"We should take him to a hospital. Maybe someone can fix him."

He shook his head. "They won't be able to."

"We have to try."

"And I told you that we might have to put him down."

Color rose in her cheeks. "You say that as if he's a—a lame horse."

"I say that because he's not alive. Not anymore. And there's no use trying to preserve it, condemn what's left to a half-life of pain." Gabe found a broken piece of tree root on the floor of the chamber. He snapped it in half, revealing a sharp, jagged edge.

Petra watched him with round eyes as he advanced on Jeff. He put his hand over Jeff's eyes. Petra looked away.

And Gabe slammed the makeshift stake up under Jeff's rib cage.

Jeff's keening stopped, as if someone had shut off a switch deep within his chest. Cold light ran up over Gabe's knuckles, soaked his sleeve. Golden fluid gushed out from behind Jeff's ruined chest, tapping out on the floor like rain.

Slowly, the Lunaria released him. The tree roots set him down gently on the floor of the chamber, with reverence. Its roots slithered away, the fingers of a lover reluctant to leave her beloved's bed.

The glowing light faded, leaving the body dark on the floor. Whatever remained of Jeff was well and truly dead.

"We'll bury him. It won't be much, but I'll see that he gets a nice view." Gabe stared down at the body. Petra's coyote sniffed it and backed away.

Petra stepped beside him. He could hear her shallow breathing in this enclosed space, like a rabbit in a trap. Tentatively, she put her warm hand on his elbow. "I think . . . I think I'm ready to go."

Gabe nodded, led her away from the body without comment. The tree roots parted above him to yield a trapdoor. He pushed it open, revealing the pale light of true dawn, not the artificial light of the world below. He knelt and laced his fingers together before her. Petra stepped into his grip, fingers lingering on his shoulder.

Gabriel tossed her up as if she weighed no more than a stone. Petra landed on her hands and knees on the grass outside the passage.

He reached for the coyote, who looked at him suspiciously. Petra whistled from above. Sig consented to being picked up and handed through the opening.

Gabriel startled her when he leapt up through the opening to land on the grass beside her. He hadn't meant to alarm her with his unusual strength and speed, but there was no point hiding from her now.

She spun around in the pink light of dawn, her salt-brittle hair lashing her face.

She was beautiful.

Gabriel put his hands in his pockets, put his head down.

"Are you immune to it?" she asked.

"To what?" There were so many ways he could answer that. Immune to loneliness? Time? Despair? The way she bit her lip?

"To life. You took Jeff's so quickly . . ." She stifled a shudder; he could see it in the way she wrapped her arms around herself. "I keep fucking up. I keep bringing chaos and disaster behind me. I'm responsible for the death of the man I loved." She wiped her nose, and her breath shook.

"No." He reached out, shoved her hair away from her face, turned her chin to face him. "You have the most precious gift the universe can bestow. You have life. Real life. Not some simulacrum of it. Do you have any idea how much that's worth? Jeff had none of that. He was just a shell."

"You don't understand. It's been more than a hundred years since you were human." Her brown eyes were leaden.

"You don't think I thought about ending it? I did. Many times."

"What stopped you?" Curiosity crawled into her voice.

"I wasn't the only one. There were other Hanged Men. They needed me."

"I'm not as strong-willed as you."

"You don't have to be. You just have to be what you are—a scientist. And keep on being that."

He had no idea what she'd do when she left; she could keep his secrets or spill them to the entire world. He willingly gave her that power over him and the Hanged Men, to do with as she wished.

She gave him a wan smile and walked away. Walked into the rose-gold dawn and Gabe's uncertainty.

But that bit of uncertainty made him feel alive.

CHAPTER NINETEEN

THE ATHANOR

Stroud was in a bad way.

Cal stood in the Alchemist's basement, clutching a bottle of rubbing alcohol. Stroud lay on one of his experiment tables, surrounded by jars and stained rags. He was propped half-up with a pair of mildewy bed pillows, shirtless, digging at the wound in his lower right ribs with a pair of forceps that Cal had just sterilized in the furnace. A gooseneck clip-on lamp illuminated his work in a hot circle of light, with a rearview mirror from a car allowing Stroud to get a better view of the wound. Not that this was the only one. Bits of birdshot peppered Stroud's arms, but Cal wasn't mentioning those. Stroud's creepy mercury intermittently spat out bits of it onto the floor. What remained of it in Stroud's flesh was not worth picking at now.

But the cop's bullet, that was serious shit. Sweat glossed Stroud's forehead as he grunted and worked at the wound, which began to soak blood through the rags that Cal had placed beside him to staunch the flow. Stroud's sweat was metallic in the light, seeming to bead and run together in crazed frost patterns on the surface of his skin.

Cal didn't want to touch him. Blood made him dizzy.

But he did as he was told.

"Can you see the bullet?" Stroud hissed.

Cal knelt and squinted. "Yeah. I think so. But it's hard to tell, on account of the blood."

The forceps fell out of Stroud's grip and clattered to the floor. Cal rushed to scoop them up and sterilize them again in the fire. When he brought them back, the tips glowed red. He offered the cool handles to Stroud.

Stroud shook his head. A runnel of mercury dripped down his pale lip. "You do it."

Cal swallowed. "I'm not a doctor."

"Play one on TV. I can't see the damn thing."

Cal screwed up his resolve. On one hand, he was flattered to be the only one Stroud would allow to tend to him, despite his many fuck-ups over the past week. On the other hand, if he fucked this up, Stroud would kill him. That was, if Stroud survived. If not, the others would.

It was a no-win. Cal grasped the handles of the forceps and stared into the wound. He mopped at it with a rag, stalling for time. The wound itself was really small, about the size of a dime, but the blood kept obscuring the surface. A bit of mercury kept welling up to gnaw at it, but it wasn't strong enough to push it out.

Stroud was losing a lot of blood. Cal flicked a glance to the trash can full of soaked cloth. He wouldn't be able to stay conscious much longer.

"Just do it."

Cal put the flat of his hand gingerly on Stroud's belly, trying to keep the mouth of the wound from moving when the Alchemist breathed. He touched the tongs to the wound, and Stroud hissed, clutching the edge of the table.

"Do it!"

Cal reached in. He could see something shiny inside, dug into it hard with the tongs. The thing was slippery, twisted, twitching.

Stroud screamed as Cal worked. Cal finally succeeded in getting the tips of the forceps around the bullet and yanked it out.

He staggered back, holding a warped piece of metal stuck to a piece of flesh in the grip of the instrument. Nauseated, he dropped the forceps and the bullet to the floor. His hands shook.

"Good." A silver tear leaked from Stroud's eye. "Now heat that bottle of mercury in the athanor."

Cal looked at him blankly.

"In the furnace," he said gently, eyes glazed. "It's called an athanor. The crucible where all purity is forged." He pressed a rag to his leaking side. He began to babble: "Paracelsus said, 'By the element of fire all that is imperfect is destroyed and taken away . . .'"

Cal grabbed the pair of tongs, grateful to have something to do that didn't involve gore. He fitted them around the neck of the mason jar of mercury, held it over the flame.

"Heat it until it boils."

Cal concentrated very hard on not dropping the jar. "Are . . . are you going to be okay, now?"

Stroud took a slug out of a vodka bottle. Cal noticed that Stroud never used drugs. And he wondered why, but never would ask.

"I think so." Stroud's gaze fixed him, then wobbled. "Thank you."

Cal squirmed. "It was nothing."

The Alchemist stared up at the ceiling. "Justin tells me that you found a body. On the Rutherford ranch."

Cal swallowed. "Yeah. I think . . . I think it was Emmett. It was wearing his watch."

"How did you find it?"

Shit. Shit. Shit. There was no use lying to him, even in his drunk and weakened and sort of poetic state. The Alchemist always found out. "I asked Petra to help me. I figured that if she was a geologist, she could find where that body the guy in the bar was talking about . . ." He trailed off, stared into the steaming jar.

Silence hung between them.

Shit.

"I thought I'd try to use her, you know?" Cal concentrated on not dropping the jar. "I didn't realize . . ."

"You may have opened a door that I can use," Stroud said finally. Sweat prickled on the back of Cal's neck. That didn't sound good.

"She said that she was looking for her father. Maybe that's why she's with Rutherford's guys." That sounded good. Like he had been out spying for Stroud and bringing back useful information. Still on the home team and shit.

Stroud shook his head. "They wouldn't know. *I* know."

Cal looked over his shoulder. "You do?"

"Our paths crossed many years ago. He and I had . . . similar goals." Stroud's gaze was distant and misty, as if he was remembering something. Or getting really drunk. Cal couldn't tell.

"He was an alchemist?"

"Yes. I worked with him for a time."

Cal noticed that the mercury in the jar was bubbling. He drew it away from the flame with the tongs and walked slowly to Stroud, careful not to spill any.

"Set it here." Stroud pointed to a vacant spot on the table.

"Was he like you? I mean, was he good?"

Stroud smiled. "He was good. Still is." Stroud pulled

on a welder's glove and grasped the jar. He poised the jar over the wound, drizzled hot mercury into it. He cried out and growled, the welder's glove shaking. Drops of mercury slid off the table and rolled away on the floor. Mercury pooled within the wound, turning black as it roiled.

Stroud set the jar aside and lay back on the table, panting. Cal got him a cool cloth from a bucket and wiped his brow.

"You okay?"

"Yes."

But he didn't look okay. Veins of mercury crept out from the wound, black under his skin. It was as if a living thing dug beneath his flesh, worming under the surface.

"I want you to do something for me, Cal," he said. He grasped Cal's collar, drew him close. The old man's breath smelled like sour vodka and metal.

"Sure. Anything."

"I want you to find Petra. Tell her that I know where her father is. I'll trade the artifact for the information. Bring her here, and we'll make the trade."

Cal licked his lips. There was no defying the Alchemist. "Yessir."

"Good man." Stroud reached up to ruffle Cal's hair. "I can always count on you. You're my number one foot soldier."

Cal suppressed a shudder as a cataract of mercury slid over Stroud's eye.

Petra sat next to Mike at Bear's deli, picking at her sandwich and thinking about how much to tell him as he conducted his fishing expedition.

"So, you gonna tell me how Stroud wound up in the trunk of his car?" Mike asked around mouthfuls of pastrami sandwich.

"I told you. That wasn't my call." Petra looked behind the counter. Bear was feeding Sig leftover bits of meat from butcher paper in a major health code violation and cooing to the coyote in a voice that seemed entirely inappropriate for such a big man. Sig wriggled in pleasure, staring up at Bear adoringly. Petra was beginning to think that Sig would go home with him.

"Whose idea was it?"

"It was Gabe's. He said Stroud was dangerous. And I kind of agreed with that assessment."

Mike sipped his coffee. "The deputy he attacked was babbling about a man in silver armor. The ER thought that Stroud might have choked the oxygen from his brain and caused one hell of a hallucination."

"Maybe," she said uncertainly. "But Stroud didn't look normal. He was leaking what looked like mercury. And Gabe . . ." She trailed off.

"You gonna tell me what one of Sal's men was doing at your place?" Mike turned his coffee cup around to inspect the Styrofoam.

"I asked him for help finding my father." Petra didn't like lying outright; half-truths were easier. She intended on telling Mike a version of events that was similar to what she told the sheriff's deputies: She was minding her own business when Stroud and the boys showed up looking for trouble for no good reason. The sheriff's office seemed to accept that Stroud's people were in the wrong and wanted little from her except a statement. Mike wouldn't be shaken off so easily, but she'd try. She changed the subject. "How's Justin?"

Mike shook his head. "Justin, the weasel, stayed long enough to demand about a gallon of green Jell-O, then split. He went out the damned window when his assigned county guard was reading the paper in the hallway."

"What about Stroud?"

"None of the hospitals within two hours' drive have reported any gunshot wounds. Between getting hit by Maria and the deputy, he's in a world of hurt. I don't look for him to survive beyond . . ."

He looked past her, through the window to the street, and began to slide off the stool.

"What's wrong?"

Mike gestured with his chin. "There's Justin."

Petra followed Mike's line of sight, saw Justin crossing the street and slinking into the Compostela.

"Stay here," Mike said. He was on his feet and banging through the door of the deli. The cowbell rattled like an alarm.

Petra was right behind him, whistling for Sig. "Not a chance."

She rushed across the street to the ornate door of

the Compostela. She tugged it open, reaching for the gun at her right hip. The bar denizens had fallen silent as a congregation at mass, turning their gazes toward Mike charging across the polished floor.

"The tweaker," he demanded of a woman stacking glasses behind the bar. "Where is he?"

The waitress lifted her hands. "I don't want any trouble in here."

Mike slapped his hands on the bar. "He's wanted for attempted burglary and assault with a deadly weapon. You tryin' to get in my way?"

The waitress pointed to the men's room. "In there."

Mike straight-armed into the men's room, and the door struck the wall with a sound like a gunshot. Fluorescent light flickered overhead, illuminating Justin leaning over a sink with a glass pipe.

"Drop it," Mike ordered.

Justin sucked air from the pipe, held it in his lungs, and released it in a curling ghost of smoke that passed over his black eye.

Petra wrinkled her nose as the smoke drifted in her direction. It was unlike anything she'd ever smelled before: acrid and sweet at the same time. Like drain cleaner and roses.

Mike snatched the pipe from Justin, who was suddenly unsteady on his feet. "What's this? Meth?"

Justin's hands balled into fists, and his eyes were dilated so black that she couldn't tell the true color of his eyes. He shook his head. "Elixir." The corners of his split lip turned upward in an expression of sublime love. He slid from his perch on the edge of the sink and oozed down to the floor.

"Great," Mike mumbled, shaking the contents of the pipe. White crystals and a rim of liquid lay in the bottom, producing a Jack-Frost pattern on the interior. "A brand new drug."

"Well, it doesn't seem to be making him violent, at least." In her few interactions with Justin, she'd known him to be fueled entirely by testosterone. Whatever the Elixir was, it was making him pretty damn agreeable.

The young man sat half-upright on the broken tile floor, looking at his battered hands in his lap.

Mike bent down. "Where'd you get this?"

"From the Alchemist." Justin looked up at him in an expression of utter peace and contentment. Petra had only seen that look on the faces of certain orders of nuns. He lifted his hands, stared at them in fascination. Maybe he was having a hallucination or was contemplating why his left pinky finger was turned in the wrong direction and an ugly shade of purple.

Maybe not.

His fingers splayed open, stretched, twisted. A splinter of bone pierced the skin on the back of his hand, dripping a runnel of blood down his wrist. His fingers turned back, freezing into claws.

"Jesus Christ," Mike whispered, reaching for his radio.

Justin's preternatural calm broke. "What's happening to me?" he whispered.

The paleness crept up his arms, like venom. Petra could see his skin stretching, hardening, breaking. Blood leaked to his elbows. His radius and ulna turned backward, and he began to scream.

" . . . Need the squad at the Compostela, right now," Mike was shouting into his radio.

Petra held Justin's shoulders, horrified as the calcination began to crackle under the sleeves of his T-shirt, bending and twisting redly under the cotton. It was like there was some terrible beast inside him, struggling to get out.

"Just breathe," she told him, because that was the most important thing, and she didn't know what else to tell him. He needed to keep doing that. *"Breathe."*

Justin twisted out of her grip, scrambled to his feet, and ran out of the men's room.

"Stop him!" Mike yelled.

Petra and Mike chased him through the bar, the patrons stunned to silence by his screams. Justin bounced off a pew like a pinball, crashed into a table, shattering glassware. He ran through the dimness of the bar, instinctively heading like a moth to the light of the outside.

The glare of noon momentarily blinded Petra. She focused on Justin, stumbling in the middle of the street.

His right leg collapsed under him like rotten wood. Petra could see the bones driven up under his kneecap, ripping apart denim and flesh. He limped forward, keening, as Petra caught up to him.

She recoiled as she saw his face. His cheekbone had

grown up over his eye, blinding him on one side. His skin had hardened and stretched to ghoulish proportions, bone breaking through his jaw. He collapsed in Petra's arms, and she could feel his ribs moving and crackling like ice as she held him.

"Just breathe," she told him, straining to feel the flex of hardening muscle under his chest.

She was conscious of Mike's cool shadow falling over her, but she strained to listen. Justin had fallen silent, just a thin whistle emanating from his ruined mouth.

"Just breathe," she pleaded. "Breathe."

He tried. Petra could feel the creak of his muscles laboring. But his ribs opened up like a flower, pulling apart flesh, and crystallized in her hands.

Petra stood in the shadow of the Compostela, watching as the volunteer firefighters took turns staring at Justin's body. They'd put a sheet over him to keep onlookers from gawking, waiting for the Feds, who were reportedly sending people from the DEA and CDC. Nobody really wanted to touch him, but everyone wanted to see. Bar patrons crowded the window, peering out and muttering.

Petra rubbed her hands against her jeans. She'd washed them three times, on the off chance that Justin was contagious, but Mike was suspecting the drugs. He paced the perimeter of yellow caution tape that blocked off this side of the street, talking intently on his phone.

"I can't believe that he's gone. Not like that."

Petra turned to see Cal standing beside her, hands jammed into his pockets and jingling his wallet chain.

"Hey, asshole," she greeted him.

"Hey," he muttered. "You, uh . . . gonna have me arrested?"

"Why shouldn't I?" She glanced around for Mike, but he had his back turned to her a half block away, quietly speaking into his cell phone and rubbing the back of his neck. He had "administrative nightmare" written all over him.

"Look, I just wanna talk."

"About you and Stroud and Justin showing up at my house wired for sound?"

"No, I . . . fuck. I didn't want that. But Stroud, he made me." The dejected line in Cal's shoulders was convincing. "You got no idea of what he can make people do."

She grabbed him by the arm and hauled him around the corner of the building, out of sight.

"The drugs. Did they do that to Justin?" she demanded.

Cal shook his head helplessly. He seemed just as at confused as she was. "We've all smoked the Elixir a bunch of times. It never did that."

"Why on Earth would you do that anyway?" Petra blurted.

Cal looked up at her. "It's hard to explain. The Elixir isn't like anything else. It makes you . . . peaceful. Very Zen. Stroud says it's the closest thing to immortality that humans can experience."

Petra gazed at the sheet-shrouded ghost lying on the pavement. "Yeah, well. You might want to stop. Just sayin'."

"I never did it all that much. Never really had the money. But Justin likes—liked—it a lot." Cal stared down at his scuffed boots. "He always had money for it, anyway."

Petra frowned. Maybe it was the cumulative effect. Or a bad batch. That would also explain the hiker with the drug paraphernalia. And the bodies on Rutherford's farm. If those were also Stroud's people . . .

"Listen, you've gotta warn people," Petra said. "This isn't the first. You recognized the watch on Sal's ranch."

"Yeah."

"And I have to tell you something." Petra blew out her breath. "There was a man and woman found on Rutherford's ranch, too."

Cal's heavily kohled gaze flicked up. "Found . . . like that?"

"Yeah. I can't say for sure it was your friends, but . . ." Petra struggled for words. "I'm sorry."

"Did you see them yourself?" His voice crackled, and he cleared his throat.

"No. Gabe—one of Sal's men—told me. But I believe him."

"Shit." Cal rubbed his nose with his knuckle and looked away, blinking. He looked as if she'd struck him. His gaze eventually turned back to her. "Hey, thanks for that. Really."

She wished that she didn't have to be the bearer of bad news. This kid, despite his transgressions, just seemed like he was perpetually in the wrong place at the wrong time, and Petra could sympathize with that.

"I do have some info for you." Cal seemed to steel himself. "About your dad."

Petra's heart stopped. "You do?"

"Stroud knew him, says he knows where he is."

The hair prickled on the back of Petra's neck. "Stroud. The Alchemist."

"Yeah. He says he'll trade you the information for the artifact. And then he'll leave you alone."

Petra's eyes narrowed. "Why does he want it?"

"Stroud's into all kinds of weird shit. Magic. He wants anything to do with Lascaris. He's kinda obsessed that way."

Petra reached into her pocket, weighed the Locus in her hand. "I want to talk to him. But only on neutral turf."

Cal shook his head. "Stroud's in a bad way after he got shot. He can't even get up to take a piss by himself."

Petra's brow's drew together. "He's dying?"

"I dunno." Cal looked away. "I took the cop's bullet out, but he looks bad. Real bad. He's still full of birdshot from that chick at your trailer. I dunno how long he's gonna last."

She bit her lip. Her heart swelled and pounded in her chest. What if Stroud knew? What if the Alchemist could give her an address, a phone number, any clue to her father? A fistful of gold would be a small price to pay.

"Okay," she said finally. She glanced down the street. Mike was still turned away, talking to one of the paramedics.

Her phone rang. She reached for it, and her heart twitched when she saw UNKNOWN NUMBER on the display.

"Hello?"

The voice at the other end sounded very far and very much like her father: "Don't go."

"Who is this?" she demanded, feeling her eyes grow hot. "Who are you?"

"Don't go," he said again. "Please."

"Then you have to tell me where you are."

"I'm not anywhere . . . not anywhere you can find me."

And the call disconnected.

Petra gulped down a mouthful of air. She needed to find out, needed to know. And the disembodied voice at the end of the line wasn't telling her.

"Everything cool?" Cal asked.

"Yeah, yeah." She rubbed her face.

Cal nodded. "I'll take you to the Garden."

CHAPTER TWENTY

THE GARDEN

The Garden was not what Petra expected.

The name conjured up an image of some secret mystical grotto where Druids and dryads danced under glittering leaves. Instead, a dilapidated house stood at the end of a long dirt road surrounded by a makeshift trailer park. White paint peeled from the structures like birch bark in winter. Sheds, tents, strung-up laundry, rusted-out car chassis and chickens sprouted among the tall grasses. The whole compound was surrounded in barbed wire. Beyond it, stalks of corn nodded their heads in a vast field.

"I thought you said that this was a garden." Petra slammed the door of the Bronco. Sig slipped out from behind her legs and immediately took off after a chicken.

"There is a garden." Cal pointed to a cluster of stringy tomato plants clinging to each other. "But Stroud says that it's more of a philosophical garden. Something about the alchemist's secret vessel. I just nod like I understand," he said sheepishly.

"Sure." Petra picked her way up the rotted steps, through the torn screen door and the lintel covered in glass beer bottles. Her heart hammered in her chest behind the necklace her father had given her, and she paused to button her shirt collar up to her chin, hiding it.

The interior of the house was strewn with trash: crushed Styrofoam cups, broken glass, and bits of aluminum foil. The walls and ceiling were yellowed and stained with smoke. The acrid smell of meth and piss clung to the drapes, the stained shag carpet, and the sagging velvet couch on which a woman was stretched. She looked to have passed out, one arm flung over her head.

"You live here?" Petra asked. She was used to tough living conditions, but this squalor was something else entirely.

Cal ducked his head and didn't answer.

She felt a pang of sorrow for him as she followed him through the kitchen stacked high with dishes and beer bottles. A roach the size of a mouse scuttled along the countertop, unafraid of people or daylight.

Cal paused before a door that Petra assumed led to the basement. The red paint was peeling off the surface in chunks, but the crystal knob sparkled. It was the only clean thing that Petra had seen in the place.

"He's down there."

Cal opened the door and descended into darkness. Petra took a deep breath and followed him down the creaking steps. The air was stale here, metallic and reeking of dried blood. At the bottom of the stairs was what appeared to be the Alchemist's laboratory. Shelves of mason jars and decanters surrounded a table made of a door propped up on cinder blocks and mismatched turned legs. The door was marred with a rusty brown stain that dribbled off the side to the concrete floor. Wadded rags, tongs, and an empty vodka bottle stood on the table. A moth circled a bare lightbulb overhead, fluttering into the glass with a futile tap.

"You came."

A voice crawled out of the shadows at the far wall. Stroud sat upon a threadbare gold-upholstered chair. He was, as Cal had said, in a bad way. The Alchemist was shirtless, his torso bound with what looked like the remnants of a bedsheet. Hair matted, he sat slouched with his pale fingers gnawing the fringe on the arms of the chair. Underneath his skin, Petra could see the mercury moving like a trapped creature. As it crawled up under the loose skin of his face, it flicked up over one eye, covering the iris and sclera. When he spoke, Petra could see it glittering on his tongue.

Petra struggled to keep her voice steady. "Cal said you had information about my father."

"Did you bring the Locus?" The mercury seethed between his ribs in a lump.

"Yes."

Stroud licked his lips, leaving a sticky silver residue in the corners. "Your father came here in search of alchemical knowledge. I remember him well. He believed that alchemy could be used to extend human life, transmute the decay of cells into perpetual regeneration. He was trying, in effect, to cheat death."

"Where is he now?"

"He wasn't successful in his quest. I did try to help him."

"You're telling me he's dead." Her voice sounded leaden to her.

"No. But the Alzheimer's chewed far into his brain. He might as well be."

"Alzheimer's?" Petra echoed. "He was too young." But her mind raced back to the postcards and letters he'd sent her, the disjointed commentary about lions and violet flames. She'd suspected schizophrenia, but . . .

"Early-onset. He knew that he'd had it for years. He was desperate for a cure. By the time he'd come to Temperance, he often forgot what year it was."

"Why would he rely on alchemy for an answer?"

Petra's nails chewed into her palms. "He was a man of science."

"And also a man of faith. He knew that modern science doesn't hold all the answers."

"Where is he now?"

"Phoenix Village. It's a nursing home forty minutes from here." Stroud extended a shaking hand. His fingernails were black, and two of them had peeled off, revealing moist nail beds the color of wet steel. "I've honored my part of the bargain. Now, you."

Petra reached into her jacket pocket for the Locus. The finish on it was dull with her dried blood.

Stroud's eyes shone when she handed it to him. "Lascaris wrote about the *Venificus Locus*. A beautiful tool. He engineered it himself to feed on blood and find magic. I've tried to reproduce it, but failed every time."

"What will you do with it?" Petra asked. "Use it in your experiments?"

Stroud grinned. "Sal Rutherford has secrets on his land. Some that not even he knows about, ones that rightfully belong to me. The Locus will lead me to them."

He gestured to the bloodstained table. A battered brown book lay open. Across two pages was an elaborate ink illustration of a tree. A gorgeous tree, reaching heavenward with its branches and deep into the earth with its roots. The Lunaria.

Petra's throat closed. *Shit*. She'd woefully underestimated the scope of Stroud's knowledge and ambitions.

At the top of the stairs, she heard the door slam shut. She reached for the guns in their holsters, whirled on Stroud. "We had a deal."

Cal twitched in alarm. "You said that you wouldn't hurt her."

Petra leveled the guns before her, backed up the stairs. The knob was locked, and wouldn't turn. She aimed at Stroud. "Let me out."

Stroud shrugged. "I can't make the Locus work. Not on my own."

"Why not?" Her grip on the gun was sweaty. She pulled back the hammer.

"I'm too much magic."

Her thoughts raced. "There are others in the Garden who can use it for you."

"Yeah," Cal said. His eyes were wide with fear. "I can try it."

Stroud shook his head. "They've taken too much Elixir. Their blood is too contaminated with magic to work." He leaned forward. "I need fresh blood, ordinary blood. There is nothing magical about you."

Petra stared over the pistol at Stroud. "Let me out or I'll shoot. I swear that I will."

"I don't think so." Stroud smiled. His gums glinted silver, lurid against his blackened lips. "You are too much your father's daughter."

Petra turned and aimed at the doorknob. She shielded her eyes and pulled the trigger, shattering the crystal lockset in a hail of splinters. The echo of the shot in the small space was deafening, and it competed with the roar of blood in her ears as she shoved the door open and stumbled into the arms of a half dozen of Stroud's people clustered at the top of the stairs. They were thin and gaunt, like ghosts, smelling like acid and sweat. She felt hands upon her, ripping away the pistols and gun belt.

Stroud crawled up the basement steps on all fours like a revenant, blinking in the light. As she struggled and howled, she saw him grab a steak knife and a mason jar from the kitchen sink.

Something slammed against the screen door. *Sig*, she thought. She hoped that he would run, not try to help her like the Good Dog he'd turned out to be.

"Hold her," Stroud hissed, and a man stretched out her arm, tore her sleeve up to her elbow. The steak knife ripped into the white, freckled flesh inside her arm, a horizontal cut that released red in a gush.

She fought, kicking, and knocked the mason jar out of Stroud's grip.

Her head slammed against the filthy kitchen floor, and a sticky darkness that smelled like blood fell over her.

Petra awoke, seeing red. Red and white.

Her cheek was pressed to something cool and moist that smelled like fresh-turned earth.

And roses.

Her vision was blurry, and rose petals stuck to her face. Around her stretched massive hedgerows over seven feet high, full of crimson and white roses, exquisitely wound in an organic wall. On her hands and knees, Petra squinted at them. These were not the fragile tea roses that she'd seen cultivated in civilized gardens. These were old-world roses, dog roses that grew wild. Blooms with flat faces and wicked spines reached out over insect-chewed leaves. It seemed like it could have been a garden that had been abandoned long ago and allowed to consume itself.

Her fingers flexed in the damp, petal-strewn earth. She reached to press a hand to her left cheek. Her eye on that side was nearly swollen shut. Perhaps a fracture—she couldn't tell, and it made her queasy to poke at it. She squinted up at the sky. It was white and opaque, and she couldn't detect the sun.

She sat up, and a grey blur immediately launched itself into her lap, licking the dew from her hands.

"Sig." She sighed, throwing her arms around him. He grinned at her, his tail slapping her chest.

"Where are we?" she muttered around his ruff. Perhaps this was some unused part of Stroud's "Garden." It was certainly less grim than the house, and might afford her the opportunity to escape. Perhaps he was done with her, and she could run, run and warn Gabe about the terrible thing she'd done . . .

A deep, bass growl emanated behind her.

Petra turned, feeling Sig's fur lifting under her fingers. It wasn't him. The coyote's lips pulled away from his teeth, and she smelled salami on his breath.

He snarled at the shadow of something moving just beyond the wall of roses. Something large. Something growling. Something with claws that she could see moving just under the hedge.

Petra scrambled to her feet, head pounding. She grabbed Sig by the collar and urged him to run. He obeyed, racing with her down a corridor of hedge roses to another wall of vegetation at the end. They could go right or left; right was closer to the growling thing. Petra chose left.

The hedgerows turned back on themselves as she ran, and she had the sinking feeling of being trapped in a maze. A maze with a minotaur. She skidded in the petals and leaves, dodging back and forth in the labyrinth with Sig at her heels. Her breath scalded the back of her throat, and her hair stuck in her mouth as she zigged, right, left, always away from the growling and the claws churning the debris behind her . . .

And then she struck a dead end. Her fingers scraped thorns and let loose a shower of petals. She briefly considered throwing her jacket over her head and trying to push her way through the hedgerow, but it was too thick to brute force her way through. She tried to shove Sig underneath it, but he resisted.

A roar that was deep enough to shake dew from the branches rattled behind her. She spun on her heel, to find herself faced with a lion.

A huge, muscled lion with a magnificent mane.

And he was green.

Petra shrank up against the thorns. He wasn't just green, like a child's cartoon. He was the color of verdigris, the patina on copper, that cold green that only came from time and a really persistent chemical reaction. The lion roared at her, showing white teeth in a black mouth.

"What the hell?" she muttered to Sig.

Petra felt like she did when she stepped off a ship and onto land after weeks at sea, the way she'd felt under the influence of Frankie's microbial water. Reality was shifting, and she didn't like it. She automatically reached down for her gun belt. To her surprise, it was still there. The pearl grips on the pistols quavered in her hands. Had Stroud's people given them back to her in the name of sport? Or was she completely out of her wits? Was she unconscious on his kitchen floor, neurons firing helplessly away in a terrible dream while they minced her up and fed her to the chickens in the yard?

"Get back," she demanded. Truth be told, she was less likely to shoot an animal than she was a person, and she knew it. But maybe the lion didn't. She tried to nudge Sig under the hedge with her boot, but he slid away, circling around to face the lion.

The lion padded up to her slowly, every sinew taut and rippling in his back, tail lashing. He ignored the snarling coyote and moved close to her, nostrils flaring.

Maybe she could scare him. Petra aimed over his

head, pulled the trigger in a warning shot. The sound echoed through the labyrinth and was quickly swallowed by the foliage.

The lion hunched down to the ground, looking over his shoulder. But he didn't flee. He reared up, his paws pressing into her chest, pushing her into a painful wall of thorns. One of the pistols fell to the ground, and Petra gasped. She heard Sig barking below her, and a squeal as the lion shook him off effortlessly.

The lion was taller than her by more than a head, and she knew that he was going to devour her. She sucked in her breath, ready to be torn apart, feeling the meat of those paws against her collar and the scrape of the claws in her flesh.

But the lion's peculiar white eyes were fixed on her throat. Not getting ready to tear it out, but staring at the gold pendant her father had given her, which had fallen over his paw.

The lion blinked. His slitted cat irises had gone round, more human. He pushed away from her and dropped to all fours.

Petra remained where she was, tangled in the roses, frozen.

The lion dipped his head. He seemed to melt, to fall into his shadow. Petra had only seen that before with Gabriel and the ravens. Fur dissolved and re-formed. The animal silhouette grew and lengthened to a man's, and then stepped out of the pool of ink, a new shape.

It was a man in a black coat, with grey hair and

brown eyes. Eyes like her father's. It was the same man from her earlier vision, beside the sea.

"Dad?" she squeaked.

He reached out to his sides, as if he walked a tight-rope and meant to steady himself. He looked about, dazed, until his gaze settled on her.

"Petra."

She threw herself into his arms. His knotted fingers came to rest on her shoulders and under her chin, turning her face to him.

"You look like your mother when she was your age," he said, the lines around the corners of his eyes crinkling "Are you dead? Is that why you've come?"

"No," she said, then reconsidered, her hand flitting up to her bruised cheek. "Well, I don't think so."

He peered at her, as if she were transparent. Hell of a mutual existential crisis.

"Stroud said . . . he said you were in a nursing home." Her mind tracked back, trying to bridge the border between reality and lies. "And you're not. You're here. Dad, you need to tell me . . ."

Her father's mouth turned down, and his nostrils flared. "Come with me."

He grasped her arm and led her back into the laby-rinth. "Where are we?" she demanded, struggling to keep up. The old man moved fast, even faster than Sig.

"The Garden," he said, seeming surprised that she asked. "No one comes here by accident. People spend lifetimes trying to find it!"

"Stroud's Garden?"

"No. The Alchemical Garden. The vessel of the great work!" Sweat glossed his brow as he tugged her along. It reminded her of the postcards he used to send—rambling nonsense about signs and symbols.

Petra tried to dig in her heels. "Where are we going?"

"To the center," he muttered. The wind was picking up, blowing the petals from the hedges. "The center is safe."

"Safe from what? The lion?" She struggled to make sense, to follow the grooves of his thoughts in the maze as he slung her behind him like a rag doll, charging ahead.

He laughed. "You have nothing to fear from the lion! You are the blood of the lion."

She tugged at his sleeve like she might have as a little girl. "Dad, stop!"

But her voice was torn from her by the rising wind, whipping dead foliage and rotten petals behind her, tearing through her coat and her hair. She stumbled with her father out into a clearing.

"I know this place," she whispered.

A massive tree stood in the center—a scarred and massive tree that she knew. The tree of the Hanged Men—the Lunaria. The wind had stripped it of leaves, and only ravens clung to it now, cawing, their wings flapping. It seemed a great living thing, churning and crying out.

"The Philosophical Tree!" her father shouted, pointing. "You'll be safe there."

Petra grasped his collar and shook him. "Dad. Are you really here? Are you really alive?"

His pale gaze wavered, then seemed to fix on her and truly take her in for the first time. "I'm not dead. But I can't get back to you. I can't help you."

"This is all in my head!" she shouted, above the rising maelstrom of leaves and thorns. Her shoulder struck the Lunaria, and she struggled to remain standing. Branches reached down for her, as they had reached for the men underground. "How do I get out?"

He grasped her hands in his, and they were cold. "Use all the tools at your disposal. Your hands and your blood."

The birds took off all at once, screaming, as the white sky blew apart.

Gabriel wasn't a man moved by pity or concern.

He was moved by pragmatic things, by expediency. By silence.

He walked soundlessly through the corridors of the county hospital. He found it to be a curious place, obsessed with disinfecting and masking pain to create the illusion of control. A pregnant woman was pushed through the tiled halls in a wheelchair, while a motionless old man was drawn away in a gurney. Life came and life went here, and it was all foreign to him, this buzz and furor over it. Like it was some rare and precious thing, when it teemed all around. Sentimental.

He went first to check on Sal. They'd let Gabe in

with no more scrutiny than signing the visitor's log in an indecipherable scrawl. He entered a glassed-in room, fringed in polka-dotted drapery and painted a sullen pink. Sal lay in a metal bed, tubes running from machines chirping around him. His face was bruised and unmoving. A mask strapped over his nose barely fogged with breath.

Gabe paused at the foot of the bed, where a clipboard with a metal cover hung. At the very least, he was curious to see how long they'd keep Sal. Gabe traced his callused fingers over records of IV fluids administered, pain medications given. His finger stopped at the bottom of the second page, snagging on the thin yellow paper of patient history notes. *Metastatic liver cancer. Cirrhosis. Elevated risk of bleeding.* The words were hastily scrawled, a quick marker in memory of something too large and complicated to be forgotten.

Gabe paged through the notes. This was not a recent development, not something that had been uncovered in the emergency room. This cancer had been flowering, hidden, behind Sal's thick hide for some time. Sal knew.

And now Gabe knew, knew why his boss had fed Jeff to the Lunaria. Sal needed to unearth the Hanged Men's secret to eternal life before his own time ran out.

Gabriel stood over him, watching. It would be very easy to end Sal's dominion over the Hanged Men, right now. It would take no more than pressing that crisp white pillow over his face and walking away. A finished job.

Gabe even went so far as to reach for the pillow, feeling the coolness of the cotton under his palm.

Tempting. It would be satisfying to do so. And if he had only himself to think of, Gabe would have done it long ago. But killing Sal would not serve the best interests of Gabe or any of the other Hanged Men. Best to wait and let things unfold. Patience had always rewarded him. Perhaps it would reward him with a natural death for Sal, and time for a suitable successor to emerge. Gabe stepped away, back into the bright lights of the hallway, to search for Frankie.

He found him on another floor, one with fewer staff and more noise. Gurneys clattered down the hall, more than one with an unwilling prisoner strapped in. Someone behind a curtain insisted that he was the incarnation of Hamlet, while a young woman stared vacantly through glass, twirling her hair, displaying vicious cut marks on her forearms. A young man stood in the corner and pissed in a mop bucket, singing a pretty convincing sea shanty:

"*Who lives in a pineapple under the sea? Absorbent and yellow and . . .*"

He found Maria at Frankie's bedside, smoothing his hair from his brow. She glanced up at Gabe's shadow in the door.

"How is he?" Gabe asked.

"I've never been this scared for him before," Maria confessed. "Not when he hit a moose while driving drunk. Not when he was found hitchhiking with a garbage bag full of dead trout. Not when he attempted snowmobiling—naked—in January. Not ever. Not even Frankie could do this to himself. That fucker, Sal . . ." She looked away.

Gabe took two steps into the room and stopped. He considered telling Maria that Sal was helpless in a bed two floors up. He imagined that she would finish what he had contemplated.

He kept his mouth shut. Instead, he asked, "Are they taking good care of him?"

Maria sighed. "They hooked him up to IV fluids and a heart monitor. He's been intubated and had his stomach pumped to keep him from choking on his own vomit again. And they hooked him up to dialysis." She gestured to a whirring machine beside Frankie, who seemed very small and very fragile in the bed. "Maybe . . . maybe this will be the time he stops drinking."

"Maybe," Gabe agreed.

A rustle emanated from the bed. Maria looked up. Frankie turned his head from side to side. He couldn't speak with the tube in. He flexed his hands that were strapped to the side of the bed.

"Why's he tied up?"

"He tried to rip his tube out," Maria said. "The ER doctor ordered him to be restrained. The sedation hasn't been going well."

Frankie turned his head to her, eyes wild.

"It's for your own good, Frankie," Maria said soothingly, rubbing his arm.

Frankie struggled, trying to talk, his arms straining against the bonds. He glared at Gabe.

"Don't try to talk," she said. "He's not going to hurt you. I promise. Just sleep. Sleep it off."

He shook his head. Frankie grabbed her hand where it rested next to his restraints. He took her finger between his, pantomined writing.

"I understand." Maria dug through her purse, came up with a pen and the back of an electric bill envelope. She ripped open the Velcro of the restraint on his right wrist.

Frankie snatched the pen from her and began scratching furiously on the paper.

Maria looked on, then showed it to Gabe. He'd written:

GREEN LION LOST IN THE GARDEN

"Who's lost?" Maria asked.

Frankie circled "*GREEN LION*" furiously.

She tried a different tactic. "What does *THE GARDEN* mean?"

Frankie underlined. "*THE GARDEN.*"

Maria frowned. "Frankie, I don't understand."

Frankie began to draw. He drew a crude shape of a creature standing on its back feet, its open mouth around a disk. It sort of looked like a lion. He drew rays from the disk in a determined fashion.

"That looks like Petra's pendant," Gabe said.

Frankie nodded furiously. Around the lion, he

began to draw something that looked like thorns. Or barbed wire.

"That doesn't look like a garden, Frankie." Maria squinted at it.

Frankie went back to underlining "*THE GARDEN*."

Maria frowned. "I last saw Petra at Sal's ranch when the Feds showed up. She promised to come by to see Frankie." Maria glanced at her watch. "She hasn't come."

Maria dialed Petra's cell phone number. It rang until it rolled over to voice mail.

Maria stared at the phone. "She's in trouble, isn't she?"

Frankie's eyes had drifted shut. She shook his shoulder, stuffed the envelope under his nose.

"Frankie. Frankie, is that it?"

The old man's eyes closed.

"Damn it." Maria stared at the crude drawing and looked up at Gabe. "Do you know what any of this means?"

Gabe's mouth thinned. "Yes. And it's nothing good."

CHAPTER TWENTY-ONE

FINDING THE GREEN LION

Petra awoke to a dull ache in her veins that grew into a tremendous pounding in her head.

She opened her eyes. The overgrown garden she'd dreamed of was gone. Instead, she was lying on her side in gravel, hands tied behind her back and feet bound with duct tape. She wiggled her fingers, and the ache in her body grew. She swallowed, throat dry, and lifted her head to take in her surroundings. The eye that had been pressed to the gravel was swollen shut, throbbing with a bruise. She felt curiously light-headed, as if she were floating, and moving her head caused yellow spots to form in the periphery of her vision.

Corroded bits of junk surrounded her, tossed haphazardly in what she guessed was a shed made of corrugated steel. Broken chairs, tires, and the dead carcasses of lawn mowers were parked amid old oil drums, broken birdhouses, empty snakeskins, and filthy mason jars. The roof was rusting through under the eaves, allowing light to penetrate. A nest of daddy longlegs watched her from the roof, pale and wispy in the golden light.

But it wasn't just the gaze of the daddy longlegs upon her. Cal squatted before her, holding a bottle of Mountain Dew.

"Hey, you're awake."

Petra cast him a murderous glare. "You motherfucking little weasel. Let me go. Now."

Cal bit his lip. He looked genuinely sorry. "I can't. Stroud would kill me."

"Yes, you can. If you let me go, you can leave with me. I won't press charges."

He extended the bottle of Mountain Dew. "I can't. But I brought you something to drink."

Petra's tongue was stuck to the roof of her mouth. She paused, torn between the urge to verbally eviscerate poor Cal, who was simply a stupid stooge following orders, and the desire to have a drink.

"I'd love to have a drink. Untie me."

"No can do." He extended the lip of the bottle to her

mouth, clumsily trying to pour the sickly-sweet liquid. A good third of it dribbled over her face to the floor before he got the hang of pouring it in small sips and giving her time to swallow.

Petra drained the bottle, lay back on the rocks.

"How are you feeling?" he asked.

"Like I've been abducted, had my ass kicked, and am tied up in a shed," Petra retorted.

Cal rolled his eyes. "No. I mean the blood loss."

Petra's skin crawled, and she stared at Cal through her good eye. She wiggled her fingers, and her arms ached. Her hands felt rubbery and swollen. She remembered the steak knife and shut her eyes.

Cal picked at a piece of gravel. "Stroud bled you so that he could start playing with the Locus."

"He what?"

"He took your blood," Cal repeated helpfully. "He says . . . he says that you should last for a long time." He tried to give her a reassuring smile.

"Where's Sig?" she demanded.

"Nobody's seen your dog since he bounced off the screen door, trying to get at Stroud."

Petra pressed her cheek back down against the ground. "You have to tell Mike. The ranger from the bar," Petra said. "Tell him where I am."

Cal shook his head. "I can't."

"Tell Gabe. Tell Maria. Tell someone who can get me out of here."

Cal rose to his feet, backed away. His eyes were full of regret.

"Cal!" Petra shouted at him, loud enough to make her head pound.

He disappeared from sight. She heard a door being dragged shut and the crimp of a padlock.

He was sorry. But not sorry enough to do anything to help her before Stroud bled her dry and left her for dead. And the way things looked, that was likely to happen a lot sooner than the sheriff's office showing up with their white horses to arrest Stroud.

Gritting her teeth, she pulled at her bonds. Rolling on the gravel, she succeeded in getting her wrists under her ass, then her feet. The effort made her dizzy, but she managed to get her trembling arms in front of her.

The sight made her nauseous. Her sleeves were hiked up past her elbows, soaked in blood. Long, seeping gashes ran across her forearms. She counted six of them, three on each. If Stroud was expecting her to last a long time, he was going to have to find other places to cut. If infection didn't set in from his filthy steak knives first. Her fingers were pale and cold.

Despair settled deep in her belly. She wished she was back in her dream, confronting a lion.

Something her father said still rattled in the back of her skull: *Use all the tools at your disposal. Your hands and your blood.*

She rolled to a sitting position and scanned the shed, looking for something sharp, and spied a broken rake in a corner.

She wormed over to it slowly, taking care not to

exert herself too much. She didn't want to pass out again. Bracing the handle of the rake between her feet, she set her wrists to it. Gritting her teeth, she began to saw at the duct tape.

She'd be damned if she'd give Stroud another opportunity to bleed her. One try was all he got.

The duct tape began to split, and she pulled it free of her wrists, then peeled it free of her ankles. She didn't dare try to stand yet, just sat with her head between her knees. There was no telling how much blood Stroud had taken from her, but it sure as hell felt like more than what the vampires at the Red Cross took for donations. She tried to count backward to the last year she'd had a tetanus shot. Two years ago? Three?

Wobbly, she climbed to her feet. Unconsciousness still gnawed at the edges of her vision, but she resolutely put one foot before the other until she reached the door of the shed. She tried the handle, shoved at it, but it was clear from the bolts on the inside that there was indeed a hasp and a padlock on the outside.

Shit. She sat down to take stock. She wasn't getting out until the next time someone came for her. Which meant that she should prepare for that eventuality.

Conserve her energy.

And maybe build a weapon.

Her gaze picked out a few items of interest: the duct tape she'd left on the ground, an old canister vacuum cleaner, a coiled garden hose, a pump garden sprayer, PVC pipe, and a red gasoline can.

She crawled to the gasoline can, shook it. The slosh suggested that it was half-full.

She grinned. It sounded like hope.

Stroud was wrist deep in blood.

And batshit crazy.

Cal was frozen in place halfway down the stairs to the basement, wishing he could melt into the moldering walls. Stroud held the gold compass he'd taken from Petra. He'd soaked it in her blood, and the red liquid spiraled around the compass's groove, a confused mass of droplets colliding and spinning against each other.

"The Locus," Stroud murmured. "Look at it, Cal. It reacts, sensing the magic in the things around it." He thrust the golden disk against the athanor, and the blood spun faster. When he pulled it toward a pile of cinder blocks, the pulse of it slowed.

And it also reacted to Stroud. When he held it close, the red quickened. "It's got to haveLascaris's living magic running through it. So much more than a simple tool."

He set the compass down on his workbench, his hands framing it. A droplet of mercuric sweat dribbled down his fingers, rolled to the Locus. The device hissed as mercury touched it. "Lascaris's notes were an incomplete set of instructions. But they will be a guide. A guide to finding the magic on Rutherford's ranch, to uncovering its secrets." His cracked lips pulled back in a grin.

Cal cleared his throat. "Stroud."

The grin dissolved into a snarl. "What do you want?"

Cal backed away. "There's someone here. At the gate to the Garden."

Stroud grimaced and limped up the stairs, past Cal and into the kitchen.

"Who is it?"

"I think it's cops." Cal offered him a set of binoculars with a shaking hand.

Stroud's eyes narrowed, and he snatched the binoculars from Cal. He crept to the kitchen window and focused on the long driveway leading up to the main road.

"Shit," he swore.

Dusty blue and black SUVs with government plates had pulled off the road next to the mailbox. Men with windbreakers emblazoned with the letters DEA were spilling out of the SUVs. They were largely interchangeable, men in sunglasses and buzz cuts. Except for the man in the park ranger uniform at the back of the group. Cal recognized him as Petra's friend.

Stroud was counting the number of men under his breath. Twenty-four. Cal knew that Stroud had at least forty people in the Garden, but these men were trained, and at least two-thirds of Stroud's garden flowers were stoned at any given moment . . .

A man in a windbreaker and bulletproof vest disengaged from the rest, walked past the gate down the quarter-mile driveway. A piece of paper was in his hand.

"Looks like they've got a warrant," Stroud mumbled. "Maybe they played rock-paper-scissors for who got to serve it."

Stroud reached up to feel along the top of the refrigerator, his wound seeping through the bedsheet bandage. Cal's stomach turned to see it. Stroud came back with a nine-millimeter handgun hidden in a crumpled bag of chips. He checked the ammunition in the clip, brushed the salt from it.

He ate a chip and turned the lights off.

And waited. Cal knitted his fingers together. When Stroud was quiet, it was bad news. He edged backward, back toward the shadows of the living room. Now would be a really good time to slip out the back and make a run for it.

A knock sounded at the front door.

Stroud walked, barefoot, across the sticky linoleum. He reached for the doorknob, opened the door . . .

And fired through the screen door at the DEA agent on his doorstep. Cal squeaked and hid behind the kitchen table.

The agent fell backward into the half darkness, blood blossoming from his right eye. The body fell to the floorboards of the porch.

Stroud closed the front door and locked it. He bent down to pick up another broken potato chip from the floor, chewed it thoughtfully.

He turned on Cal. Cal could barely hear him over the ringing in his ears. "Get the guns from the upstairs bedrooms. And assemble everyone for the disaster plan."

"Yessir."

"I've prepared for war for years," Stroud mused. "Expected that it would be war with Rutherford. But I'll start with the law."

Petra gently blew on the spark she cradled in her hands.

The flame intensified under the power of her quavering breath. She'd found an abandoned bird nest in a flowerpot in the back of the shed and had struck pieces of flinty gravel together until she'd finally summoned a spark that caught and held. She needed a fire soon; it was growing too dark to scavenge for more materials without it.

And she needed it to breathe life into her weapon.

The bird nest in her palms smoked and began to glow. She blew on it again, encouraging the tongue of fire to lick at the brittle walls of the nest. The nest would burn quickly; she had to work fast.

She set the nest down on the gravel and broke a tendril off. She chased a bit of flame with the twig and caught it. Shielding the burning twig with her cupped hand, she moved it to the awkward contraption she'd assembled to defend herself.

The metal vacuum cleaner tank lay beside her, laced

with bits of seat belt from a riding lawn mower. The tank sloshed when she moved it, the guts of the garden sprayer swimming in gasoline within. Garden hose snaked from its side, secured with bits of brass pipe fittings. A gun-shaped device made of PVC pipe scraps, half-rotted twine, and a hose nozzle was secured with the same duct tape that had held her prisoner. In the flickering light of the nest, it looked like a pathetically jerry-rigged piece of shit. Like a high schooler's science experiment. But it was all she had.

She partially depressed the trigger on the gun, got the flow of gas going, lit . . . *okay, okay, good* . . . and set the spark to the twine pilot light. With shaking hands, she released the trigger, hoped that the damn thing wouldn't burn her to death. She'd checked for leaks as best she could, but . . . she still held her breath.

The pilot light caught, held with a steady flame.

She let out her shaking breath, released the handle of the homemade flamethrower, and set it carefully down on the ground before her, afraid to breathe too hard on the pilot light. It should theoretically burn until she ran out of fuel. As for the rest of it . . . maybe it would work. It had to.

She heard scratching against the wall of the shed. It didn't surprise her that there would be rats here, but she didn't want to waste precious fuel on toasting rodents.

The digging intensified, and a whine and a muffled bark sounded.

"Sig?" She rolled over onto her hands and knees

and crawled to the side of the shed. The scraping noise was coming from where the wall met the gravel floor. She saw a tiny crack of less-than-perfect pitch blackness at the seam and heard paws scrabbling in gravel and dirt. A nose squeezed into the void, followed by Sig's head and shoulders. Petra grabbed his flea collar to haul the coyote through the tiny crack in the dirt, which looked barely large enough to accommodate a cat.

Sig shook filth from his coat and tumbled into Petra's lap. His hot tongue washed her face, and she weakly wrapped her arms around him. He sniffed at her arms, licking at them like a worried mother over a puppy. She let him, figuring that Sig's mouth was cleaner than Stroud's cutlery.

"I'm okay," she said into his ruff, but her voice caught in her throat. She looked over his shoulder at the open seam of grey light. Perhaps she could widen the hole that Sig had started, find a piece of metal or wood to make a makeshift shovel . . .

A metallic sound tore at the front of the shed, and the door began to open. Petra scrambled for the flame-thrower, throwing it over her shoulder by its seat belt strap. Cool air trickled into the closed space, and she could make out a tall silhouette against that lighter patch of night. Too tall to be Cal, her mind registered an instant before she pulled the trigger.

Flames erupted from the nozzle of the device with a *fwoosh*. The light wreathed the silhouette, and Petra let up on the trigger with a yelp.

Gabe stood before her, his sleeve on fire. He looked at the flames and slapped them out with his hat.

Petra wobbled to her feet, one hand clapped over her mouth. "Shit. I'm sorry."

Gabe crossed the space between them in two quick steps. He grasped her shoulders, and she sagged against him. His shirt smelled like earth and char.

"Nice toy."

"Thanks. I made it myself."

He pushed her hair out of her face. "Are you all right?"

"Yeah. How did you find me?"

"Frankie and Maria. He had a vision that the 'Green Lion' was in danger. I got the Hanged Men, and we came the back way, through the fields. Sig led us the rest of the way." He frowned at the blood on her sleeves. He took her wrists and turned her arms over to view the cuts across her arms. "What happened?"

She looked down. "Stroud has the Locus. He . . . he needed blood."

Gabe's amber gaze darkened. "I will find him."

"Gabe, I'm sorry, I didn't . . ." He was furious. She hadn't meant to lose the Locus, had no idea that Stroud would try to use it to find the Lunaria. "He said he knew what happened to my father."

"Never mind the Locus," he said, and her jaw dropped. "The other Hanged Men are in the field. They'll take you back."

"But Stroud . . ."

"I will take care of Stroud." He slipped his arm

around her waist to lead her from the shed. "Where is he?"

"In the basement of the farmhouse. He's wounded."

A gunshot roared from the direction of the house, and Sig whimpered.

"What was that?" she whispered.

Gabe's jaw was a hard line in the gloom. "Maria called your friend Mike. He rustled up some friends in law enforcement. The DEA is here."

He pushed open the shed door into the falling darkness, looked right and left before pulling Petra into the cool night air. No lights were on in the house or trailers. Petra thought she saw fireflies swimming in the distance. But as her eyes adjusted, she could see that the lights were in pairs: the Hanged Men walking in from the field, climbing over the barbed wire at the back of the compound. Ravens perched on the fence, clotting like blood.

Gabe handed Petra off to the nearest Hanged Man. "Take her to the hospital."

"Leave Stroud for the DEA," Petra said. She reached out and put her hand on his charred shirt.

Gabe shook his head. His gaze was bright and murderous. It was the most feeling she'd ever seen in him. "No. Stroud's gone too far."

He reached out, curled his cold hand around the back of her neck and kissed her with cool lips that tasted like winter.

Petra blinked, stunned, as he drew away.

He gave her a half smile. "What, it's only okay if you kiss me?"

She was speechless as he turned and walked away toward the house, the remaining Hanged Men soundlessly falling in step behind him.

Gabe strode across the ragged grounds of the Garden, seething. Rage was a sensation that he had not experienced in many years. When he had turned over Petra's arms, had seen what Stroud had done, he felt it rise deep within his chest, thaw some of the coldness that lay there. He could almost hear that frost crackle and break.

As he circled around to the front of the house, he could see the DEA advancing behind plastic shields. They had pushed past the gate and a pair of body-armored men were dragging a fallen officer off the front porch to safety. The officer's face was a mask of blood. From the upstairs windows, Stroud's people were firing down on them. The muzzle flashes sizzled bright as lightning in the darkness.

This was clearly not the best way in. Gabe returned to the rear of the house and plucked the paneled back door from its hinges. The Hanged Men moved past him into the acrid gloom of the house. He directed them upstairs with a jerk of his chin, toward Stroud's gunmen. He heard their steps on the stairs, then screams and shouts.

Gabe's gaze swept the dim kitchen. Light leaked out from under a red door that he supposed led to the basement. The lockset was shattered, hanging by its stem. He shoved the door open and plunged down the stairs.

He smelled the sharp bitterness of sulfur, the metallic softness of mercury, the tang of salt. And over it all, the copper scent of blood. He knew those odors: the stench of an alchemist's lab. And the reek of death, gathering close.

The basement glowed in light from an athanor burning at full blast. The heat made the air thick and muzzy, shimmering like noon on summer pavement. The Alchemist stood before his table, on which the Locus and ruddy jars of blood glistened. He was shirtless, his skin the color of slate and twitching over the tide of mercury roiling beneath it. He was packing an ammunition bag of items—Gabe assumed that he was preparing to flee.

"I was expecting the DEA," Stroud said, glancing up at him. "After me for selling Elixir."

Gabe cocked his head. "You've done more than sell poison."

Stroud shrugged, and the motion sent his grey skin rippling over his shoulder. "I didn't intend for it to be that way. I was trying to create a sense of timelessness. A piece of the Philosopher's Stone. The illusion of forever in a crystal." He sighed, and the mercury in his skin slumped. "But I've created an incomplete process."

"Calcination."

"Yes. Too much of my Elixir, over time . . . they become the calyx, the body of stone."

"That's not why I'm here. You took something that doesn't belong to you," Gabe said.

Stroud glared at him. "The bulletproof man. Perhaps you'd like to give me your secret?"

"I think you've had enough of secrets. You've poisoned yourself on them."

Stroud snarled, lips pulled back from his blackened gums, and threw a bottle at Gabe. He felt the glass explode against his chest, the sizzle of acid against his skin and clothes.

He lunged over the table at Stroud, turning it over and shattering the jars of blood. He slugged Stroud, sending him sprawling on the floor. The Alchemist spat out a glob of mercury and a few teeth, but his fingers skittered in the debris and came up with a table leg. He thrust it at Gabe, slamming it into his belly with all the force his gaunt body could muster.

Gabe gasped as the wood broke his skin and tore. Luminescent blood gushed from the wound. He staggered backward, crashing against a shelf. Bottles shattered against the floor, leaking on the cement. The pain was bright, excruciatingly brilliant, a fever of sensation. He fell to the ground, holding his gut. A string of luminescent blood worked free of his lips. Stroud stood on Gabe's neck, reached down.

"I'll force you to give up your secrets." The mercury dribbled from his hand, slithered along the ground like a force with its own volition. It began to creep into Gabe's wound. Gabe howled.

Through blurring vision, he saw the trail of liquid from the broken jars running toward the athanor. A panicked salamander scuttled out of the furnace. He could smell the vapors steaming along the floor.

A spark escaped from the furnace, jumping to the volatile compounds on the cement.

And a blinding roar rolled over Gabe that eclipsed all that luminous awareness of fire and pain.

The Hanged Men were determined to follow orders.

Two of them led Petra away into the darkness as gunshots flared. She twisted to look behind her. Men were shouting, and Stroud's people were fleeing into the fields in the wash of high-powered flashlight beams.

She couldn't leave Gabe to face Stroud alone. She struggled against the grip of the Hanged Men, but they held her in their cold, viselike hands.

Petra took a deep breath and went limp, allowing her head to sag forward and her knees to buckle. One of the Hanged Men let go, and the other loosened his grip long enough to try to put her over his shoulder to carry her.

Petra slipped out from under his arm and ran.

Blood pounded unevenly in her chest, and her breath was ragged as she charged back toward the house. She was conscious of Sig running beside her, following her back into the fray.

She could make out the figures of DEA agents in body armor storming the garden, tearing down strings of laundry, trampling the pathetic tomato patch and shouting orders. The denizens of the Garden who hadn't already run were returning fire, fighting back with guns and even rocks.

She spied a familiar figure: Mike had a young man down on the ground, handcuffing him. Behind him, she saw another man bearing down with a rifle. A man in ragged jeans and a sweatshirt that didn't say "DEA," a cigarette dangling from his lips.

She shouted for Mike to look behind him as she disentangled the nozzle of her makeshift flamethrower from the garden hose. Mike couldn't hear her over the fracas, seeming to be busy yelling orders at the man he was handcuffing.

She aimed and pulled the trigger at the rifleman. Gasoline washed over him, and he was engulfed in a plume of flame. He shrieked, dropping the gun and rolling around on the ground beside the farmhouse. The conflagration spread along the dry brush, sparks leaping from the broken tassels of grasses.

Mike looked up at her, stunned.

The fire moved like waves on the ocean did—inexorable and roaring. From the grass, it spread to the clothesline, turning laundry into burning ghosts. It slipped up the siding of the house, curling and shattering the paint, rushing into the open windows with orange tongues. The flames licked at something shimmering beyond the blackening curtains, some hazy fume that she'd barely tasted before in the kitchen.

The farmhouse exploded in a deafening roar. The concussion hurled Petra to the ground. She rolled over, stunned, staring up at the house that was bursting at its seams in flames that blotted out the stars and the glow of the moon.

She screamed. Gabe was in there.

No. Not again.

And it was all her fault.

CHAPTER TWENTY-TWO

BURNT THINGS

Cal couldn't explain why he felt drawn to return to the Garden after the fire destroyed it, but he did. He felt pulled in the way that metal is drawn to a magnet, or the way a vulture is compelled to circle carrion. Maybe it was because the Garden was the only life he'd ever really known.

Maybe it was because he wasn't quite done with that life yet.

When everyone was gone, he ventured out of the grasses and crickets to absorb the devastation. Under a full moon, Cal paced the grounds with his hands in his pockets. He kicked at a piece of hot rubble from the ruined house. The heated metal melted a smudge in the toe of his boot. A few blackened beams reached to the sky, like charred fingers. The chimney still stood, though the cap had begun to slide down the back. It was as if everything had simply been scribbled over with a marker.

He wasn't the only one who'd come back. He'd stayed in the fields overnight and all of the next day, watching the DEA and volunteer firefighters comb the site while the ravens harassed them.

His life, as it had been, was gone. No more being the footman of the local meth lord. He wasn't sure what he was going to do next. Hit the road, he guessed. There was nothing keeping him here.

He stood in the shadow of the broken chimney, remembering how this seemingly tiny pile of broken timbers and scattered shingles used to be a house that smelled like acid and piss. He hated to admit it, but he was relieved that Stroud was dead.

Sort of.

He spied something shiny, glimmering in the darkness like a sliver of moonlight. He knelt, wondering if it was something he'd be able to sell. So far, he'd found about ten dollars in change, a rusted key, and a melted fishing lure.

Cal touched the ground. This section was cool. He dug in the dirt, brushing away the ash and burned clay bricks. But his excitement turned to a cold pit in his stomach as something soft and metallic squished under his hand.

Mercury.

He yanked his hand back, but the mercury stuck to his fingers. This shit was poison; Stroud's madness was evidence of it. He shook them, trying to flip the drops away, but the metal still clung.

He wiped his hand against his jeans, trying to scrub the liquid off. But the droplets crawled up his sleeve, scurrying like ants.

In a panic, Cal yanked off his jacket and began to rub his arm on the ground. The beads of mercury congealed and began to seep into his skin. Jesus, he could feel it soaking through his pores, worming under his flesh. It was hot as liquid metal in his veins, and he gasped, clawing at his body. His nails dug deep bloody welts in his skin, but they summoned only blood. He couldn't dig the mercury out.

He could feel it settling, leaden and heavy in the marrow of his bones. He shook in fear, wondering if he should try to get to a hospital. Maybe they could get it out of him.

A rustle emanated from the far side of the field. Cal dragged his gaze away from his crawling flesh and saw glowing eyes advancing on him over the dark terrain.

Shit.

He'd seen them before, that first night alone at the ranch and again as the Garden burned. Sal Rutherford's ranch hands had come, silent and unflinching, to tear the remains of the farmhouse apart. Stroud had been right: They were unnatural. Magic.

And Cal wanted no more of magic. He scurried away, running to the safety of the road.

Looking behind him, he could see that they had stopped at the ruins of the house, carrying shovels over their shoulders. A raven cawed softly at them, as if in greeting.

With silent determination, they began to dig.

Nothing and no one was indestructible. She knew that, now.

Petra returned to the Garden days later. The sky overhead was a clear blue, feathered with cirrus clouds. The house fire had burned itself out, leaving a pile of charred and broken timbers behind.

She was still bandaged from shoulder to wrist on both arms. Stroud's experimentation would leave her with scars that would never disappear entirely. She'd cut her hair off at the shoulder to remove the ends charred in the explosion, but it still smelled burned whenever it fell over her face. Her gun belt, retrieved by the DEA from a tweaker fleeing the scene, was slung around her hips, feeling more natural than she cared to admit.

But she was alive.

Sig walked at her side. He wore a real dog collar now, with tags for his name and the address of the trailer. His fur felt soft and shiny, thanks to a bottle of shampoo and three types of hair conditioner.

She'd left the Bronco behind the police tape at the gate and walked slowly to the pile of skeletal junk. Ash stirred in the breeze. A backhoe was parked beside the ruins of the house, ready to be pressed into service soon. Mike had told her that the DEA would be excavating for weeks, but they expected that the heat from the meth lab explosion had likely incinerated any useful evidence or human remains. There was no way to reconstruct Stroud's formula for the calcinating Elixir. The members of the Garden who had been captured didn't know any of Stroud's recipes. DEA was considering the deaths to be a freak accident, a bit of mad science gone wrong.

She stared at the pile of blackened wood: ceiling joists, wall framing, shattered sheets of floor. Even if Gabe had been able to survive fire—and based on what she'd seen, she thought that there was a fair chance that he could—there was no way that he could survive the weight of that much wood crushing him. Her heart sagged.

On the way, she'd picked a bouquet of red fireweed. She laid it down on the crumbling chimney. She felt as if she should say something.

"I wish . . ." More words wouldn't come. She couldn't compress what she felt into a phrase. *I wish that you hadn't come back for me. I wish I had known you better. I wish I hadn't fucked it up, because I was beginning to feel something again, and it scared the hell out of me.*

Her attention was arrested by something writhing in the shadows behind the ruin of the chimney. She climbed to her feet and squinted at the shadow. Sig scuttled toward it.

"Sig, leave it alone."

A wing, moving. Petra plunged her hands into the ash to free the raven. She blew ash from its face. It blinked up at her through a filmy eye, its beak parted in stress. She carefully ran her fingers over its feathers, pausing over singe marks on its body. Its left wing had been burned and crumpled. Its tail was a charred nub. But it lived.

Petra sat back on her heels, pressing the bird to her chest. She wondered if this was one of Gabe's, keeping vigil. Maybe, in its own way, it haunted this place. Maybe it was a hand or a foot separated from his destroyed body, searching for the remains. Hope flared in her as she gazed down at the bird.

"Are you part of him?" she asked.

The bird didn't answer.

She wrapped the bird carefully in her denim shirt. It took three tries to get out of the sleeves without causing the wounds under her bandages to howl. The bird's talons chewed into her tank top, leaving smears of soot on it like charcoal in a sketchbook. His head jerked to and fro, searching for the sky beyond her shoulders and the confines of his denim straitjacket.

Whistling for Sig, Petra returned to the Bronco.

Sig was suddenly shy. The coyote clambered solemnly into the backseat, leaving shotgun for Petra's burden.

The bird remained silent as Petra cranked the engine. She had a momentary fear that the raven would go batshit and flutter around the car in a panicked escape attempt, but it simply lay where she'd put it, watching her with a marble-like eye. As the Bronco crunched down the gravel road, late afternoon sun poured through the bug-smeared windshield. She tried to convince herself that there was some intelligence glimmering in the raven's eye, that she had something more than a half-roasted and exhausted bird in her truck.

"I know it's stupid," she told Sig. "I know that it's stupid to think that part of Gabe is still alive . . . that he could be restored."

Sig glanced back they way they'd come and whined.

"But I have to take the chance. I have to. And if the Hanged Men never came back for him, never brought his body to the Lunaria . . . then at least this part of him can be home."

The coyote huffed and paced the pleather seats.

Taking the back road to the Rutherford ranch, she exited to the west through a gap in the barbed wire fence and plunged the truck into the sea of golden grass. The axles creaked and groaned at the off-road terrain. At this hour, the cattle grazed peacefully under blue sky. All seemed ordinary and unenchanted. There was no sign of the Hanged Men.

The Lunaria stood, magnificent at sunset. Gold

streamed through the reach of its branches, illuminating bits of grass and dust motes floating in the air, like fireflies. No breeze or birds rustled the branches, like they had in her dreams. The tree was still. But when she looked closer, she saw that part of the tree had begun to wither, as if early autumn had bruised it. Several thick branches were studded with rusty leaves that had once been green.

Petra shut off the engine. She hopped out and waded through the grass. It took her three passes around the tree before she found the ring of the trapdoor. Lifting it open, she peered into the blackness beyond.

Sig whined.

She stared down at her bandaged arms. There might be a possibility that she could get down there unaided, but climbing back out without any help would be impossible.

Returning to the truck, she popped the back tailgate and rummaged about. She came up with jumper cables and returned to the hatch. Tying one end of the jumper cables around the hinge, she threw the other end into the dark.

Petra gathered the singed bird from the truck and crossed back to the hole. Sig was making awful faces, pacing before the entrance to the catacombs.

"You can't go," she said. "I can't lift you back out."

He parked himself on his rump, resolved to watch her as she awkwardly grasped the bright yellow cable with one hand, balancing the bird in the crook of her other elbow. Her right foot swung around, probing until she found the cable. Clasping the cable between her knees, she took a deep breath and lowered herself.

The cable turned and twisted as she descended. She slid down, forgetting the clamps at the other end. A clamp ripped into her shin, and she hissed, nearly letting go. The cable was short, and she kicked the darkness with her left foot, feeling nothing below her.

"Damn it."

Gripping the bird tightly with her left arm, she let go with her right.

She landed on her feet after a short drop, but lost her balance and fell forward onto one knee. She caught herself with her free arm, fingers flexing in the dirt. The bird squirmed at her chest, but she could see nothing until her vision adjusted.

For a moment, Petra dared to believe in the tree's magic. She hoped that Gabe had somehow survived, that the Hanged Men had dug him up under the cover of night and brought him here to regenerate. More than anything, she wanted to find him sleeping in the loving grasp of the tree's roots. She hoped that this bird was one of his, that she could return it and awaken him with this offering.

Sucking in her breath, she took a step forward.

Out of the glare of the light above, she could make out a shimmer of gold before her. The roots of the Lunaria dangled from the ceiling like icicles, gleaming in the shifting shadows. It was daytime, so no phalanx of silent men dangled here. But something was nestled in the brightest part of the roots, an orb that shone like a harvest moon.

She touched it, and it dimmed. The otherworldly shine faded to something she recognized—the Venificus Locus. The compass was set in a nest of roots that curled around its edges. It still held a drop of her blood, spinning crazily inside it like a wasp in a mason jar, scraping against the gold with an insectile whine.

Unthinking, she reached for it. Some part of her knew that this was hers, that no matter if the Hanged Men had retrieved it in Stroud's Garden, *it belonged to her.*

It came loose as easily as plucking an apple, and she stumbled backward with the compass in one fist and the bird in her other arm. The compass was thick and sticky with a luminescent fluid that trickled over her wrist, as if she'd opened some great and terrible wound in the tree.

The bird started screaming.

Clutching the struggling bird close to her chest, she looked up, up into the seething shadow. The roots were moving, shifting. *Shit.* She'd disturbed something badly in here, and the tree was awake.

Mighty roots turned toward her, and she saw a face hovering above hers, just above the cavity where the compass had lain.

"Oh, my God," she breathed.

It was Gabe's head—his face had gone slack in a death's mask of pale horror, his hair wound in the tendrils of roots. His eyes were closed, and his mouth stretched open. He was frozen in a scream—screaming with the raven's voice.

"Oh, no . . ."

The shifting light illuminated him—what was left of him. His chest cavity was open and shining, roots winding through the pale fingers of ribs, searching for the compass she'd just removed. His hands hung above him, an impossible distance away from his shoulders—one pale and unmarked, the other like a clutch of finger bones sewed together with a glowing spiderweb. She couldn't see any feet, or any of the rest of his body in the seething mass of roots and broken bones.

Perhaps only this had survived, this incomplete horror. She remembered what Jeff had been, how the magic of the tree had been unable to re-form him. Any thoughts she had about Gabe being older and stronger and more magical disintegrated.

Tears ran down her cheeks. "Oh, Gabe . . ." She stuffed the compass in her back pocket and reached out to touch his face with her fingertips. He flinched away. One eye opened, and it was black as obsidian. Inhuman.

He drew breath to scream again, and out of his mouth came the raven's shriek. Luminescing blood dribbled down his lip.

She reached for her belt to fumble with a gun. Her sweat-slick hands shook so hard that it took two tries to pull the hammer back. She aimed the gun at a spot just between his eyebrows. If she had any bit of mercy or ethics about her, she should shoot him in the head until the raven stopped screaming. That would be the humane thing to do, wouldn't it? That had been what he'd done for Jeff.

But a bullet wouldn't kill him. Only wood could end his pain. "Damn it, damn it . . ." Her vision blurred to gold shadows and charred feathers. She couldn't leave him. Not like this, in pieces. But she couldn't end him either, this howling shadow that remained.

The bird in her arms continued fight against its denim straitjacket.

She stepped back, and the raven clawed loose of the prison of her arms. It flung itself at Gabe, clambering up the ruin of his chest with its talons, until he found the hole in his chest where the compass had been set. In a flutter of soot and feathers, it dove into that hole.

And then there was silence.

Gabe's face went slack, and his eyes shut. The sudden quiet . . . it terrified her more than the screaming.

She put the gun away and edged close to him, reached for his neck. She felt nothing. Not that she'd expected to feel the beat of a pulse, but she expected to feel that odd staticky hum of his. But the silence was unbroken.

With shaking fingers, she dug the sticky Locus out of her pocket. The Locus was unmoving.

No more magic.

She stared at Gabe, in pieces, for a long time. Only when the sunshine drained out of the hatch in the ceiling did she turn to leave. She jumped up to reach the cable, then hauled herself, fist over fist, up into the twilight middle world. Her arms ached, and stitches in her skin beneath the bandages split, oozing rusty red blood over her elbows and between her fingers.

She crouched at the edge of the hatch, staring down into the darkness. Sig sat beside her, solemn and steady as she dragged the door shut. The illusion of a perfect field was now complete.

"I'm sorry," she said. She kissed her hand and pressed it to the earth.

She had the sense that Gabe hadn't wanted to live forever, that he had simply been trapped in a terrible machine he'd been unable to escape. There had been something human there.

Something she'd begun to love.

She pressed her hands to her face and sobbed.

Petra smoothed the dress she'd borrowed from Maria as she walked through the automatic doors of the Phoenix Village Nursing Home. The place smelled of disinfectant and mashed potatoes, that unmistakable odor of civilized death.

She walked through a small, shabby lobby with plaid couches and a plastic flower arrangement that an elderly lady was trying to take apart. A young woman in a smock was trying to keep the old woman's hands occupied, carefully taking the flowers from her fingers and pushing a soft rag doll into them. Petra's borrowed heels clacked on the green checkerboard tile, and she wobbled up to the front desk.

"Hello. I'm here to see Joseph Dee," Petra said.

The middle-aged woman in a nurse's uniform behind the front desk frowned at her clipboard. "I'm sorry, ma'am, but we don't have a—"

Petra shook her head. "I'm sorry. I think he's listed in your system as John Doe Number Three."

The nurse nodded. "We have plenty of John Does. Sign here." She passed a sign-in sheet across the desk, and Petra scribbled her name.

"He's in room 113, hon."

Petra swallowed and nodded. She sucked in a deep breath and walked past the desk down the hallway. Her fingers gnawed at the itchy bandages under her calico sleeves. She was excited to find her father, but also afraid. She wondered if he would look like he did in her hallucinations. On the phone, the facility administrator had said that John Doe Number Three was the right age and general physical description to be her father. But he hadn't spoken for years. His bills were paid every month, on time, but the administrator couldn't say by who—the payer's identity was shielded by a legal trust.

She paused before an open door with the number "113" stenciled on it. Steeling herself for disappointment, she knocked on the doorframe.

"Hello?" Her voice sounded very small, as if it belonged to a little girl.

A room with two beds in it had a television running at low volume. A man in a wheelchair sat facing the window, and Petra could only see the back of his head. The view was just of the parking lot, but she supposed that it was more exciting than the game show on the fizzling black and white television.

Petra forced herself to put one foot in front of the other until she was beside the wheelchair. She squatted and looked up at the man's face.

The man in the chair stared vacantly outside. His face was unfamiliar, saggy and lined. His hair had been shaved with clippers, probably to make him easy to wash. His fingers were gnarled and tangled in his lap, and he was dressed in a faded hospital gown with a blanket covering his lap. He seemed utterly foreign.

But this man had her father's eyes, opaque and distant. She recognized that look, the look that he had when thinking of distant places. She recognized the amber color from her dream.

"Dad?" she whispered.

The eyes didn't flicker, didn't move from their intense focus on a trash can just outside the window.

Petra reached out to touch his hand. "Dad? It's me. Petra."

He didn't respond.

Her eyes filled with tears. Perhaps Stroud had told her the truth; that he'd lost himself to Alzheimer's a long time ago. She choked back a sob.

The old man's eyes turned to her. But they weren't looking at her. They stared at the pendant around her throat. Petra followed his gaze, unfastened the necklace. She pressed the pendant into his hand. "Dad, do you remember this?"

Her father stared at the glittering lion devouring the sun in his palm. His thumb slowly traced the arch of the lion's back. Then he reached out with his other hand and touched Petra's freckled cheek.

She smiled and blinked back tears. Some small part of him was in there. A flicker, some bit of that spirit that she'd encountered in the otherworld. "Yeah, Dad. It's me."

It wasn't much, but it was a new start. Maybe she could grab onto it with both fists and pull it back through sheer force of will.

"**S**ig. Stop that."

Petra sidestepped a stream of urine issuing forth from the coyote onto a telephone pole. She was determined to remove the flyers she'd put up all over town, and Sig had taken this as an invitation to mark the entire town of Temperance as his territory, from the post office to the hardware store and every pole and parked car in between.

Sig ignored her and kept watering the dead tree.

"Jesus. You must have a bladder the size of a basketball."

Sig snorted. He stopped pissing long enough to stand back and sniff at his handiwork.

Petra snatched her flyer from the telephone pole, tucking it under her arm with a stack of others destined for the recycling bin. She knew where her father was—at least, she knew what space his physical body was occupying. She'd worry about where his mind was next, but she was pretty sure that her homemade signage wasn't gonna help with that.

A familiar pickup truck rumbled past her, then parked at the hardware store just up the street. The Hanged Men piled out of the back as a group, heading inside without discussion. She watched them, wondering. Who was directing them, now that Gabe was gone? Were they just doing what they always did on the farm, or had Sal tightened the reins on them?

The driver's side door of the truck opened, and Petra's heart fell into her stomach.

It was Gabe. He swung out on two legs, his body seeming as whole and normal as she remembered. Both hands were attached to flannel-covered arms, and no wounded ravens nested in his chest. He looked down the street, gazed past her, and reached inside the truck for a white hat on the dashboard.

"Gabe!"

She dropped her stack of flyers in the middle of Sig's puddle and ran down the street to him.

She reached out to grasp his arms. "Gabe, you're alive!"

He looked at her blankly. When he did so, his head twitched a bit, like a bird's.

"Gabe. It's me. Petra." His skin felt cold and unyielding under the flannel.

There was no recognition on his face. None. His eyes seemed to go through her, barely registering her presence.

She released him, stepping back. "Don't you know me?"

He said nothing, just looked at her with that infuriatingly empty gaze. He didn't blink. She'd seen that mechanical look before, in the rest of the Hanged Men. The ones that he'd called automatons.

A lump rose in her throat. "The Lunaria . . . it worked, didn't it? It made you whole, but . . . it didn't have enough power. It made you . . . like them." She gestured at the men carrying bales of wire to the pickup.

He put the white hat on his head. This hat was new and crisp and completely unlike the old black one he used to own. He turned away from her, as if she was entirely irrelevant to his existence, to pick up a bale of fence wire. His arms jerked a bit as he loaded the bale into the truck. A puppet working with tangled strings.

He left her standing there, dumbfounded, as the Hanged Men loaded up their supplies. They moved around her as if she were no more than a lamppost, climbed back into the truck, and drove away.

She watched them go, unbelieving. Sig, ever the Good Dog, sat down beside her without offering to pee on anything new.

Petra looked up at the sky, blinking back tears, and spotted a raven perched on a telephone wire.

The raven peered down, staring her full in the face. It saw her . . . really saw her . . . and then winged off to join the Hanged Men and their trailing cloud of dust.

ACKNOWLEDGMENTS

Much gratitude to my wonderful editor, Rebecca Lucash. Thank you for your boundless enthusiasm, keen eye, and glowing encouragement. Under your wing, this story found its own darkly perfect ending. Thank you for making this book a reality!

Many thanks to my superhero agent, Becca Stumpf, who I am quite certain wears her cape and Wonder Woman boots twenty-four/seven. Thank you for being in my corner with your magic bracelets.

Thank you to Marcella Burnard, for the late-night reading, head-desking, and moral support. Thanks also for the glow-in-the-dark fairy dust and catnip, which are equally magical at my house.

ABOUT THE AUTHOR

Laura Bickle grew up in rural Ohio, reading entirely too many comic books out loud to her favorite Wonder Woman doll. After graduating with an MA in Sociology-Criminology from Ohio State University and an MLIS in Library Science from the University of Wisconsin-Milwaukee, she patrolled the stacks at the public library and worked with data systems in criminal justice. She now dreams up stories about the monsters under the stairs. Her work has been included in the ALA's Amelia Bloomer Project 2013 reading list and the State Library of Ohio's Choose to Read Ohio reading list for 2015–2016. More information about Laura's work can be found at www.laurabickle.com.

Discover great authors, exclusive offers, and more at hc.com.